THE PLATYPUS PLOY

CLAIRE MCNAB

Other Bella Books by Claire McNab

Under the Southern Cross
Silent Heart
Writing My Love

Carol Ashton Series:
Lessons in Murder
Fatal Reunion
Death Down Under
Cop Out
Dead Certain
Body Guard
Double Bluff
Inner Circle
Chain Letter
Past Due
Set Up
Under Suspicion
Death Club
Accidental Murder
Blood Link
Fall Guy
Lethal Care

Denise Cleever Series:
Murder Undercover
Death Understood
Out of Sight
Recognition Factor
Death by Death
Murder at Random

Kylie Kendall Series:
The Wombat Strategy
The Kookaburra Gambit
The Quokka Question
The Dingo Dilemma
The Platypus Ploy

THE PLATYPUS PLOY

CLAIRE MCNAB

BELLA
BOOKS

2022

Copyright © 2007 by Claire McNab

Bella Books, Inc.
P.O. Box 10543
Tallahassee, FL 32302

This is a work of fiction. Names, characters, businesses, places, events and incidents are either the products of the author's imagination or used in a fictitious manner. Any resemblance to actual persons, living or dead, or actual events is purely coincidental. The publisher does not have any control over and does not assume any responsibility for author or third-party websites or their content.

Printed in the United States of America on acid-free paper.

First published in 2007 by Alyson Books
First Bella Books Edition - 2022

Cover Designer: LJ Hill

ISBN: 978-1-64247-360-5

Always Sheila

An emphatic thank-you to my bonzer editor, Joseph Pittman, for his support and especially for his sense of humor

CHAPTER ONE

"G'day," I said. "I'm Kylie Kendall. Would you mind telling me where the administration office is?"

The Clarice Turner Evenstar Home was much grander than I'd expected. Set in a sea of manicured lawns and gardens were three buildings, each in a distinct architectural style—the first, Gothic, and the second, neo-Mayan. The third modernist structure's metal walls dazzlingly reflected the morning sun.

I'd left my car in the landscaped parking area and set off hoping to see a sign of some sort, but so far there'd been nothing to indicate where to go. I'd asked the first person I ran across for directions—an old bloke apparently having an animated conversation with a clump of flowering bushes.

"Do you mind?" he said. "I'm rehearsing." He spoke in the strangled vowels of an upper-class English accent.

"Oh, sorry. I didn't mean to interrupt."

He inclined his head graciously. "One isn't always to know. Your name again?"

"Kylie Kendall."

Taking my hand in both of his, he said in a rich, fruity tone, "Good morning, Kylie Kendall?" He flashed a set of chalk-white teeth—surely dentures—and raised his snowy eyebrows. "I imagine I need no introduction. You will know who I am."

Crikey, I didn't. I knew that there were many retired show-business celebrities at the Clarice Turner Evenstar Home, but I couldn't place him, although with his strong hooked nose and determined chin he looked vaguely familiar. I decided that was probably because he was dressed like a classic British gentleman with a deer-stalker hat, silk cravat, tweed jacket sporting leather patches at the elbows, and tan slacks with knife-edge creases. Becoming aware that the bloke was staring at me expectantly, I gave him a rueful smile. "You'll have to give me a bit of a hint."

My hand was dropped like a hot potato. "A hint? Sir Rupert Martindale doesn't give hints." He regarded me narrowly. "Your voice—Australian? And from the outback, I fancy." When I nodded, he added, "Hah! A gel from the Colonies. Ignorance not surprising."

That really got up my nose. I felt like snarling, "Typical Pommie comment," but managed to stop myself in time. "Sorry, Sir Rupert. Now I recognize you. You're the famous Shakespearean actor."

Somewhat mollified, he said, "Rather more than simply famous, don't you know? My Lear is widely regarded as the interpretation for the ages. Why, even Larry Olivier himself said to me, 'I came to your performance a colleague, and left a student.'"

"Blimey," I said, "that's a crash-hot compliment."

A regal nod. "One becomes accustomed to praise, but one is particularly delighted with the unfettered admiration of one's peers." His good humor restored, he went on, "But enough of my storied career. What do you do, Kylie Kendall?"

"I'm a private investigator. Well, more a trainee PI."

Sir Rupert recoiled a little. "A private investigator?" His thick white eyebrows formed a disdainful V. "I imagine you handle grubby little divorces and matters of that ilk." He gave, appropriately, a theatrical shudder. "I myself would feel besmirched, sullied."

"Kendall & Creeling are more into security consulting and industrial espionage," I observed. "Plus undercover investigations and skip tracing."

"*Creeling?* Would that be Ariana Creeling?"

"You know Ariana?"

"Our paths often crossed when she was visiting her friend in the Evenstar special-care facility. Ariana is a charming woman. And those eyes! Of deepest azure! Sapphire-hued!"

"Ariana has got bonzer blue eyes?"

Sir Rupert frowned. "Kendall & Creeling? Are you saying you're Ariana's business partner?"

"I reckon so?" *And much more, I hoped and prayed.*

"A mere slip of a gel like you?"

I had to grin. No way could I be described as slender.

His frown deepening, Sir Rupert said, "In all the times I've spoken with her, Ariana has never mentioned her participation in the private detecting profession." It was obvious that she had abruptly gone down in his estimation. He flung out one hand and pronounced, "The cruelest lies are often told in silence."

This was obviously a quote, but I had no idea where it came from. There was an awkward pause, then Sir Rupert, his disapproval plain, went on, "So, Miss Kendall, you're here at Evenstar to investigate some malfeasance?"

Actually, I was. Someone had been embezzling considerable sums of money, and the company owning Evenstar wanted a hush-hush undercover investigation with no police involvement.

"Not at all," I assured him. "I'm here to volunteer for the extravaganza's fundraising committee."

"Indeed?" His expression appreciably warmer, Sir Rupert declared, "Excellent! Have you been privy to a performance of *Swan Song for the Luminaries?* Last year my selected soliloquies from *Hamlet* received a sustained standing ovation."

I had to admit I hadn't even heard of the extravaganza until quite recently.

He sighed and muttered something about Philistines. Then, in the tone of one speaking to someone who was a bit of a nong, he said, "Once a year the extraordinarily talented individuals at Evenstar provide an invaluable opportunity for the ordinary citizens of Los Angeles to see the stellar heights quality entertainment can reach. The modern so-called star is but a pigmy when compared to the giants of the stage and silver screen, such as myself."

Sir Rupert paused, then made a sweeping gesture. "'He doth bestride the narrow world like a Colossus.'"

"*Julius Caesar.*" I spoke with confidence, having been given the part of Brutus in Wollegudgerie High School's staging of Shakespeare's play, when it became clear that there was a shortage of males auditioning for fear of being called sissies.

It seemed I'd redeemed myself, because Sir Rupert gallantly offered me his arm. "Let me escort you to the administration office."

This suited me, because I'd decided to cultivate him as a source of information. I'd just grit my teeth and smile if he made any more snide remarks about Aussies.

"There are no signs indicating which building is which," I said.

"That's to maintain a friendly, neighborly atmosphere," said Sir Rupert. Indicating each as he spoke, he told me that the Gothic-inspired building housed administration offices and special-needs patients, the massive Mayan building was entirely residential units, and the modernist structure held the most luxurious of the apartments plus a theater, meeting rooms, and a dining hall.

As we walked along at a leisurely pace, he said, "I'm delighted you'll be involved in *Swan Song of the Luminaries*. You'll find it an enriching experience that will nourish your very soul. It's more than quality entertainment. It's more than mature star power incandescently glowing. *Swan Song* is, not to put too fine a point upon it, a vital necessity in this cultural desert."

I thought of the old belief that swans sing before they die. Personally, I thought mentioning a swan song in the title of a show starring rather ancient celebrities was a touch morbid, as if the audience expected performers to fall off the perch at any moment.

Sir Rupert broke into my thoughts by inquiring, "Do you yourself have any facility in the performing arts?"

"'Fraid not. Except I can carry a tune pretty well."

"Carry a tune? Pretty well?" He gave a scornful snort. "My dear gel, that's more *American Idol* than the top-notch performance art to which I refer." He patted my hand indulgently. "But I'm asking too much of you, Miss Kendall. You are an Australian, after all, with every element of artistic impoverishment that entails."

I gritted my teeth and smiled. Fair dinkum! Wouldn't it rot your socks?

CHAPTER TWO

The waiting room of the administration office was very luxuriously appointed, with thick maroon carpet and elegant furniture. Oddly, I thought, two of the walls held full-length mirrors. I realized why when Sir Rupert paused to check his reflection and give himself a pleased little nod.

Catching me watching him, he smiled complacently. "One must always keep up one's appearance for one's public. It is expected of one."

"Must be a bit of a trial, always having to worry about how you look?"

"Not at all, not at all. Fame has its demands and responsibilities. I believe I fulfill my duties in that area to the full."

A derisive snort sounded from one corner of the room. Sir Rupert cast a look in that direction, and his face hardened. "Ignore him," he said to me, turning his back on the snorter. "Now, where the dickens is Glenys Clarkson?"

There was no one sitting behind the mahogany desk. On the wall behind it hung a portrait in a heavy golden frame lit by concealed lighting. A nameplate indicated this was an oil painting of Clarice Turner, founder of the Evenstar Home. If the artist had got it right, she'd been a tough-looking sheila built like a wrestler, with a gimlet glare and a tight mouth.

Sir Rupert peered behind the desk as if expecting the missing occupant to be crouched there. Finding this not to be the case, he clicked his tongue in irritation. "Glenys Clarkson spends far too much time away from her appointed place. I've had occasion to complain before. Remain here, Kylie. I'll locate the woman and send her to you."

"Right-oh."

As Sir Rupert swept out with the air of a man on a mission, the bloke who'd been lounging in one of the leather chairs in the corner got to his feet. He beamed an incandescent smile at me. "*Kylie.* What a very beautiful name. Melodic, sweet-sounding to the ear."

He'd obviously been extremely handsome when younger and still looked pretty good for an old cove, tall, with a thin body, thick steel-gray hair, and tanned skin. I don't usually like mustaches, but his suited him. The contour of his jaw was suspiciously firm and there was hardly a line on his face. Thrusting out his hand, he declared, "Cory Grainger at your service."

"G'day, Mr. Grainger," I said, extricating my fingers from his warm, insinuating grasp.

"Please, call me Cory." He sent me another electric smile. "Kylie, you have a lovely name, and a charming accent too. An enviable combination."

"Thanks," I said, thinking he was laying it on with a trowel. Although I hadn't tumbled to who Sir Rupert was right away, I immediately knew who this bloke was from old movies on TV. Cory Grainger had been the romantic lead in any number of Hollywood Golden Age dramas. "*Heaven Indefinitely Postponed,*" I said, mentioning one of the most successful of the tearjerkers. "You starred with Ina O'Neil."

"Oh, poor Ina." He gusted a sigh. "She was far too old for that part. Plummeting towards career oblivion, I'm afraid. Vaseline on the lens, soft lighting, the best makeup artist in the business—nothing really could disguise the relentless, unforgiving march of time. Of course it's different for the male of the species."

"It is?"

"Nature's unkind little trick on womankind is to limit her best years to the bloom of youth." He smoothed his mustache with a manicured forefinger. "In contrast, men become more distinguished as they age, like fine wine."

Checking his appearance in one of the full-length mirrors, he continued, "One has to keep fit, of course. The ladies appreciate a taut body." He and his reflection shared a close moment together, then he turned to me. "Surely, my dear, there's no argument that the passing years treat the genders differently, unfair though it may be."

"Crikey," I said, "I'd better get cracking, as I reckon I'll hit my use-by date any day now."

"I believe you can rest easy for the moment," he said gallantly. "You appear to have excellent skin. It so happens that I can recommend an exclusive beauty clinic specializing in maintaining radiant complexions. Clients are accepted by reference only. Would you be interested?"

I was saved from replying by Sir Rupert's return. He was followed by a pleasant-faced, middle-aged woman with a comfortably plump body swathed in a deep purple dress. Her hair was an extraordinary pinkish-beige color, which I reckoned couldn't be natural.

"I found her indulging in elevenses," announced Sir Rupert with a frown. He ostentatiously checked his watch. "And it's barely ten, Mrs. Clarkson, barely ten."

"Oh, Sir Rupert," she said with a sweet smile, "you do go on."

"And why shouldn't Glenys have as many coffee breaks as she desires?" Cory Grainger asked. "After all, dear lady, you work punishing hours. Punishing."

Sir Rupert's lip curled. "Balderdash, Grainger," he said. "Of course I value the work Mrs. Clarkson does, but it's merely office duties. Thespians such as myself, for example, know only too well what punishing hours involve."

Cory Grainger rolled his eyes. Undeterred, Sir Rupert continued, "I can call to memory many times when I was so utterly fatigued that I had to make a superhuman effort to literally drag myself from my dressing room to the wings, knowing that when the curtain went up on the stage, my public would be waiting."

Cory laughed unkindly. "What a total ham you are, Martindale."

"I've a mind to give you a good thrashing."

A look of alarm crossed Glenys Clarkson's face. "Gentlemen, *please!*"

"'O villain, villain, smiling damned villain!'"

Cory's iron-gray mustache bristled. "Don't quote Shakespeare at me, you old fraud."

"Sir Rupert! Cory! May I remind you what happened last time?"

"Calm yourself, Mrs. Clarkson," said Sir Rupert. He shot a look of intense dislike at Cory, then turned to me with a smile. "Until we meet again, Miss Kendall."

"It's *Ms.*," I said.

"I don't hold with these modern nomenclatures," he declared.

"Typical," said Cory. "You're an old fogy who doesn't move with the times."

"Gentlemen, please continue this discussion outside." Glenys Clarkson's tone was brisk and businesslike. To my surprise they both meekly obeyed her, Cory Grainger managing to seize my hand for a quick, clammy squeeze before following Sir Rupert out the door.

"What happened last time?" I asked.

She shook her head. "They actually came to blows. The police had to be called. Fortunately Emory was able to persuade the officers not to arrest either of them."

Emory would be Emory Hastings, the administrator of the Clarice Turner Evenstar Home, and the person employing me to suss out the embezzler. I was here to meet him for the first time, under the pretense that I was volunteering to join the *Swan Song* fundraising committee.

"I'm Kylie Kendall. I've an appointment to see Mr. Hastings," I said.

She went behind her desk and tapped at a keyboard. Peering into the screen she said, "Ah, yes, ten-thirty. You're a few minutes early, but I'll check if he's available."

She disappeared through a paneled door obviously leading to an inner office. In a moment she was back. "Emory will see you now. Do your require refreshments? Coffee, perhaps? Spring water? A bagel with cream cheese?"

"Not a sausage, thanks."

A slight frown creased her forehead. "I don't believe I mentioned any type of sausage."

"I meant that I need nothing at all, thank you."

"Then come this way, please."

The inner office was fully as luxurious as the outer area, but here the plush carpet was a deep blue and the walls held what appeared to be framed diplomas, certificates, and other qualifications. As outside, there was a portrait in an ornate golden frame, but this was of a beautiful woman, and someone I recognized: television personality Zelda Webber. She was also Emory Hastings' wife.

Hastings came out from behind his large antique desk. He wasn't tall, but he held himself as though he was. He had olive skin, very black hair, and dark eyes. His mouth was full-lipped and sensuous. He would have been seriously handsome but for the fact that his head was just a little too big for his slight body.

He greeted me warmly, dismissed Glenys Clarkson, and ushered me to one of two cream leather lounge chairs set by the full-length window. "Ariana Creeling has told me all about you," he said.

I grinned. "That could be a bit of a turn-off."

"Not at all, Kylie. I may call you Kylie? And you must call me Emory." He leaned forward confidingly. "We don't stand on ceremony here at Evenstar. We pride ourselves on being a warm and friendly community, a place providing a safe harbor for every guest, famous or not, to enjoy to the fullest every moment of their latter years." His expression grew serious. "And, of course, we have a special facility for those whose cognitive faculties are failing." He paused, then asked, "Did you know Professor Natalie Ives?"

Natalie Ives had been Ariana's lover for many years. She'd been stricken with early-onset Alzheimer's. The disease had progressed to the point where Ariana realized she could no longer look after her. Evenstar Home included a state-of-the-art facility devoted to the care of Alzheimer's and dementia patients. Fortunately cost had not been a factor, as Natalie had carried substantial insurance.

"I never met her." I said.

"Tragic, Natalie's death, but in some sense, a merciful release. I always think the disintegration of personality is worse than watching a loved one suffer a potentially fatal illness." His dark brown eyes were swimming with compassion as he added, "It came near to breaking Ariana's heart to see Natalie in such a state of mental confusion."

This wasn't a subject I was comfortable with, so I said briskly, "I don't like to take up too much of your time, Mr. Hastings."

"Emory."

"Emory. How many people know the real reason I'm here?"

"Just two. Apart from myself, the head of the Evenstar board, Oona Turner, is aware of your undercover role."

"Would she be any relation to Clarice Turner?"

"Oona is her granddaughter," he said, a fleeting expression of distaste crossing his face. "Oona sees herself as carrying on a proud family tradition of golden-years care."

My trusty reference book, *Private Investigation: The Complete Handbook*, emphasized the importance of noting any signs of conflict between personalities when investigating a case.

I was about to probe this area when Emory said, "No doubt Ariana would have told you that Evenstar's accountant, Vincent Yarborough, initially brought the shortfall to my attention, blaming it on sloppy bookkeeping associated with *Swan Song for the Luminaries*. At the time Vincent had no idea of the true extent of the problem, and since then I've taken care to keep him in the dark. It would be an unmitigated disaster for the good name of the Clarice Turner Evenstar Home, should word get out that our funds had been compromised in any way. Naturally the forensic accountant I had examine our financial records will maintain professional confidentiality."

"I've seen a summary of the forensic accountant's report," I said. "Would it be possible to see the report itself?"

I was interested in the details, as the summary made it clear that the slapdash recording of donations and outgoings for the extravaganza each year provided many opportunities for someone larcenous to redirect funds to dummy companies and untraceable accounts.

Emory Hastings sat back, raising his emphatic black eyebrows. "I'm afraid the full report would mean very little to you, unless you're well-versed in such matters."

"I reckon I am," I said. I didn't add that most of my expertise had been gained back in Australia, where I'd set up the computer system and run the financial side of my mum's pub, The Wombat's Retreat.

Clearly not too chuffed at the idea of giving me a gander at the report, he said, "I'll see what I can do."

"How about your assistant, Glenys Clarkson? Does she know about me?"

"Glenys? Definitely not."

Could this be true? In my experience it was difficult to keep secrets in an office environment. "I noticed a receptionist's desk in the lobby of the building. Using my superior detecting skills, I'm guessing you have a receptionist."

Emory didn't smile. "Nancy," he said. "Nancy McDuff. An excellent employee who's been here with us at Evenstar for many years. Utterly reliable."

Like personal assistants, receptionists were in a unique position to pick up bits and pieces of information that could be used to make a shrewd guess as to what was going on in a company. I'd experienced firsthand the astonishing reach of the receptionist network, through which a sensational story could spread like lightning.

"Receptionists usually have a finger on the pulse of an organization," I remarked. "It can be amazing how much they know."

"Nancy does her job superbly, but as for substantive matters, she wouldn't have a clue," he said dismissively.

"Right-oh," I said, but I wasn't so sure.

CHAPTER THREE

When I walked back to the parking area I saw, with a familiar tingle of anxiety, that there was a folded sheet of paper wedged under the driver's side windscreen wiper.

I looked around carefully, not expecting to see anyone lurking in the bushes, but checking anyway. Then, after making sure no one was sitting in any of the nearby vehicles, I unlocked my car, Zellsteind in the back to reassure myself an intruder wasn't crouched on the floor, then went through the routine of getting latex gloves and a plastic bag out of the glove box and retrieving the sheet of paper. All of the other notes had been free of fingerprints and I reckoned this one would be too, although there was always a chance that whoever the anonymous writer was, he or she would get careless and leave some trace behind.

Before sliding it into the plastic bag, I unfolded the note. The first message I'd received under my wiper three weeks ago had said baldly: "Go home, bitch. You're not wanted in my country." There'd been three others along the same lines, but this one contained a more direct threat: "Leave now while you have the option, or be sent back to your family in a body bag. Your choice."

What made it worse was that I had absolutely no idea who was sending me these messages. As far as I knew, I had no enemies. Examining the few cases I'd been involved with since coming to LA failed to turn up any likely names.

I hopped into the car and locked the doors. I'd already entered the Evenstar Home office number into my cell phone. The cheerful voice answering was probably Nancy McDuff, the receptionist Emory Hastings had described in such glowing terms. I identified myself and asked for Glenys Clarkson. In a moment she was on the line. "Ms. Kendall? Have you forgotten something?"

"It might sound an odd query, but I'm a bit paranoid about going to places, particularly at night. Since the fundraising committee will be having lots of meetings, I was wondering if there are security cameras set up to cover your grounds and parking areas.

"We employ an excellent security service. The buildings and grounds are patrolled, night and day?"

"And cameras?"

Glenys sounded puzzled at my insistence, but she answered freely, "There's camera surveillance covering the entrances to our three buildings, but we've not found it necessary to extend that to other areas."

I thanked her, burbled on for a moment on how thrilled I was to be accepted for the committee, then rang off. It had been a long shot that there'd been a camera recording the person placing the note on my car, but it was worth checking out.

These days, turning the key in the ignition made my skin prickle. I couldn't believe whoever was trying to get rid of me would go so far as to plant a bomb, but my overactive imagination insisted on visualizing being-blown-to-pieces scenarios.

To keep my mind on other things, I reviewed my fruitful morning at the Clarice Turner Evenstar Home. I was driving back to Kendall & Greeling's offices on Sunset Boulevard a bona fide member of the volunteer committee for *Swan Song of the Luminaries.* I'd rather thought someone would have asked why I, an Aussie recently arrived in LA, would want to be on the fundraising committee, and had rehearsed a convincing starstruck story along the lines of how thrilled I'd be to be part of this celebration of show-business history.

Disappointingly, this effort was wasted, because when I met the head of the committee, former movie queen Heidi Brandstett, she had only seemed interested in my past experience in fundraising—which would be none—and how many hours a week I could devote to the cause—oodles. Heidi had been gratifyingly pleased with my availability.

She had to be in her seventies, but she looked twenty years younger. She was a pocket Venus, diminutive, but with ample curves. Her blond hair—an expensive wig?—was piled on her head in artful curls. Her eyelashes were so long they had to be false. She had a slightly husky voice and a soft, insinuating laugh.

There was to be a meeting of volunteers for the committee the next evening and I assured Heidi I'd be there. At that point she'd given me a speculative look. "And what does an attractive young woman such as yourself do with her spare time?"

My gaydar is often unreliable, but in this instance when it shrilled an alert I reckoned it was spot-on. I recalled at the height of Heidi Brandstett's career there'd been scandalous rumors that her romantic inclinations were directed mainly towards women—Greta Garbo and Katharine Hepburn had been mentioned.

"Oh, this and that," I'd said vaguely. "Strewth, is it eleven-thirty already? Sorry, I'm afraid I have to go."

Before I could escape, Heidi had seized my hand, given it a gentle squeeze, and, looking up at me, batted her eyelashes. "Kylie, I can't tell you how much I'm looking forward to tomorrow night."

Driving along, I grinned to myself. I couldn't wait to tell Ariana all about it. She was in Phoenix on a case, but would be back this evening.

As I turned off Sunset into our parking area, I saw that Bob Verritt was about to fold his tall, skinny self into his new silver Lexus. He waited for me to pull into my spot, then called out, "How did it go at Evenstar?"

"No probs. I'll give you the good oil later." It would be soon enough then to tell him I'd received another disturbing note.

As a trainee, I had to report to Bob, who was a licensed private investigator, and therefore qualified to supervise me. To become a PI myself, I had the onerous task of accumulating a total of six thousand supervised hours spread over three years. Once I'd accomplished this, I would have to sit for a challenging exam, but that was a long way off.

"I'll be back in a couple of hours," Bob said. "By the way, we have a new member of staff. Hope you approve."

Since I was co-owner of Kendall & Creeling Investigative Services with Ariana Creeling—my dad in his will had left me his 51 percent share—any addition to our staff was my business. "We do? Who? Does Ariana know?"

Grinning, Bob slid into his car. "Not yet." He waved a farewell and took off.

This was intriguing. I hurried across the little courtyard and headed for the black, copper-studded front door. Our offices were in a converted Spanish-style house with fat, red terra-cotta tiles on the roof and pinkish-ocher stucco walls. At first the building had seemed glaringly colorful, but now I was used to it.

Inside, Melodie was seated at the huge, black pseudo-Spanish front desk. She was our receptionist, at least until her always-about-to-burgeon acting career finally took off in a big way.

As she handed me my messages, I said, "I ran into Bob in the car park. He mentioned about a new member of staff."

"He must mean Rocky," said Melodie, flashing her perfect teeth and tossing her long blond hair. She had wide green eyes, great skin, and a bonzer figure. Fair dinkum, I could almost hate her at times.

"Who is Rocky?" I asked.

Melodie reached down behind her desk, then straightened up with a pug puppy in her arms. "Isn't he just the cutest thing you've ever seen?"

I had to agree the puppy was totally adorable. A deep cream color, he had a velvety black muzzle and a quizzical expression on his wrinkled face.

"He's yours?"

"I wish, but you know I can't have pets in my apartment building. He belongs to Bob."

Rocky wriggled his compact little body until Melodie put him down, then he negotiated his way around the desk and approached me with a purposeful air, his tightly curled tail held high.

"G'day, Rocky," I said.

"Bob says Rocky's too young to be left alone at home, so he's going to bring him to work every day." In a tone of deep foreboding, Melodie added, "The problem is, Julia Roberts doesn't know yet. She won't be pleased."

"Crikey," I said, "you're not wrong there."

With her usual uncanny timing, Julia Roberts' tawny feline form came sauntering down the hallway towards us. Rocky, who'd been investigating my shoes, was riveted. He gave a tentative wave of his curly tail.

Julia Roberts halted. She peered at Rocky, then her green eyes narrowed into slits and her ears folded back. Her tail became a bottle brush. She made a sound somewhere between a snarl and a hiss.

The puppy, having no idea of the peril he was in, gave a high bark and crouched in play position, his bottom in the air.

"Uh-oh," said Melodie.

I decided to appeal to Julia Roberts' better nature. "Jules, get a grip. It's a pug puppy, just a baby. Not worth a moment of your time."

Julia Roberts' hissing snarl morphed into an outraged yowl.

"Do something, Kylie," said Melodie, wringing her hands. "I sense a dreadful tragedy pending."

"Fair dinkum, Melodie! It's just a cat and dog sorting things out."

"It's not just a cat, it's Julia Roberts. You know what she's capable of, and that was a full-grown standard poodle."

"You've got a point?" I got ready to scoop Rocky up and out of danger.

Julia Roberts advanced snarling, in a half-crouch. From Rocky's point of view, she must have looked more than intimidating—try terrifying. He lost interest in any idea of playing, gave an anxious whine, and before I could snatch him out of danger, he rolled over on his back to display his stomach in a submission posture.

Jules abandoned her I'm-coming-to-maim-you attitude. Her tail became sleek again, her flattened ears became erect and her bared teeth disappeared. She sauntered over to inspect Rocky, sniffed, then stalked off.

"I told you he wasn't worth your time," I called out after her. A snap of her tail was the only sign that she'd heard me.

"Poor baby Rockykins, did the big, bad pussycat scare the widdle man?" cooed Melodie, rushing around her desk to pick Rocky up. "Don't you worry. Auntie Melodie wuvs you itsy bitsy—"

"Oh, *please!*" Fran slammed the front door behind her. "Anything but baby talk." With deep loathing she added, "Can't hack that kitchy-kitchy-coo rubbish?"

"Fran, isn't Rocky gorgeous?" Melodie held him out for inspection.

"I suppose," Fran said grudgingly. I thought her flinty expression softened a bit when Rocky wriggled wildly in an attempt to reach her.

Fran was a little thing, with a warrior-queen mind-set and the bleakest views of life in general. She had porcelain skin, dark red hair, and an arresting bustline made more emphatic by her tiny waist. As I was tall, with olive skin, brown hair and eyes, there was quite a contrast between us.

"What's a puppy doing here?" she demanded of Melodie.

"He's Bob's. Rocky's going to stay in the office during the day."

Fran's mouth tightened. "Bob failed to check with me."

She was Kendall & Creeling's self-appointed office manager. As Fran was also Ariana's niece, she'd not only held on to the title she'd bestowed upon herself, but had also taken to throwing her weight around as far as anything to do with the office was concerned. This led to Fran and me being in a state of constant low-key skirmishing.

"Why should Bob have to check with you?" I asked.

Fran gave me a condescending look. "As office manager, and disaster coordinator, it's my duty to be constantly on the alert for potential health and safety problems."

"*Disaster coordinator?*" It seemed that Fran had added another title to her resume.

Fran held the firm conviction that any minute now Los Angeles would suffer major cataclysmic destruction—earthquake, tsunami, fire, hurricane force winds, or possibly a meteor strike.

Alternatively, the city could be the focus of a deadly terrorist attack. Germ warfare was her current preoccupation, with a dirty bomb not far behind.

In anticipation of such dire events, Fran had accumulated enough disaster supplies to equip a fair-sized field hospital. She'd commandeered the office-supplies room to store them all, having the office stuff relocated to a shed at the back of the building.

I'd been seriously miffed, as secretly I had had my eye on that room for myself. My bedroom and bathroom were adjacent, and with the dividing wall knocked down my living space would expand to include a comfortable sitting area. It was not to be, although I hadn't given up all hope. The trick would be to find some other location for Fran's blasted disaster supplies. So far I'd drawn a blank.

I became aware that Fran was still talking. "In an emergency situation, having a dog underfoot could lead to unnecessary injury or even a fatality."

"Like, that's so unfair, Fran," said Melodic, rocking the puppy in her arms. "Rocky wouldn't hurt anyone. How could he?"

"Imagine a devastating poison-gas attack," said Fran, cheering up now that she was discussing a catastrophic situation. "One should immediately shut any windows and outside doors, then get to the disaster-supplies room as quickly as possible, where I'll be distributing gas masks and further instructions."

Melodie made a face. "*Not* attractive, gas masks. When I put one on I look like a big fly."

Fran frowned at this frivolous interruption. "As I was about to say, unfortunately in these situations *some* people—I'm not naming names—tend to panic and run wildly about. It's very clear that tripping over the dog is a very real possibility in these circumstances, and those lost moments could be the difference between life and death."

Melodie shot out her lower lip. "Are you saying I'd panic in an emergency? That is *so* not true!"

Fran's smile was grim. "You can say that now, Melodie, but when the terrorists strike, or the Big One hits, overwhelming terror and paralyzing dread will sweep through your body."

"If Melodie's paralyzed with dread, she won't be able to trip over Rocky," I remarked helpfully.

Fran narrowed her eyes. "Thank you, Kylie, for your contribution. I'm sure I can count on you to attend the earthquake emergency drill I've scheduled for five-thirty. I left a reminder note on every desk."

"Stone the crows," I protested, "it seems we have a safety drill every second day."

This did not go down well with Fran. "Let me get this straight. Rather than spend a few minutes in earthquake-preparedness training, you'd prefer to be totally unprepared?"

"Well—"

"When the Big One strikes, you won't have a clue what to do. More than likely you'll be trapped in the rubble, listening to the screams of the dying."

"So tragic!" Melodie squinched up her face. Rocky took this as an invitation to lick her chin. "Entombed! Like *The Poseidon Adventure*, only on land."

Fran and I shared a look. Sometimes, admittedly rarely, we thought as one.

Before Fran could say something cutting to Melodie, the front door opened and Lonnie Moore, Kendall & Creeling's technical wizard, shuffled in, his shoulders sagging and his head down.

He usually had a cheeky little-boy smile, complete with dimples. This was so unlike his usual plump, cheerful self, that I said, "Blimey, Lonnie, what's eating you?"

"Eating?" he said bitterly. "It's more like gnawing away."

"You're not well?"

He shook his head violently. "Don't want to talk about it."

"Meet Rocky," said Melodie, holding the puppy out for inspection. "Isn't he adorable?"

"Adorable," Lonnie said listlessly, barely glancing at the pug.

Even Fran looked surprised, as Lonnie was a pushover for dogs. "What's the matter?" she asked. "Don't tell me your car's broken down again? Face it, Lonnie, you'll have to give in and take that rust bucket to a mechanic. You can't fix it yourself."

Formerly reliable, if noisy—to me it sounded like a crop-duster taking off—Lonnie's battered vehicle had lately developed the bad habit of suddenly stalling. On LA's freeways, where obstacles to traffic flow frequently caused multicar pile-ups, losing power this way could be a lethal proposition.

"It's not the car," Lonnie said. He gave a woebegone little moan. "I'll be in my office if anyone's looking for me."

Watching him drag his feet down the hallway, Fran, who had very little patience with sooks, snapped, "What the hell's got into him?"

Melodie gave us a smug smile. "It just so happens that I know." Rocky, who'd dozed off in her arms, woke when she hugged him tightly. "What do you say, widdle man? It's real heartbreaking, isn't it?"

"*Widdle man!*" hissed Fran.

"So what's up with Lonnie?" I said before Fran could build up a head of steam.

"It's Pauline Feeney." Meaningful pause. "You'll never guess what she said to Lonnie last night at the Golden Spatula Awards banquet…"

"Spit it out," Fran growled.

Melodie frowned. She hated to be hurried while delivering one of her dramatic presentations. "It was right before the Golden Spatula was presented to the Chief Chef. Like there was this hush, and everyone at their table heard Pauline say, "Lonnie, this isn't fair to me—it isn't fair to you. It's simply not working for either of us. I must have a relationship with more pizzazz. I'm going to have to let you go."

"I could have told you it would never last," Fran declared with dour satisfaction. "From the start, Lonnie was way over his head with that Glowing Bodies crowd."

"He's real popular there," said Melodie stoutly. "They're saying in the office that Pauline's made a big mistake—that guys like Lonnie don't come along every day."

I didn't ask how Melodie had gained all this information. I already knew. Once again I was seeing the awesome power of the receptionist network in action.

CHAPTER FOUR

I felt bad about poor Lonnie, so I called by his office to say hello and maybe cheer him up a bit. Sitting outside his door was the garish garden gnome that had been a gift from Pauline Feeney. Taped to its head was a note to Luis, our cleaner. It was in Spanish, so I wasn't sure what it said, but had a fair idea it would tell Luis to get rid of the gnome any way he liked.

I knocked, then popped my head through the door. "Lonnie?"

He was slumped in a chair in front of his monitor gazing blearily at the screen. "Yeah?"

I took that as an invitation to come in. His room was its usual indescribable mess, with papers and electronic gear strewn haphazardly from one end of the place to the other. Lonnie claimed to know exactly where every separate item was. He called it filing by chaos. So far I'd never caught him out. I'd ask him for a particular document or file, Lonnie would look vaguely around, then fossick in the clutter until he emerged triumphant.

The only thing he never could locate was Julia Roberts, who, although she was banned from the area because Lonnie was violently allergic to cats, frequently managed to sneak in and hide herself. It was a game to Jules, but a constant aggravation to Lonnie.

"I'm so sorry about Pauline," I said.

He looked at me with bloodshot eyes. "I suppose just about everyone in the entertainment industry knows she dumped me last night."

"I reckon they do, but I get the feeling that plenty of people are on your side." I added with a pulse of indignation, "It was rotten of Pauline to say that to you in public."

He sighed. "It was what Pauline felt. She's always very direct."

"You're making excuses for her?"

He sagged even further into his swivel chair. "I think Pauline cares for me a little, but I *love* her, Kylie. And no matter what she says or does, I'll keep on loving her."

"Oh, Lonnie…"

What to say to that? I knew very well you could love someone totally and not be equally loved in return.

I patted his shoulder. I couldn't think what else to do.

* * *

When Bob returned in mid-afternoon, I dropped into his office to bring him up to date on my experiences at the Evenstar Home. I reckoned he'd be a beaut source of background info for some of the senior stars I'd be encountering in the days to come because he was a longtime fan of the Golden Age of movies.

Rocky was installed in a puppy-proof enclosure, taking great pleasure in making a squeaky toy squeak. It had a particularly shrill sound, and Rocky was working up to a crescendo when Bob reached into the pen to take the squeaky toy away. The puppy looked miffed for a moment, then flung himself enthusiastically at the rawhide bone Bob was offering him.

"He's a bonzer little bloke," I said.

"Always loved pugs. Had one when I was a kid." Bob sat down behind his desk, which was overflowing with files and folders, and said with a grin, "No doubt you've managed to cause your usual turmoil at the Evenstar Home, so shoot."

Before I started my report, I handed him the plastic bag with the latest note I'd received. "When I went back to my car in the parking lot I found it under the windscreen wiper. And I checked—there are no surveillance cameras to catch the bloke, if it is a bloke, red-handed."

Bob's thin face was no longer amused. "This is number five, isn't it? The threats are escalating. Maybe it's time for you to get out of town for a few weeks."

"What? Now that I've just started a new case?"

"Your safety's more important than any case. I don't like you alone here at night."

"Crikey, Bob, I'm safe as houses. Lonnie's got cameras set up on both entrances, front and back, the car park's floodlit and so's the building, and a security company checks for intruders at least twice a night. And if all else fails, I'll do a John Wayne and spray bullets in all directions."

Bob, being a total worrywart, had insisted on taking me to a shooting range to teach me how to use a handgun. Being brought up in the country, I was quite a good shot with a rifle, but I'd never fired a small weapon, so it was a new experience for me. Bob had given me one of the handguns registered in his name—a Smith & Wesson 9 mm semiautomatic—along with a leather holster. He'd quite seriously suggested that I keep it by my side at night when I was alone in the building, and hadn't been pleased when I'd hooted at the very idea.

"Don't treat this as a joke, Kylie. This could be serious. We need a strategy meeting with Ariana."

I put up my hands. "If you insist."

"I do." He looked at me narrowly. "Anything else you're not telling me?"

I told him about Lonnie's breakup with Pauline Feeney.

Bob's face darkened. "She's shallow and artificial, like everybody in that business."

Pauline was a so-called star wrangler, working for the well-known event coordinator, Glowing Bodies. For considerable sums of money, the company guaranteed to supply appropriate celebrities—A, B, or C list—for parties, charity functions, product launches, and so on.

Lonnie and Pauline made an odd couple, but maybe it was true that opposites did attract, because the two of them certainly had nothing in common in personal style, life experiences, or personality. Even so, just days after plunging into the hectic social whirl that was Pauline's world, Lonnie had declared that he was in love with her and that their differences were not important. It seemed he'd been wrong.

"After we finish here," said Bob, "I'll find Lonnie and give him the bracing man-to-man spiel about there being plenty of other fish in the sea. Now, tell me about this morning."

When I got to the part about meeting the head of the committee, a delighted smile spread across Bob's endearingly homely face. "So you met Heidi Brandstett, eh? She make a pass at you?"

"She was very friendly."

"Very friendly?" Bob brayed his nasal laugh. "I betcha! Heidi's famous for being *very* friendly to anything that has a pulse."

"Blow it! And here I was thinking it was my overwhelming Aussie charm."

Bob gestured to one of the framed posters on the wall behind him. Under the scarlet-lettered title, *Insatiable*, a young, voluptuous Heidi Brandstett gazed with hungry passion at a suave-looking bloke with a pencil mustache. In the background was a group of vaguely familiar faces, supporting actors I'd seen in various old movies on late-night TV.

"Never was a title more appropriate," he said. "The gossip was that Heidi seduced the director, followed by most of the cast and crew—male and female—without breaking a sweat. Then she set her sights on Morgan Zellstein, the studio head, which turned out to be somewhat of a miscalculation."

"Heidi came a cropper?"

"She ran up against Vanessa Banning, Zellstein's wife, a star in her own right, and not at all inclined to have Heidi bed her husband. One of those delicious Hollywood feuds followed, with Vanessa and Heidi at each other's throats and the gossip columnists having a field day."

"Did anyone win?"

"Both of them. You just can't buy publicity like that. Vanessa Banning went on to headline a series of movies with the theme of a wronged wife fighting to keep her man. The best of them was *He's Mine!*, for which Vanessa even scored an Academy Award nomination. As for Heidi, she burnished her reputation as a sex machine who would have put Mae West in her heyday to shame, starring in movies such as *Unquenched*, *Voracious*, and my favorite of all time, *The Need and the Greed*."

"Crikey," I said, "and this is the woman who's looking forward to seeing me tomorrow night."

"My advice is to be a moving target. Don't let Heidi back you into a corner." Bob chuckled at my glum expression. "My money's on you, Kylie."

"I feel better already."

Grinning at my wry tone, he went on, "You do have a fallback position. You can always become second-best friends with Vanessa Banning. That'll turn Heidi off fast."

"Vanessa Banning is a resident at the Evenstar Home too?"

"She is, and though Morgan Zellstein has long gone to the big movie studio in the sky, her feud with Heidi burns as brightly as it ever did."

Bob's phone rang. He located the handset under a pile of papers. "Ariana for you, Kylie."

My heart gave a pleased little jump at her name. "I'll take it in my office."

I skipped down the hail, said a cheery "G'day" to a young woman coming out of the kitchen with Melodie, and shot into my office.

"Ariana?"

"Hi. I'm at the airport in Phoenix waiting for my flight to board. Are we still on for tonight?"

I found myself stupidly grinning. "Too right."

A picture of Ariana as I'd first seen her rose in my mind—her pale hair pulled back from her still, cool face, her eyes an intense blue. That day she'd been wearing a black shirt, black pants, and black high-heeled boots. I'd since discovered that black was her favorite color for clothes.

Ariana hadn't been at all pleased to learn that I had no intention of selling her the controlling interest in Kendall & Creeling my father had left me. And her detached control had taken quite a hit when I'd announced I was aiming to stay in LA and become a PI.

Ariana jolted me back to the present by asking, "Anything I should know?"

I tossed up mentioning that I'd found another note on my car, and decided to wait until I saw her. "Nothing urgent. Lonnie's heart has been broken—smashed, really—and Bob has a pug puppy called Rocky, who's adorable. What else? I've made my first visit to the Evenstar Home and got appointed to the Swan Song committee, no worries. Oh, and you'll be upset to learn you're going to miss Fran's earthquake preparedness meeting at five-thirty."

"So disappointing," said Ariana dryly.

* * *

Speaking with Ariana had put me in an excellent mood. Last night I'd watched *Saturday Night Fever* on a classic-movie channel, so I found myself humming "More Than a Woman" while on my way to the front desk to see if Melodie knew anything about the receptionist at Evenstar.

The person I'd seen coming out of the kitchen was curled up in one of the visitors' chairs chatting with Melodie. Taking the advice of *Private Investigation: The Complete Handbook* that a detective's observational skills require constant polishing, I gave the stranger a quick once-over.

She was wearing a long brown dress patterned with signs of the zodiac in gold. On her feet were golden sandals. Her toenails were painted gold, too. She had a thin face with heavy-lidded, pale blue eyes. Her nose was long and elegant, her mouth a pouting rosebud and her chin decidedly pointed. Thick honey blond hair cascaded in ringlets to her shoulders. She wore many enamel bracelets and silver rings on almost every finger. I noticed that the elaborate silver pendant resting on her flattish chest was actually a timepiece.

"Meet Yolanda," said Melodie. "She's my new roommate."

Lexus, real name Cathy, had been sharing an apartment with Melodie, but had recently shot through with my cousin Brucie, who had temporarily put off returning to Australia to embark on a cross-country drive "to discover the real America." I suspected the real reason he hadn't gone home was that he hoped my resolve would weaken and I'd agree to give him a job at Kendall & Creeling. Brucie had a snowball's chance in hell of that ever happening.

Melodie had not been pleased when Lexus announced that she'd be accompanying Brucie. Not only had Melodie lost a roommate, she rather fancied Brucie herself. In fact, Brucie had invited Melodie along too, but she'd been forced to refuse, pointing out that her acting career must come first, no matter what wrenching personal sacrifices she had to make.

A small group of us had watched Brucie and Lexus clamber into the second-hand Volvo Brucie had picked up for a song. As they departed with a clattering roar and a cloud of diesel smoke, Melodie had put a hand to her throat and said with resolute bravery, "My art is a harsh, harsh mistress, but if true love is something I have to forgo"—she drooped her head—"so be it."

I recalled Lonnie had quite spoilt the moment by snickering, an insult Melodie had still not forgotten, nor forgiven.

"G'day, Yolanda," I said, putting out my hand. "I'm Kylie Kendall."

She uncurled herself from the chair and stood up. I'm quite tall for a woman, but she had a good half-head on me. "I know many things about you," she said in a soft half-whisper. "I've received messages from the Other Side."

"You have? Who do you know in Australia?"

Melodie tsk-tsked. "The *spirit* world, Kylie. Yolanda's, like, a professional medium."

"My card," said Yolanda. She handed me a midnight blue business card. Next to a picture of a crystal ball wreathed in wisps of mist, in silver lettering the words *Cassandra Smith-Jones, Full-Service Psychic Medium* appeared.

"Aren't you Yolanda?" I said.

"Cassandra is my professional name," she breathed. "*Cassandra,*" she repeated with drawn-out vowels. "Tell me, do you not discern how the very sound of the word has otherworldly vibrations?"

"Isn't Cassandra the ancient oracle who always told the dinky-di truth, but no one ever believed a word of it?"

Yolanda/Cassandra frowned at me. "The truth is out there," she intoned.

This sounded familiar—some TV show? "I'm sure it is," I said agreeably.

Her pale blue eyes gazed deeply into mine. "I perceive secrets in the very heart of you, Kylie Kendall. Hidden secrets and longings. Deep longings."

Right now I was deeply longing for a cup of tea. When I told her so, she nodded understandingly. "You're using a classic deflection technique. I see it constantly. Most people are frightened of the paranormal the first time they encounter it."

"Crikey, I've just encountered the paranormal? Stone the crows! I didn't even notice."

Her rosebud mouth tightened, then relaxed. It seemed Yolanda had decided I wasn't mocking her, but was just a rather simple Aussie.

Yolanda checked the time on her silver pendant. "I have packing to do," she said to Melodie. "I'll be moving my things in this evening. See you around seven?"

"Seven's fine."

"I do have some valuable mystical equipment that will need special care."

"Mystical equipment," repeated Melodie, clearly very impressed.

Yolanda gave her an indulgent smile. "I believe you mentioned you had some degree of psychic talent yourself."

Blushing a little, Melodie said, "Nothing compared to you, Yolanda, but I have to admit I'm very sensitive to the unknown. Sometimes it creeps me out."

"I believe I can help you develop that sensitivity."

"Awesome!"

Yolanda paused at the front door and gave me a long, significant look. "Until next time, Kylie. And a friendly warning—prepare to be startled."

"Awesome!" said Melodie again as the door closed behind her new roommate.

CHAPTER FIVE

Fran's earthquake-preparedness meeting was held in Ariana's stark black-and-white office, the largest—and tidiest—room. No one in the building escaped: Fran had rounded us up like an irritable sheepdog dealing with wayward sheep.

She positioned herself behind Ariana's desk and the rest of us sat in a semicircle of chairs. I was at one end and next to me was Lonnie, looking morose. Then came Melodie, tugging vainly at her micro skirt, which had ridden up to display the full length of her excellent legs. I brooded for a moment on how I'd look in a micro skirt, and concluded not half as good as Melodie. Then I wondered why suddenly I was worrying so much about my appearance.

Next to Melodie was Bob, with Rocky snoozing on his lap. Melodie leaned over to coo, "How's the widdle Rockykins?" before Fran silenced her with a laser glare.

The last person, smoothly handsome as ever, was Quip, Fran's husband, who'd been unlucky enough to have dropped in just as the meeting was about to start.

Fran tapped a pen on the desk for attention. "It's very unfortunate Ariana and Harriet chose to miss this opportunity to be earthquake-proofed," she began.

"Fair go," I said, "Ariana's in Arizona on business and Harriet's just had a baby."

Harriet Porter worked for us part-time while putting herself through law school. She and her partner, Beth, had decided to have a baby, so now Harriet was on maternity leave, although she was still available for legal advice by phone or e-mail.

"Whatever," said Fran. "Now let's start with a quiz."

"Like on *Jeopardy?*" Melodie asked with a practiced toss of her long, blond hair. "You give us the answer and we give you the question? I'm real good at that."

"Nothing like *Jeopardy*," snarled Fran. "It's a simple quiz to assess your individual preparedness level."

Lonnie let out a loud groan. "A quiz? You've got to be kidding."

"I am not kidding."

Lonnie folded his arms and sank down in his chair, a mutinous scowl on his face. "Count me out."

Fran's answering scowl beat Lonnie's hollow. I mused over why this should be so. Perhaps it was because Fran, if you could ignore her pit-bull nature, was actually very good-looking, which meant her scowl had something attractive to be contrasted against. Not that Lonnie was ugly. He had a cheeky little-boy smile and—

"Kylie? We haven't got all day." Fran gave an exasperated snort. "Do you want me to repeat the question?"

Since I hadn't heard it the first time, I indicated this could be a good move.

With elaborate patience, Fran said, "You're indoors when the Big One strikes. At that desperate, life-threatening moment, what do 'D, C, and H' mean to you?"

"Crikey…"

"They mean 'Duck,' 'Cover,' and 'Hold,' Fran snapped. "*Duck* under a desk or table, remain there under *cover*, and *hold* on tight to avoid being thrown around. And remember to stay away from doors and windows."

"So that would be 'S, D and W,' " interjected Lonnie.

"What?"

"Stay away from *doors* and *windows."*

Bob brayed a laugh and Quip hid a smile.

Fran's eyes narrowed dangerously. "Are you trying to be funny?"

Teasing her had quite cheered Lonnie up. "Just being helpful," he said virtuously.

"Don't be." Fran switched her attention to Melodie. "Okay, Melodie, what do you do if you're outdoors when a major earthquake occurs?"

"Nothing," said Melodie with confidence. "Like, there's no windows or doors."

"That's your answer?" Fran was plainly incredulous.

Melodie gave it some thought. "You could lay down, I s'pose. Yes, that would be a good idea, so the shaking wouldn't knock you over."

"What about power lines? Walls? Trees? Buildings?"

"Um..."

"You stay away from them, Melodie! They could fall and kill you. You should move to the nearest open area."

"I knew that," Melodie declared.

Fran looked to the ceiling. "Give me strength!"

"Steady, sweetheart," said Quip.

"I know what to do if you're in a car," Bob volunteered. "You stay in the vehicle, slow down, and stop, taking care to avoid overpasses or bridges."

"Excellent, Bob," said Fran, at last pleased with a response. "At least one of you is prepared for a major earthquake."

"What happens if you're in a vehicle that's already driving across a bridge when the Big One hits?" Lonnie inquired. "Or, for that matter, on or under an overpass?"

"There are casualties in every major disaster," said Fran with a shrug. "That's only to be expected."

"So it's stiff cheddar, old cheese?" I said.

Fran glared at me. "I haven't a clue what you're talking about, which, I must say, is often the case."

"I'm saying that you're saying it's too bad those people were in the wrong place at the wrong time."

"I don't think that's correct," said Lonnie. "Shouldn't it be in the wrong place at the *right* time? When you look at it logically, it's the right time for the earthquake, but the wrong time for the victims."

Fran's store of patience, never very large, was exhausted. "Shut up, Lonnie!"

Her raised voice got through to Rocky, asleep on Bob's lap. His eyes popped open and he gave a small yelp of alarm.

"I'll have to ask you not to frighten my pug," Bob said.

Fran's normally porcelain complexion was a shade of mottled puce. "Your pug? That totally unauthorized animal you've brought into the office without even checking with me first?"

Bob, usually the mildest of men, sat bolt upright in his chair. "You're not pulling your office-manager stunt again, are you? If so, I might just have to set you straight on a few things."

I was about to intervene to prevent a full-scale brawl when Quip said, "Fran, honey, have you told them about the book you're writing?"

Fran writing a book? This was astonishing news, as she had never shown any interest in such a thing. Quip was the writer in the family, having penned many screenplays—none had yet been produced—and one very successful biography, still on the bestseller lists, of a corrupt, larger-than-life real-estate magnate.

Fran's red cheeks now indicated blushing modesty, not rage. "I haven't liked to mention it," she murmured.

"What sort of book?" Melodie asked. "A romance? Are you writing a romance? With lots of sex? Sex sells, you know."

"More likely chick lit," said Lonnie knowledgeably.

"All wrong," said Quip with a proud smile. "My Fran's writing nonfiction, tackling a very important subject."

"I knew it!" Melodie exclaimed. "A diet book. That's *so* cool. Or cellulite. Cellulite's a *big* problem." She added quickly, "Not that I have cellulite myself, but I know people who have—"

"Enough with the cellulite. My book's title says it all, *Imminent Cataclysm: Be a Survivor.* And the subtitle explains it further—*Tips on saving loved ones from lingering death.*"

"Catchy title, Fran," said Bob, a sardonic note in his voice.

"No chance it won't sell a million," said Lonnie, matching Bob's tone. "Or maybe I'm thinking too small. I mean, who wants their loved ones suffering a lingering death? So how about megamillion sales?"

Quip frowned at them both. "It's a timely subject, and who better to write it than Fran?" He paused to give his wife an admiring look. It was bonzer, the way Quip and Fran always supported each other. "And it's all her own work. Fran won't even let me read the manuscript."

"It's my creation," said Fran with dignity. "My name will be on the spine, not Quip's, so every word in it must be mine."

"But Quip's a writer," Melodie pointed out, "so he'd know what he was doing."

"Are you saying I *don't?*"

"Well…"

Leaping lizards! There could be blood on the floor any minute. "Fran," I said, "have we covered earthquake preparedness? I've got an urgent appointment." I tapped my watch for emphasis.

"Thanks to some people getting completely off the subject," said Fran, giving us all an equal-opportunity glower, "we haven't covered the subject adequately. You can all hope and pray the Big One doesn't strike before the follow-up meeting you're forcing me to schedule."

"Having lived in LA all my life," Lonnie declared, "I know all I need to know about earthquakes."

Fran indicated she found that hard to believe. Lonnie indicated what he found hard to believe—that Fran had the creative talent to write a book.

"I declare this meeting closed," I said hastily. "It's time to go home."

This was a magic phrase that cleared the room fast. Melodie lingered to say to me, "I've checked up on Nancy McDuff for you."

When I'd asked her earlier about the Evenstar Home's receptionist, Melodie had said she didn't know her personally, but would call around and get back to me.

"Evenstar Home being a retirement place," said Melodie, "Nancy McDuff networks mainly with receptionists at AARP and health funds and funeral services and all that elder stuff?"

It hadn't occurred to me that the receptionist network would have subnetworks, but of course that made sense now that I thought about it. "So I reckon you couldn't find out much, right?"

Melodie gave me a pitying look. "You don't get it, Kylie, do you? Nancy's a fellow receptionist. That means she's in our system, so there are people out there who know all about her."

Nancy McDuff appeared to be quite a woman. She'd buried two husbands and divorced one. At present she was living with a retired rocket scientist whom she'd met at a ballroom-dancing contest. She'd dumped her dancing partner and waltzed off with him. They were well-suited, Melodie said, as he shared Nancy's interest in professional boxing—they rarely missed a championship match in Vegas.

"You're making this up," I said.

"I am not!" snapped Melodie. "It's like Crystal at Heavenly Shores Cemetery says, 'Nancy talks the talk of a retirement-home receptionist, but she doesn't walk the walk.'"

* * *

I drove up through the now-familiar narrow, winding roads to Ariana's Hollywood Hills home, feeling my customary anticipation mixed with a measure of apprehension. The physical side of our relationship was intoxicatingly exciting, but the emotional side was out of balance. There was no disguising the fact that I absolutely adored her, but as for Ariana…? I knew she was fond of me, cared about me, but she had never said, "I love you," and perhaps she never would.

To be realistic, I didn't expect Ariana to commit to me, at least not yet. On the surface she appeared to have adjusted, but there was a thread of sadness and loss underneath. It hadn't been long since Natalie had died, and even though Alzheimer's had finally robbed her of all memories of Ariana, she was still the woman Ariana had loved and shared her life with for many years.

Ariana's house was perched on the edge of a cliff, which gave it stunning views of Los Angeles spread out below. It was particularly beautiful at night, but I preferred it in daylight when, smog permitting, you could see all the way to the Pacific Ocean.

Gussie, Ariana's delightful German shepherd, barked as I drove through the open gates and pulled into the parking area behind the house. Gussie stayed with Ariana's sister, Janette, when Ariana had to be away overnight, so her presence here meant Ariana definitely was home.

I knew a tiny, inconspicuous closed-circuit security camera was on me as I rang the doorbell. When Ariana opened the door barefoot and in jeans, her hair still wet from the shower, I had my usual moment of indecision. I wanted to seize her tightly in my arms and say, "I've missed you so much. I'm only half-alive without you." Instead prudence had me say, "Hello," and kiss her on the cheek.

"G'day, gorgeous," I said to Gussie, who, tail wagging gently, was waiting patiently to be acknowledged.

"Bob called me," Ariana said as she stood aside to let me past. "If it's okay with you, we'll meet Bob and Lonnie in your office at ten tomorrow to discuss the situation. Unless we can nail your stalker, Bob believes you'd be safer out of LA, and I agree."

"They're just stupid notes," I protested. "Some galah's having a laugh at my expense. I'd feel like a galah myself, if I ran away."

"Someone's been following you around. If he or she—it's not necessarily a male—puts a message on your car, the person can just as easily wait for you to come back and attack you."

"I'm being supercareful, Ariana."

Obviously impatient with me, Ariana said, "Being supercareful doesn't cut it. You're not taking this seriously, and you should."

I hated the way this conversation was going. I knew there was some truth in what Ariana was saying, but I didn't want to think about it now. "Can we give it a rest?" I said. "I'd rather discuss this tomorrow morning, and forget about it tonight."

"Okay, it's a deal, as long as you promise to listen to reason tomorrow."

"I'll try." Catching her dubious expression, I added, "Really, really hard."

She laughed and shook her head. "I suppose I'll have to be satisfied with that."

As I followed her down the hall to the living room's spectacular view, she said, "Are you staying the night?"

As if she needed to ask! "I did tell Julia Roberts not to necessarily expect me home."

Ariana grinned. "At a wild guess, I'd say she wasn't pleased."

"Jules was brave about it, especially since her fave dinner, liver and chicken in savory gravy, was on the menu."

"That reminds me, I haven't eaten since lunch. If you don't mind, let's order in right away."

"I don't mind," I said, thinking Ariana could ask anything, demand anything, and I would agree. Well, actually that wasn't true. If Ariana were to tell me to leave and never see her again, I'd buck at that. And I couldn't, wouldn't stop loving her, no matter what she said or did. And if—

"Kylie?"

"Sorry, did you say something?"

Amused, Ariana said, "Where do you go?"

"Pardon?"

"Sometimes I feel your body's here, Kylie, but you're miles away in some other world."

That made me think of astral travel, which brought Melodie's replacement for Lexus to mind. "I've got scads of things to tell you," I said. "For one thing, Melodie's new roommate is a professional psychic."

"You're kidding," said Ariana with a disbelieving smile.

"I'm not. Yolanda's her name, but she calls herself Cassandra Smith-Jones when she's working as a medium. I'm pretty sure she's not fair dinkum, but Melodie's totally convinced."

"Melodie would be." Ariana's tone was dry.

I was about to tell her how Yolanda was offering to develop Melodie's supposed psychic talents, when the phone rang. I wandered off with Gussie while Ariana took the call.

"That was Emory Hastings," she said when she put down the receiver. "He's asking me to join the Swan Song fundraising committee."

"What did you say?"

She grimaced. "I told Emory I'd be glad to make a donation, but it was too soon for me to visit the Evenstar Home."

Before I could speak she added with stinging emphasis, "I never want to see that place again!"

CHAPTER SIX

I left Ariana sleeping and drove down the winding roads to Sunset Boulevard in the dawn light. It was Thursday morning, and traffic on Sunset was already heavy. As I often did, I wondered where all these vehicles could be heading, especially at this early hour. Some would be driving to work, as commuting in LA was such a nightmare that the best option if you had any distance to drive was to leave before the traffic became impossible. Others would be coming off night shifts and heading home to sleep the day away.

And I reckoned there'd be a few like me, leaving a lover's bed. If they were lucky, they wouldn't have my mixed feelings. I was both sated and unsatisfied. Ariana was a wonderful lover, passionate and mercurial, her cool, controlled persona burnt away by the urgency of desire. I could be so close to her, yet know there was something in the core of her I could never touch.

Although I'd never done this with anyone else in my life, I trusted Ariana with my whole self, not just my eager body. Last night, when we lay spent in each other's arms, I'd said to her, "Ariana, I'm yours, body and soul."

She didn't move, but I felt her withdraw from me. "Kylie, please don't ever say that."

Although nothing more was said on the subject, there was a palpable change in her. I wished I'd never spoken those words, but it was too late now. I slept badly, and woke very early. Breakfast with Ariana was usually a delight, but this morning I didn't want to even try to cope with the barrier I'd created between us. So, like a coward, I'd slid out of bed, dressed quickly, and left her still sleeping.

* * *

It had become automatic for me to carefully check the surroundings before I left the safety of the car. Kendall & Creeling's parking was empty, apart from the pick-up truck belonging to Luis, our office cleaner.

"G'day, Luis," I said, meeting him coming out the front door as I was coming in.

He was carrying Lonnie's garden gnome and nearly dropped it in alarm. Then he murmured something in Spanish, probably an appeal to whatever saint it was whose job description included protecting cleaners.

Luis had never got over our first encounter when I'd just lobbed in from Australia. I'd gone to sleep alone in the building, and wakened to alarming noises. Convinced there was an intruder, I'd confronted a startled Luis with a golf club at the ready. Since that unfortunate incident I'd tried to make friends, even going to the trouble of learning a few soothing Spanish phrases, but Luis had clearly decided that I had psychopathic tendencies.

"Beaut gnome," I said to him cheerfully. "Good quality. Going to keep it yourself, are you?"

Lonnie's now ex-girlfriend, Pauline Feeney, hadn't picked a mass-produced garden gnome for her first gift to Lonnie. It had the traditional garish colors of red and green, but it had obviously been made by a craftsman.

Luis stared at me, clutching the gnome tighter to his chest. I held the front door open for him, and he scuttled past, taking care not to turn his back on me.

"Fair dinkum, Luis," I said, "you've got to admit that if I were totally bonkers, I would have attacked you long ago."

Luis sped up. A few moments later, I heard the sound of his pick-up truck taking off.

I shook my head as I closed and locked the door behind me. My education at Wollegudgerie High had not included Spanish. Apart from English, the only language I had a passing acquaintance with was French, and in heavily Hispanic LA, that was no help at all. I'd have to get Lonnie or Bob, both of whom did speak some Spanish, to intercede for me with Luis.

Julia Roberts, yawning, came sauntering to greet my arrival. "Anything interesting happen while I was away, Jules?"

Another wide, pink yawn. Apparently not.

I was thinking breakfast; so was Julia Roberts. She led the way to the kitchen, checking several times to make sure I was following close behind.

While Jules wolfed down her tuna bities, I put the kettle on for a cup of tea. Checking the time, I decided it was too late to call my mother at her pub, The Wombat's Retreat, as it was now the middle of the night in Australia. I had to admit I was a bit concerned about Mum. She usually called me at least once a week to bring me up to date on the local news and to complain how Jack, her fiancé, had made some total balls-up while attempting to help run the pub.

Invariably, then Mum would beg me to come home to help her out, saying the place had gone to rack and ruin without me. As a closer, she'd go on to lament how she couldn't understand how her own flesh and blood could possibly prefer to live in the hellhole that was Los Angeles, especially as it broke a mother's heart to see her child in such constant danger.

When I hadn't heard from Mum for a week, I was relieved. Now it was a fortnight, and I was worried. I promised myself

I'd call when I got back from the first Swan Song committee meeting this evening, when it would be late afternoon of the next day in the 'Gudge, as Wollegudgerie was affectionately known.

* * *

I was in the kitchen making my second pot of tea when a flurry of dot-dot noises in the hallway indicated that Melodie in her extremely high heels was heading my way.

"Kylie, you'll never guess!"

"What?" I said warily. Melodie was notorious for finagling people into filling in for her at the front desk while she zipped off to auditions.

Melodie clasped her hands to her breast. "It's fate moving in mysterious ways. That's what Yolanda says."

"She, being a psychic, would know."

Melodie didn't seem to notice my dry tone. "Yolanda senses that there's someone looking out for me from the Other Side."

I managed not to smile. "Sort of a guardian angel?"

"I guess. Anyway, Yolanda says it wasn't an accident that Lexus suddenly decided to go with Bruce on his cross-country trip. It was sort of divine intervention, so Yolanda could become my roommate."

I was well on the way to deciding this Yolanda sheila was more than a bit suss. "Why would some spirit on the Other Side give a brass razoo who your roommate happened to be?" I asked.

"Because Larry-my-agent says it's the most vitally important audition of my whole acting career. And it's a TV show about psychics, would you believe? And"—Melodie paused dramatically—"Yolanda is a psychic!"

Melodie referred to her agent so frequently that in my imagination I always saw *Larry-my-agent* with hyphens.

"Which show is Larry-my-agent so chuffed about?" I inquired.

"Oh, Kylie, you *must* know about the one with all the supernatural stuff. It's been in the trades for months?" Melodie was referring to *The Hollywood Reporter* and *Variety*, published every week day and obsessively read by everyone in the entertainment industry.

"*Paranormality Incorporated*," said Bob Verritt from the doorway. Rocky was wriggling in his arms. As he put the puppy down to explore, he added, "Surprised you haven't heard all about the show, Kylie. It's had enough press. Supposed to be a sure-fire hit in next fall's schedule."

"Crikey, must have slipped by me. What's it about?"

Melodie frowned at my ignorance. "There's this detective agency called Paranormality Incorporated, because everyone in it has a different psychic ability, like knowing something before it happens, or seeing ghosts, or reading people's minds, that sort of thing. Then they all work together to solve the crime."

"It's a comedy?"

"It's a *drama*, Kylie. It's real serious. And Yolanda, being an expert about the paranormal, says she'll help me prepare. Like, it's destiny! Yolanda gets to be my roommate just when I need her the most."

After checking on Rocky, who had snuffled his way into the laundry annex that I'd had constructed in a corner of the kitchen, Bob perched his tall, skinny body on a kitchen stool. "Which part are you auditioning for?"

"Larry-my-agent says I was made to play Chilley Dorsal?"

I had to laugh. "Chilley Dorsal? Pull the other one."

Melodie didn't smile. "I don't know what you mean. Chilley Dorsal's a major character. She gets these creepy premonitions."

"Like a cold finger down her spine?"

"Something like that. Yolanda says I'll totally ace the audition because with her help, my interpretation of Chilley Dorsal will be real authentic."

"How did you trip across this woo-woo roommate?" Bob inquired.

"She's not any kind of woo-woo," said Melodie, affronted. "Cassandra's a professional psychic medium."

Bob looked puzzled. "I thought her name was Yolanda."

"It's Cassandra when she's working as a medium. Like, it's her professional name."

"I've got to meet this woman," said Bob, grinning. "If I cross her palm with silver, will she tell my fortune?"

"You can find out tomorrow night," Melodie said. "I'm having a welcome-roommate party and everyone's invited."

"I'm in," Bob declared. "What about you, Kylie?"

"Wouldn't dream of missing it," I said, thinking that I'd like to observe Yolanda Smith-Jones in action. Then I could decide what she was—a con artist, sincere but deluded, or a genuine psychic. I was betting on the first of the three.

Exhausting the delights of the laundry annex, Rocky had wobbled his way back into the kitchen and discovered the water and food dishes belonging to Julia Roberts. He was enthusiastically gobbling up the tuna treats left over from breakfast. This wouldn't have been so bad, but for the fact that Jules had just appeared, no doubt planning to polish off the remaining food.

"Gawd!" said Bob. "Rocky, come here."

Julia Roberts had everything under control. She didn't snarl, she didnt even fluff up her tail. She merely marched over and whacked Rocky a mighty blow with her paw.

The little pug was knocked completely over. He yelped, scrambled to his feet, and shot out the door.

"Oh, poor Rocky," cried Melodie.

"That's discipline," said Bob admiringly. "I guarantee Rocky won't touch a dish belonging to Julia Roberts ever again."

"A triumph, Jules," I said. "Quick, decisive action without wasted energy."

It was clear Jules agreed with me. She inspected her dish, flicked a Zellstein in my direction to indicate she expected me to clean it of offending puppy odors, then sat and washed her disciplinary paw to remove all traces of an inferior life form.

* * *

My office had been my dad's, and I hadn't liked to alter the furnishings because he'd chosen them, so the room was rather stark and masculine, with charcoal gray carpeting, and gray metal desk, bookcase, and filing cabinets. I had added my personal touch with photographs of Aussie wildlife I'd taken in the bushland around Wollegudgerie.

Ariana arrived for the meeting first. I looked up from my computer monitor as she came into the room. For once, she wasn't all in black, but was wearing a red silk shirt and white jeans. She was too thin, having lost weight in the last few months. Her blue eyes burned in her pale face. With a pang of alarm, I thought she might be ill. "Are you all right?"

She gave an offhand shrug. "Of course. I'm a little tired, perhaps."

Feeling awkward about sneaking away from her bed without a word, I blurted out, "This morning...I'm sorry—"

I broke off as Bob and Lonnie came trooping in for the meeting.

"Anything new?" said Bob.

"Too right. I've just discovered my stalker's switched to e-mail?"

Ariana's mouth tightened. "Show me," she said.

I swiveled the flat screen so everyone could see it. The line indicating the sender was a mix of letters and numbers. The subject was: "I've been watching you 24/7." The text in the body of the email was brief: "I warned you, but you didn't listen. You're forcing me to take action. Crying time coming."

"There's no mystery how he got your e-mail address," said Bob, "it's on our website."

"Can you trace the sender?" I asked Lonnie, who could do remarkable things with anything relating to computers and communications.

"I'll try, but can practically guarantee I won't get anywhere. This e-mail will have been bounced around the electronic world through a series of anonymous mailers."

"Ted Lark needs to see this," said Ariana, "although the LAPD won't get involved unless something more concrete occurs."

I'd met Detective Lark on another case. He'd been a colleague of Ariana's during her career with the LA Police Department and they'd kept in touch. When the first of the messages had appeared on my car, she'd passed them on to Lark to put on the record that I was being stalked. However, unless something more overt took place, such as a physical attack, there'd be no official response. As Lark had put it, "Threats are a dime a dozen, and only a tiny percentage of perps progress to anything more serious."

I had my fingers crossed that I belonged to that majority of victims who eventually had their stalkers lose interest and fade away.

"Let's get this show on the road," said Bob, pulling up a chair. He flipped open the folder he'd brought with him. "Here are the five notes left on Kylie's car over the last three weeks. Just to summarize, the first and second were delivered overnight when the car was in our parking area. Possibly because Lonnie set up a surveillance camera, the perp switched to following Kylie as she drove around, so the third note turned up when she was shopping in a supermarket, and the fourth, Tuesday this week while her car was in a public parking structure."

"Hair cut," I said by way of explanation. "Luigi of Beverly Hills."

"And the fifth note," Bob went on, "appeared like magic yesterday morning at the Evenstar Home."

"Could be no one's going to the trouble of actually following you," said Lonnie. "You may have a GPS device hidden underneath the car. I'll check it out after the meeting."

The thought that a global positioning device might be revealing where my car was at any given moment was almost as upsetting as the hateful messages were. It made my skin crawl to think that someone who wished me harm could know I'd spent the night with Ariana, perhaps putting her in danger too.

Bob doggedly continued his summary. "The notes themselves are not much help. No fingerprints, identical cheap copy paper, printed by hand using a mass-produced ballpoint pen. English speaker, educated."

"It seems to me we should be asking what the perp's motivation is," said Lonnie. "What's he gain from forcing Kylie to leave the country?"

"Simply can't stand Australians?" Bob suggested with a grin. "Or maybe it's as obvious as this—the person's basically nuts."

"I reckon even someone nutty as a fruitcake would have what seems, at least to them, to be a logical reason," I said.

Bob rubbed his beaky nose thoughtfully. "We could be looking at this the wrong way. Maybe it's someone in Australia who wants you back there at any cost."

"That would be my mum. She's been working hard to get me to return to Wollegudgerie pretty well from the time I lobbed into LA."

"Enough to hire someone to scare you home?"

I shook my head. "Not in a million years, Bob. Besides, Mum doesn't know anyone in the States."

"She knows your cousin Bruce," Bob pointed out.

The thought of Bruce doing Mum's bidding made me smile, as they really didn't get on too well, partly because Mum always referred to him as Nephew Brucie, which drove him bonkers. Besides, as I reminded everyone, my cousin had ambitions to join Kendall & Creeling, so he had every reason to want me to stay in Los Angeles.

"Great guy," said Lonnie, who'd got on well with Bruce.

Plainly impatient, Ariana said, "Let's get to what's important here—the escalating threat level."

"There's nothing specific," I pointed out.

Bob raised his eyebrows. "To my way of thinking, the reference to sending you home in a body bag seems very specific."

"Still not the faintest idea who it could be?" Lonnie asked.

I shook my head. "Not a clue."

"Maybe it's one of your many ex-lovers?" Lonnie suggested. "Someone who believes you done 'em wrong?"

"Being as I'm so irresistible," I said, laughing, "you'd think I'd have scads of cast-off lovers. Can't imagine why I don't."

Not amused, Ariana said coolly, "Your safety is the paramount issue. It seems we're no closer to identifying who it is, or why they want you to leave the States. The logical thing is to move you out of harm's way. Don't worry that you're on a case. We can negotiate something with the Evenstar Home."

"I agree," Bob chimed in, while Lonnie nodded.

I'd thought this through and made the decision not to cut and run, no matter what happened. "You lot have got Buckley's chance of getting me to budge. I'm not going anywhere."

Lonnie frowned. "Remind me again who this Buckley guy is."

"Poor bloke was notoriously unlucky," I said, "so to have Buckley's chance is to have no chance at all."

* * *

Emory Hastings had given me two sets of names, the first detailing employees of Evenstar Home and the other the current residents. I was busy making a preliminary list so that Lonnie could start running background checks, when Ariana came back into my office.

"I was just about to come and see you," I said. "I've been thinking, what if this campaign to get rid of me is really aimed at someone else?"

"And that someone would be...?"

"You."

Ariana gave me a long, blue stare, then she said dismissively, "I don't think so."

I was ready to discuss it, but Ariana sat down across from me and changed the subject alarmingly by saying, "Things aren't quite right between us, are they?"

"Ariana, if it's about me leaving this morning—" I broke off, not knowing how to continue.

"The problem's with me, Kylie, not you."

"As far as I'm concerned, there's nothing wrong," I said with hope rather than confidence, "but if there is, we can work it out."

"I don't think we can." She let out her breath in a long sigh. "Please try to understand. Essentially, I lost Natalie long before she died, at the point when she stopped recognizing me. That's why I didn't expect her death to hit me as hard as it has."

What comforting words could I say? A platitude my mother often quoted came to mind: "Time heals all wounds." "Give it time," I said, feeling inadequate.

Ariana rubbed her forehead. With a rueful smile, she said, "I've always prided myself on dealing with anything that was thrown at me. It embarrasses me to admit I'm not coping very well with this situation?"

"What can I do to help?"

"Nothing. It's for me to work out." Then, in a horrible parallel of Pauline Feeney's words to Lonnie, Ariana added, "The way things are—it isn't fair to you."

"I don't care about fair."

"I do."

I found myself holding my breath. My skin prickled with sudden cold. "What are you saying?" I said at last.

Ariana's expression became remote, implacable. Like last night, I felt her withdrawing from me. "It's too soon—too soon for us, I mean."

Sudden tears stung my eyes. "So what do you want to do?"

"Kylie, you must know how much I care—"

"Don't tell me how much you care!" A self-protective anger surged through me. "Just say what you need to say."

There was a long silence between us. At last Ariana said, "Our relationship—can we cool it for now?"

"How cool?"

Ariana looked away from me. "I was thinking friendship."

"So being lovers is off, is that it?"

"This is not forever…"

"Promises, promises," I said resentfully.

The words were hardly out of my mouth before I was bitterly ashamed of myself for being so selfish. Ariana had had years of grief, helplessly watching as Natalie's Alzheimer's inexorably progressed. Her death hadn't ended Ariana's love for her. And here was I making self-centered demands, having known Ariana such a comparatively short time.

"Forgive me," I said. "I was thinking only of myself. Of course we can cool it."

"Thank you."

I couldn't resist adding, "But don't think I'm giving up, because I'm not."

"Why am I not surprised?" said Ariana dryly.

CHAPTER SEVEN

Heidi Brandstett whacked the gavel hard enough to send a sharp crack throughout the room and exclaimed in a voice seeming too large for such a small frame, "As chairwoman, I take great pleasure in calling the Swan Song committee meeting to order!"

Heidi's exalted position was indicated by her red leather chair, which was larger than any other and elevated so she could look down on mere committee members.

This was one of the Zellstein Turner Evenstar Home's sumptuous meeting rooms. In truth, I couldn't ever remember seeing a meeting area more luxurious. The cream carpet was practically ankle deep, the walls covered with artwork that I reckoned was genuine. The surface of the table around which we sat was covered in black leather, embossed along the edges with a geometric design in gold. Every place had a crystal water flask and matching glass, plus a red leather folder upon which each person's name appeared in gold lettering. There was also an inscribed gold pen. Of necessity, the lettering was tiny to fit in the words. Squinting, I made them out to be: "The Zellstein Turner Evenstar Home presents the *Swan Song for Luminaries* extravaganza."

Apart from Heidi, I already knew three others in the room. Emory Hastings had greeted me warmly at the door. His assistant, Glenys Clarkson, had the job of guiding each person to his or her appointed seat, taking the opportunity to say to me, "I do hope you don't mind, but Sir Rupert *insisted* he be placed next to you."

Sir Rupert Martindale, dapper in a dark suit and regimental tie, had made straight for me the moment he'd come through the paneled double doors. "You'll be delighted to know I've arranged for us to sit together," he'd announced.

"I didn't know you were on the committee, Sir Rupert."

"One does one's duty, don't you know? Besides, perhaps it's a touch of immoderate pride on my part, but I do believe that when potential benefactors realize it is not some unknown lackey, but Sir Rupert Martindale himself soliciting their financial assistance, their wallets will open so much wider."

Once we were seated, he'd scanned the room, frowning. "I was rather hoping Ariana Creeling might put in an appearance. I understood from Hastings she was to be asked to join the committee. Damn shame if she's reneging, after all Evenstar has done for her.

I'd muttered something about it being too soon after Natalie's death. Sir Rupert had raised his snowy eyebrows. "No excuse, I say. Face up to things. Stiff upper lip and all that. As the Bard said—"

I was not to learn which quotation from Shakespeare Sir Rupert had selected, because at this point Heidi called the meeting to order.

Frowning, she eyed two vacant chairs. "Unfortunately not everyone values punctuality. We'll proceed with the meeting. First, a warm welcome from the committee to Emory Hastings, Evenstar's inestimable administrator. We are so very fortunate to have a man of Emory's caliber at the helm."

He was seated directly to her right, and she paused to incline her head in his direction—the absolute perfection of her blond hair had convinced me it had to be a wig—and to bestow on him a smile so incandescent that it sizzled.

Emory seemed uncomfortable, running a hand over his thick, black hair and murmuring a low-key thanks.

With a more moderate smile, she continued, "And next to Emory is someone without whom Evenstar would literally grind to a halt—Vincent Yarborough, our invaluable accountant. Vince will be handling all the paperwork associated with the pledges you wonderful people will be soliciting from our donors."

Vincent Yarborough half-rose from his seat and ducked his head in acknowledgement. He was a neat, balding man wearing a gray suit and subdued tie. His most prominent feature was his nose, which was long and narrow until it suddenly splayed out widely at the nostrils.

Heidi's smile faded as she added perfunctorily, "And Glenys Clarkson, administrative assistant, is welcome too."

"I'll second that!" A grossly overweight man with a gray crew cut, who was sitting on the other side of the table, applauded enthusiastically, then, embarrassed to find himself the only one clapping, stopped. His many chins continued to tremble.

Sir Rupert leaned over to say to me, "Would you believe Frank Franklin was a Tarzan back in the forties? Body of a young god. Rumor has it he ate his way out of the role." He went on in a stage whisper, " 'O! that this too too solid flesh would melt.' "

"Fair go," I said, hoping the bloke hadn't heard him.

"*Hamlet*, Act One," Sir Rupert advised me.

"Sir Rupert, if you don't mind…" Heidi didn't wait to see if he minded or not, continuing in ringing tones, "As you've no doubt discovered, each one of you has a personalized folder. This contains an outline of your duties and responsibilities, a brief history of The Clarice Turner Evenstar Home, details of past *Swan Song of the Luminaries*, and, finally, a list of targeted individuals and corporations you will be approaching to solicit funds for our extravaganza. Those of you who are new to the committee will be paired with a more experienced member to facilitate the process."

Emory broke in to say, "The target names are the fruit of many hours of labor by my very able assistant, Glenys, plus other members of staff, including Nancy, our outstandingly efficient receptionist." He rose to his feet. "Let us show our appreciation."

I noticed Franklin, the ex-Tarzan, waited for everyone else to start clapping before he joined in.

Heidi, apparently irked to be upstaged, pounded with her gavel until silence fell. "I'm going to ask each of you to introduce yourselves." She put up a hand. "I fully realize that many of us are so famous we are instantly recognizable, but for those who are new to our little group"—she paused to beam at me—"it will be of great help. Oona? Let's start with you."

I looked down to the end of the table to have a gander at the Evenstar founder's granddaughter. She bore a striking resemblance to the woman depicted in Clarice Turner's portrait outside Emory Hasting's office, having the same squat figure, hard eyes, and steel-trap mouth. She wore a dark gray, shapeless dress. Around her neck were many strands of pearls. Stone the crows! If they were genuine, she was wearing a fortune.

"Oona Turner," she said in a gravel voice. "Clarice Turner, the visionary who founded Evenstar, was my grandmother. That's all anyone needs to know."

"Perhaps you could add some personal details?" Heidi prompted.

"No. I don't do details."

"Thank you, Oona. Nancy?"

"Nancy McDuff. I take all calls coming into Evenstar Home during business hours. Heidi has invited me to sit in on your first meeting because as fund-raisers, you may need to use me as a resource for contact numbers and addresses."

So this was the three-times-wed, ballroom-dancing receptionist, who was a dedicated boxing fan. She looked disappointingly average, a middle-aged woman with reddish brown hair, a well-cared-for body and a sweet, helpful expression.

I couldn't visualize her ringside at a boxing match shrieking for blood. Maybe someone had been pulling Melodie's leg.

The introductions went on. There was a sprinkling of ordinary citizens. I'd say some of them had volunteered to help a worthy cause, but I was guessing most were there because of the opportunity to rub shoulders with celebrities.

One stocky woman with stringy, fair hair had certainly joined the committee for that reason, because when she introduced herself she stood and held up her autograph book. "Carrie Wentworth here," she wheezed, pink in the face. "I get asthma when I'm excited, and I can't think of anything *more* exciting than being in the same room as so many wonderful, wonderful stars. I'm hoping everyone will sign my autograph book, so if I can just pass it around the table—"

"You may not," snapped Heidi. "You can collect autographs at the reception after the meeting."

Chastened, Carrie sat down.

I noticed Sir Rupert was industriously doodling. When I surreptitiously checked what he was doing, I found he had written his own name several times and was busy embellishing each attempt with elaborate swirls and flourishes.

"Kylie?" said Heidi. It was my turn.

"G'day, everyone. Kylie Kendall's the name. I'm an Aussie who hasn't any talent myself, but I admire anyone who does. That's why I volunteered for the committee."

Sir Rupert was next. He leapt to his feet. "It may be that I need no introduction, but—"

"I don't believe you do," said Heidi, interrupting. "Does everybody here know Sir Rupert Martindale? Yes? There you are, Sir Rupert, you may consider yourself introduced."

He flung himself back into his seat. "She's held a grudge against me for decades," he whispered to me as he glared at Heidi. "She didn't take it well when I rejected her advances while we were on the movie set of the musical version of *Titus Andronicus*—horrendous bastardization of Shakespeare, but it paid well. Understandable, I suppose, that Heidi was upset when I turned her down, as certainly I would have been a wonderful feather in her cap. Pitiful, isn't it, that she's still pursuing the unattainable after all these years."

"Blimey, she's still after you?"

"I sense that she is. Pray you're never the object of her desire. Heidi never gives up."

Across the table a thin, intense man had caught my attention earlier because he was so restless. He was constantly moving in his seat, checking his pockets, fiddling with his folder and pen, and taking sips of water. I wondered how long it would be before someone sitting close to him snarled, "Stay still, will you!"

When it was his turn to introduce himself, he said in a strained whisper, "Wendell Yalty. You won't know me, but all the world knows my mother, Quintina Ladd—"

He broke off as his eyes filled with tears. "Excuse me." He blew his nose, gulped, then continued, "My mother, Quintina Ladd, radiant star of Hollywood musicals and comedies in the forties and fifties, with a voice like an angel and a dancing ability that surpassed description…"

He trailed off with a muted sob. Sir Rupert advised loudly, "Get a grip, old boy. Quintina high-kicked her way to Hollywood Forever Cemetery years ago."

Wendell Yalty shot him a furious look. "Her passing is nothing less than an abiding tragedy for the world of entertainment. We shall not see her like again."

"Quintina was one of a kind," Sir Rupert conceded.

Addressing the whole table, Wendell continued, "Surely I don't need to remind you that my mother's appearances in previous *Swan Songs* set a standard so high no one has ever been able to come close to matching it."

He switched his attention to Heidi, who had her gavel poised. "Therefore, Madam Chairwoman, I am formally requesting the name of the Evenstar extravaganza be changed to *Quintina Ladd's Swan Song for the Luminaries.*"

"Like that's going to happen," somebody muttered.

"So very, very sorry to be late!" a feminine voice rang out. "Unavoidable, naturally."

All eyes turned to the meeting room's double doors, which had been flung open. Posed there was an attractive duo, Cory Grainger, looking like a cross between a mature Cary Grant and Errol Flynn, accompanied by a petite woman with flowing dark hair and a pale, oval face. She wore a tight scarlet dress which displayed to perfection her remarkable hourglass figure.

Sir Rupert sniffed, "Vanessa always did know how to make a grand entrance."

"Vanessa Banning?"

"Who else? Can you tell her present husband is a Beverly Hills plastic surgeon? Face slick as glass. And that body? Extensive liposuction."

Followed by Cory, Vanessa advanced to the table. "Do forgive us, dahlings," she said soulfully.

From Heidi Brandstett's irate expression, forgiveness appeared to be not an option. "Is it too much to expect punctuality?" she ground out.

"Heidi, sweetie, so sorry for the inconvenience. I beg you, don't bother repeating a single word. Cory and I will concentrate hard and catch up. Are these our seats? Please, pay no attention to us. We'll be as quiet as little mice, won't we, Cory?"

"How fitting that you compare yourself to a rodent," Heidi observed icily.

"Cat-fight alert," someone said.

Emory Hastings stepped into the breach. "Madam Chair," he said, rising, "I believe we should move on to consider the most important issue facing the meeting, namely the necessity of raising sufficient funds to cover the ever-rising expenses of producing *Swan Song of the Luminaries*."

While additional papers were being distributed, I said to Sir Rupert, "Cory Grainger gave me the impression he's only interested in younger women, but Vanessa Banning has got to be about his age."

Sir Rupert snorted a laugh. "My dear gel, they're not involved romantically. Cory and Vanessa are brother and sister. Even for a cad like Grainger, dating Vanessa is out of the question."

While I was trying to discern if there was any facial resemblance between Cory and Vanessa—I couldn't see any, but that could be the plastic surgery—Sir Rupert revealed the reason he'd insisted on sitting beside me.

Out of the blue he declared, "Ariana Creeling's a damned fine looking woman. Damned fine! Any man would be proud to have her on his arm. I don't mind telling you, she's gained many admirers here at Evenstar. I count myself among their number."

"Hmmm," I said, not sure how to respond to this revelation.

Sir Rupert leaned forward confidingly. "I've been respecting Ariana's grief at losing her friend, don't you know, but time is a-wasting." He clapped his hand to his heart. "As Andrew Marvell wrote, 'But at my back I always hear Time's winged chariot hurrying near.'"

"Hmmm," I said again.

"Ariana has to pick herself up and face life again, and I'm delighted to be of assistance. As I have, understandably, special skills in the area of written communication, I'm making my initial approach via letter."

He fossicked around in his jacket pocket and came up with a heavy cream envelope. "If Ariana had been present tonight, I would have taken the opportunity to give this to her personally." He passed me the envelope. "As it is, fate has made you my courier. If you wouldn't mind putting this missive in her hand, I'd be most grateful."

"I don't think—"

"I'm begging you for this favor. Throwing myself on your mercy, as it were."

Strewth! I'd be delivering what probably amounted to a love letter from Sir Rupert to the woman I loved, who didn't love me. Wouldn't it rot your socks?

CHAPTER EIGHT

At the conclusion of the meeting we were all ushered into an adjoining room, where refreshments were to be served. Evenstar certainly knew how to put on a spread. Two long tables were loaded with various cold meats and salads as well as delicious-looking desserts. Apart from wine, there were fruit juices and, of course, coffee. As I expected, there was no chance of a decent cup of tea. All that was provided was a selection of yucky flavored teabags.

People descended on the food like a plague of starving locusts. I was rather peckish myself, having been too down in the mouth after my conversation with Ariana to have any appetite earlier. When I could get through the crush to the food, I made a selection, then looked for somewhere to sit.

Emory Hastings beckoned to me from a nearby table, where he was seated with one other. "Oona is eager to meet you," he said. I reckoned this was because she was the only person at Evenstar, except for Emory himself, to know the real reason I was on the committee.

"G'day, Ms Turner."

Oona Turner, whose jaws were moving rhythmically as she chomped her way through the contents of a heavily laden plate, gave what I took to be a welcoming grunt.

Emory rose to pull out a chair for me. "Kylie's a new member of our committee, as you know."

Another grunt. Crikey, this sheila was a real charmer. No doubt this was why Emory didn't sit down again. "I must circulate," he said, "so I'll leave you two ladies to get acquainted."

Left alone with Oona, I gave her the once-over. In looks she clearly took after her grandmother, and genetics hadn't been kind. If at a distance she wasn't attractive, in close-up she was fair dinkum repulsive. The luster of the many strings of pearls around her thick neck contrasted with the grayish caste of her skin. With her thickset body and mean expression she reminded me of an Aussie cane toad, ugly, ungainly, and malevolent.

There was silence at the table apart from the sound of Oona chewing with her mouth open. If she'd been there, my mum would have been appalled. She always maintained that table manners showed a person's true personality. Oona was falling far short of Mum's standards.

Sharing a table with Oona has meant I'd lost any desire to eat; however, I gestured towards her plate and said, "Beaut tucker," by way of making conversation.

She swallowed a mouthful, took a large swig from her wine glass, then announced, "Enormously costly. I've told that SOB countless times we don't need to provide catering at this level at functions like this, but of course Emory always goes his own sweet way."

She stabbed a chunk of chicken with her fork and held it out for me to examine. "Breast," she said. "White meat. The most expensive. No reason to pamper people." After casting a contemptuous Zellstein around the room, she added, "Freeloaders, all of them."

I reflected that cane toads were poisonous, which made it even more appropriate that Oona Turner resembled the creature. "I believe the committee raises a lot of money," I said mildly.

"A drop in the bucket. Do you have the faintest idea how much it costs each month to run Evenstar Home, let alone the astronomical sum to cover a year?"

I confessed I didn't.

She leaned towards me. "And some bastard's siphoning off thousands," she hissed. "As I said to Ariana Creeling, your company is being paid good money to find out who that person is." She stabbed a sausage finger at my face. "I want fast results. Fast. You got that?"

"Got it," I said.

Apparently that was to be the end of our conversation, because Oona's full attention returned to the contents of her plate. Fortunately she soon polished off the food in front of her. When she lumbered to her feet to go in search of dessert, I made my escape.

Getting to know these people was an integral part of my undercover assignment, so I looked around for targets. Some people were sitting at tables scattered around the room, others were standing in small groups chatting. Nearby Nancy McDuff was in animated conversation with Glenys Clarkson. Nancy was definitely on my mental list, so I grabbed a glass of wine to look convivial and drifted up to them.

"The tango," Nancy was saying, "is so *very* sexual. Unbelievably stimulating. Barry's like an animal afterwards."

Glenys gave an unhappy sigh. "You can't know how much I wish my Dave was like that. The spark in our marriage has gone out, if you know what I mean."

"Introduce Dave to the tango, Glenys," Nancy advised. "I tell you, it's better than Viagra any day. Get him tangoing and you'll score more action than you know what to do with." She cast a reflective Zellstein at Glenys' rather plump form. "And I guarantee you'll drop a few pounds."

"Hello, Kylie," said Glenys, blushing a little when she realized I'd overheard their conversation, "have you met Nancy McDuff, Evenstar's irreplaceable receptionist?"

Face to face, Nancy gave a much more lively, mischievous impression than the one I'd got during the meeting.

"G'day, Nancy. Pleased to meet you."

She shook my hand with a firm grip, saying with a grin, "Just love that Aussie accent."

"I like your accent too."

Puzzled, Nancy said, "But I don't have one."

"You do. American."

Emory came striding up to us with the manner of one bearing urgent information. He was wearing a dark suit that must have cost an arm and a leg. I wondered what sort of salary someone in his position earned. If he had expensive tastes, perhaps Emory himself might be tempted to help himself to easily available money. After all, he was the administrator, so although I imagined the accountant covered the day-to-day expenses, everything to do with large financial outlays would go through Emory's office.

"Excuse me, Kylie," he said. "Sorry to break up your conversation, but Vincent has some important procedural issues we need to clear up immediately. Glenys, Nancy? Come with me."

Emory set off at a rapid pace with Glenys and Nancy hurrying to keep up. I jumped when a voice behind me said, "Officious little squirt, isn't he? Everything's urgent this and urgent that, just to make him seem important."

I turned around to find the speaker was the fat bloke Sir Rupert claimed had once played Tarzan in a movie.

"Frank Franklin," said the purported ex-Tarzan. I hadn't realized when he was sitting at the table during the meeting how tall he was. He towered over me, a huge mass of flesh supported by a normal-sized skeleton. I looked at his spherical body and tried to visualize a muscular Tarzan concealed somewhere inside him, but my imagination wasn't up to it.

"G'day, Frank. I'm Kylie."

"I saw you talking with Glenys," Frank said, gazing longingly over to where she stood in close conversation with Vincent Yarborough, Emory and Nancy. "She's a wonderful person."

"She seems very nice," I said diplomatically.

"Nice?" he said, offended. "Then you don't know her. Glenys is so much more than *nice*."

"It's true I don't know her," I pointed out. "I met Glenys yesterday for the first time."

Embarrassed, he brushed his hand over his crew cut. "Sorry, I tend to be rather protective where she's concerned. For one thing, Hastings takes total advantage of Glenys. The guy would be completely lost without her professional skills, not that he's been willing to admit that. He doesn't appreciate her and never has."

He Zellsteind at me to see my reaction—I was wearing my sympathetic-interest face—then went on with rising anger, "Emory Hastings can be quite unreasonably demanding. A perfectionist who goes to ridiculous lengths. Many times Glenys has had to delay going home because Hastings has found fault with some task she's completed, only to find there's nothing wrong with it at all."

"So you're close friends, you and Glenys?"

Frank shifted uneasily from one foot to the other. I had a disconcerting image of his joints compressing from the crushing pressure all this weight would have on his knees and feet.

"Not very close," he admitted. "At least, not yet. But we *are* friends. I don't know Glenys as well as I'd like to in the future."

"She mentioned a Dave. Is that her husband?" I asked, all innocence.

Frank Franklin's chubby face flushed. "That deadbeat," he said between clenched teeth. "Why she sticks with him I'll never know."

Over the other side of the room, Sir Rupert had joined Vincent Yarborough, Emory, Glenys, and Nancy. Observing this, Frank said scornfully, "That washed-up little English creep thinks he's God's gift to women. You were sitting next to him during the meeting. Did he make a pass at you?"

"Not that I noticed."

"Oh, you'd notice." Frank put an unpleasantly meaty hand on my shoulder. Drawing me closer, he dropped his voice to a murmur. "I heard on the grapevine there's an arrest for stalking in his past."

"Fair dinkum?" I said, astonished.

Frank frowned at me. "What'd you say?"

"Can it really be true Sir Rupert's a stalker?"

"He was never charged. Sweet-talked his way out of it."

* * *

Dumped by Frank Franklin the moment Glenys Clarkson left Emory's little group and headed for the door—he muttered something about seeing Glenys safely to her car—I continued my circuit of the room. I wasn't the only one in motion, as Carrie Wentworth, perspiring face set with determination and autograph book in hand, was trolling for prey.

When our paths crossed, she halted and peered at me closely. "You're not anyone, are you?" she wheezed.

"Nobody at all," I said cheerfully.

This aroused Carrie Wentworth's suspicions immediately. "I get it. You're one of those Australian actors, aren't you? Like Nicole Kidman or Cate Blanchett. What's your name, then?"

"Kylie Kendall, but I'm no one you'd know."

Not at all discouraged, she said, "I've definitely seen you somewhere."

I spread my hands. "Beats me."

She squinted at my face. "I've got it! You're one of those new talents, waiting to be discovered. Am I right?"

"You couldn't be more wrong."

Carrie Wentworth was not to be denied. She shoved the autograph book and a pen at me. "And write your real name. Kylie Kendall sounds *so* false." When I didn't take the book immediately, she pushed it into my hand, declaring, "I'm not moving until you do."

"You've caught me out," I said. "I am pre-famous."

"I knew it!"

With a quick mental thank you to my English teacher, Ms Banks, who believed a good vocabulary was essential for success in the world, I carefully wrote: "For indubitably prescient Carrie Wentworth, with felicitous wishes always, Melodie Davenport."

She read my words, then shoved the book back under my nose. Stabbing a forefinger at "indubitably prescient" she said, "And what the hell does *that* mean?"

"Simply that there can be no doubt you are perceptive, and see things others don't."

"Well, that's all right, then." I could tell she wasn't wholly convinced, however she snapped her autograph book shut, gave me a long, doubtful look, then stalked off in search of more reliable quarry.

I had quarry myself: Vincent Yarborough, Evenstar's accountant, whose job would give him a better opportunity than anyone else to indulge in a spot of embezzlement.

Emory had disappeared, along with Glenys, but Nancy McDuff was still talking with Yarborough. I had set off in their direction when I was brought to a halt by a hand gripping my arm.

An alarming, husky voice purred in my ear, "Kylie, where've you been hiding yourself?"

"G'day, Ms Brandstett."

"*Heidi*, please!"

"G'day, Heidi."

She looked up at me with a slow, meaningful smile. "How about coming to my room for a nightcap?"

Yerks! Feeling like an actor in a bad forties movie, I dredged up what I hoped would be appropriate dialogue. "Thanks so much for the invite. Normally I'd like nothing better, but tonight I'm afraid I'll have to take a rain check."

Heidi batted her abundant eyelashes. "I can promise you it will be more than worth your while," she breathed. "Never-dreamed-of experiences await you. I won't take no for an answer."

Hell's bells! I was trying to think of how to discourage her when my salvation swanned by on the arm of her brother, Cory Grainger.

Remembering Bob's advice, I called out, "Vanessa Banning! For so long I've been such a keen fan of yours! I never dared to think I'd ever meet you in person."

Vanessa, gratified, changed course to head our way. Beside me, Heidi made a sound of deep disgust. "You're a fan of that no-talent bitch? Tell me it isn't so."

"Why, yes," I said, being careless with the truth, "for as long as I can remember I've idolized Vanessa Banning."

Saved! Heidi Brandstett muttered something under her breath, turned on her heel, and left me standing there.

* * *

After devoting fifteen minutes to telling Vanessa Banning and Cory Grainger what a wonderful actress Vanessa was—a bit of a challenge since I couldn't remember a single movie I'd ever seen her in—I managed to extricate myself and make my way over to Vincent Yarborough, who was now alone, Nancy having disappeared.

Plate in hand, he was eyeing the poor pickings that remained of the spread. "Not much left," I said.

He nodded slowly, while regarding me thoughtfully. He looked like an accountant, conservatively dressed in a dark gray suit, white shirt, and carefully knotted, bland tie. He was balding, and had a smooth, even-featured face. His thick rimless glasses magnified his slate gray eyes.

When he spoke, his voice was as mild as the rest of him. "Miss Kendall, isn't it?"

"I'd rather be called Kylie."

His sudden smile lit up his face. "Then you must call me Vince."

"Right-oh, Vince it is."

Vince and I were good mates in no time. He wasn't like my picture of a boring accountant at all, having a ripper sense of humor and scads of funny stories about Evenstar and celebrities in general, so it was with surprise I noticed that we were almost the last people in the room.

"Beaut time talking with you, Vince," I said, "but it's getting late, so I'll be off."

"I'll walk you to your car."

I was delighted he'd made the offer, because otherwise I would have had to locate a member of Evenstar's security staff to escort me. This afternoon Lonnie had declared my vehicle clear of any global positioning devices, but of course I could have been followed when I left the office.

The landscaped parking area was nearly empty and not well-lit, so Vince Yarborough was a comforting presence. "This is mine," I said, stopping beside my sedate Toyota sedan, not my favorite ride, the red classic Mustang my father had left me.

Vince looked past me to the corner of the lot. "Oh, dear," he said.

Beside a car two people were passionately embracing. "Oh, dear," said Vince again.

There was an urgent exclamation, then they broke apart. The woman got into the car and slammed the door, the momentary flash of the interior light revealing her to be Nancy McDuff. The man had melted away into the shadows. I've always had excellent night vision. I couldn't absolutely swear to it, but would almost bet my boots it had been Emory Hastings locked in a clinch with Nancy McDuff.

* * *

Being sociable for that many hours was exhausting. When I got back home the last thing I wanted to do was to talk to anyone, but I had to check that Mum was okay, so I made myself a pot of tea, gave Julia Roberts her chicken treats, then punched in the sequence of numbers that would connect me to the pub half a world away.

I got Jack, my mums fiancé. "Kylie? Can't talk. It's pandemonium here. Hold on, I'll get her for you."

When Mum came on the line she sounded het up. "Look, darl', the Wombat's full to bursting. I'm flat out like a lizard drinking, so I can only spare a mo'."

"I was a bit worried because I hadn't heard from you for a while."

"For good reason, darl'. I've got tourists coming out of the woodwork."

"That's good, isn't it?"

"Demanding tourists. Yanks, mainly. Don't get me wrong, I get on with them like a house on fire, and they're big tippers, but it's a challenge keeping them happy, I can tell you. We've even got a bunch calling themselves the Platypus Posse who insist they've come to see platypuses in the wild. Uncle Ernie's taking them on an expedition to Dead Man's Creek, but you know how shy a platypus can be, so it's a toss-up whether they'll see one or not. It's just another headache, and of course it's all your fault, Kylie."

"My fault? How's it my fault?"

"You know the Wombat website you set up before you left for the big smoke? It was good publicity to begin with, but now it's too bloody successful. Some American travel group got wind of it, and put us on their schedule of tours to discover the real Australia. We've got Yanks coming out our ears and even Jack, who's the second-laziest bloke in Oz, is so busy he doesn't have time to scratch himself."

"Look on the bright side," I said. "This has to be good for your bottom line."

"There's no bright side unless you come home," said my mother grimly. "I need you, Kylie. The books are a mess, Jack's worse than useless, and every bed's booked solid for months. Your place is here, my girl, helping me run the Wombat, not gadding about LA getting into God knows what trouble."

I had a ludicrous vision of Mum using my cousin to hire a shady character to frighten me into coming home. It was disloyal of me to even think my mother would consider such a thing, but I heard myself ask, "Have you spoken to Bruce lately?"

"Nephew Brucie? No. And don't try to change the subject. Now, as I was saying, your place is here, in Wollegudgerie, where you'll be safe from car jackings, freeway shootings, and God knows what else."

"Mum, I—"

"And don't tell me you haven't risked life and limb, trying to be a private eye. I know better."

"Mum—"

"I've said my piece. Now I want you to sit down and have a long, hard think about where you should be and what you should be doing. Is that too much to ask?"

When I didn't reply immediately, she said, "Well, is it?"

"It's not too much to ask, but—"

"Good!" said Mum, suddenly cheerful. "Well, that's settled. Gotta go, love. Talk with you in a few days."

I put down the receiver with a sigh. "Great galloping goannas," I said to Julia Roberts, "Heidi Brandstett's not the only one who won't take no for an answer."

CHAPTER NINE

I woke up early on Friday morning with the feeling something was horribly wrong. Then I remembered with a flood of misery that I was facing my first full day no longer Ariana's lover, but simply her good friend.

"I've just got to tough it out," I said to Julia Roberts, who'd slept on the end of my bed. "Would that be your advice?"

Jules, well into her morning ablutions, made quite a disgusting sucking noise while grooming the fur on her stomach.

"You're ignoring me? My heart's breaking here, Jules."

Ridiculously, as I said this my eyes filled with tears. Julia Roberts stopped washing and gave me a look that seemed to blend concern with a touch of surprise.

"You're absolutely right," I said to her. "I'm falling to pieces. It's total self-indulgence to sob before breakfast."

Although I'd showered last night, I had another long, hot one to cry in earnest, before I pulled myself together and faced the day. Julia Roberts waited impatiently as I dressed. She liked her breakfast early, and often. She'd been known to fake starvation so effectively that at times she'd scored multiple breakfasts from unsuspecting people coming into the kitchen to find her emitting pitiable meows.

I'd provided salmon pieces for Julia Roberts, and started on my own porridge and tea, when Lonnie came shuffling through the kitchen door. He usually arrived in the office early, almost always clutching something in a paper bag from a fast-food restaurant. Today he was empty-handed.

"G'day," I said.

"There's nothing good about it," he declared mournfully. "I barely made it here—couldn't even chance a drive-through breakfast."

"Trouble with your car?"

"Stalled three times. Damn thing just managed to get me to work, then it died out there in the parking lot. Can't even get the engine to turn over."

"Flat battery?"

"Name any part of the blasted thing—whatever it is, it's failing." Flinging himself on a kitchen stool, he gusted a sigh. "Is there anything to eat around here?"

"I could make you porridge."

"Aaugh!"

"Perhaps not, then."

"This is the beginning of a perfect day," Lonnie said bitterly. "Pauline's out of my life, my car's expired, and there's nothing for breakfast."

"I've got plenty of bread. How about toast and honey?"

"I suppose."

As he listlessly plunked slices in the toaster, he said, "Are you going tonight?"

"To Melodie's? I thought I might put in an appearance."

"Me, too. Take my mind off things. No sense in brooding alone at home." He looked up as Fran came into the kitchen holding a clipboard. "Morning, Fran."

"What does 'cataclysm' mean to you?" she asked, pen poised to write his response.

"I dunno. Something bad happening?"

"How about 'imminent cataclysm'?"

"Something bad happening sometime soon?"

Fran clicked her tongue. "Dammit! Quip could be right. He said the title of my book might not get through to the typical ordinary person."

"Watch out who you're calling ordinary," said Lonnie with the first sign of spirit I'd seen for days.

"Are you going to ask me what 'imminent cataclysm' means?" I inquired.

Fran shook her head. "I know you'd know."

"Crikey," I said, "is that a compliment?"

She shrugged. "If you want to take it that way." Switching her attention back to Lonnie, she asked, "What does 'catastrophe' mean to you?"

Lonnie mused for a moment. "I dunno," he said with a ghost of a grin. "Something bad happening?"

"This is not a joke," Fran snapped. "My book will save incalculable numbers from agonizing pain and death."

"It has to be published first," Lonnie observed.

"Not a problem. Quip's New York literary agent is working on it."

Lonnie opened his mouth to say something further, but Fran waved him to silence. "Okay," she said, referring to her clipboard, "what do you think of this for my new title: *Looming Catastrophe: Save yourself and your loved ones from dreadful suffering?*"

"I rather liked the lingering death of your first version," I remarked.

"Lingering death is excellent," said Lonnie, "but I'd lose the 'catastrophe.'" He thumped his chest. "'Cataclysm' gets me right here. 'Catastrophe'? Frankly, I could take it or leave it."

Fran gave him a look of deep suspicion, obviously thinking he was sending her up. Before she could voice this, Lonnie went on, "You need an entirely new approach, Fran. Something short and snappy. I'm suggesting *Fran's Disaster Almanac.*"

"That's utterly ridiculous," she snarled.

Lonnie put a hand to his forehead and tugged at the lock of hair that always fell over one eye. "Wait," he said, "a new title is bubbling up from my unconscious. Yes! It's here." He flung his arms wide. *"Fran's Plans: Buy this or die!* Not gruesome enough? Then how about *Buy—or Die Screaming in Agony?* No? Then how about…"

* * *

"Tell me again why Fran beat Lonnie over the head with a clipboard," Bob said between guffaws.

Ariana came into my office as he was wiping his eyes. "Did you hear about the scene in the kitchen this morning?" he asked her.

"Fran gave me her version." Her tone made it clear she didn't intend to discuss it further.

Taking his cue from her, Bob immediately sobered. "Let's have your Evenstar report then, Kylie."

Before I'd gone to sleep last night I'd jotted down brief notes and later today I'd expand them into a detailed written report. What was required now was an outline of the evening, with emphasis on anything that struck me as important. I started with the committee meeting, and when I mentioned how Sir Rupert had insisted on sitting with me, Ariana grimaced.

"I got the letter from Sir Rupert you left on my desk, Kylie." With a sardonic smile she added, "It appears he sees himself as my suitor. There was much quoting of lines from *Romeo and Juliet,* plus a love sonnet or two."

Bob was amused. "You've got to be flattered, Ariana. It's not everyone who has a knight in hot pursuit."

His smile vanished when I said, "That might not be such a good idea. Last night one of the residents, Frank Franklin, told me that Sir Rupert had an arrest for stalking in his past. Lonnie's checking it out."

"Be careful," Bob said to Ariana. "Even a geriatric stalker can be dangerous."

She gave the slightest shrug. "I don't imagine I'm in any danger from Sir Rupert. I'll gently discourage him. Without the opportunity for high drama, he'll lose interest in me."

Bob still looked troubled. "You're taking Kylie's stalker seriously, so why not this guy?"

"He's a joke, that's why?"

"Nevertheless," said Bob, "I think you should keep an eye out for anything unusual. How many times have we advised clients to treat a stalker as a genuine threat? You know very well what obsessive personalities are capable of when they're fixated on someone."

Ariana put up her hands. "Enough, already. I'll be careful, all right? Now let's get back to Kylie's report."

From Bob's expression he was as surprised by Ariana's edgy, impatient tone as I was. In the office she always displayed a cool, unruffled composure.

I started off again, describing the meeting and then the reception afterwards. Ariana nodded when I explained how Oona Turner had demanded fast results.

"Oona called me first thing this morning to complain about your attitude," she said with a faint smile.

"What attitude might that be?" I asked, indignant. "I was very respectful to the woman, which is more than she was to me."

"She didn't feel you were treating your assignment with the appropriate gravity. Oona said you seemed to be enjoying yourself chatting with different people."

"Fair crack of the whip," I said, "that's what I'm supposed to be doing, getting to know everyone."

"I made that clear."

"From all I hear," said Bob, "Oona Turner is a piece of work."

"Noxious," I said, "like a cane toad."

Bob wanted to know all about cane toads, but Ariana was irritated by the digression. "Let's keep to the point, shall we?"

I went through the events of the evening, thanking Bob for his advice for dealing with Heidi Brandstett. I knew Ariana so well that I noticed the subtle change in her expression at this mention of Heidi's name.

"What?" I said. "What about Heidi Brandstett?"

She looked taken aback, then she smiled. "An A for observation, Kylie."

"What about her?" Bob asked.

"Let's just say Sir Rupert isn't the only Evenstar suitor I have."

"You're a regular femme fatale," said Bob, chuckling.

Anger flickered across Ariana's pale face. "I visited Natalie at Evenstar for years, so naturally I got to know people, but I never indicated the slightest romantic interest in anyone."

"The lure of the unattainable," said Bob. "That's your problem, Ariana. You're a blue-eyed, blond ice princess. That makes you irresistible."

This was too close to home for me. I felt my throat tighten. Stone the crows! Any minute now I'd be snuffling. Somehow I had to get everyone onto another subject fast.

"It's on the cards that Emory Hastings and Nancy McDuff are having an affair," I said.

"You're kidding," said Bob. "He's married to the delectable Zelda Webber."

I explained what Vince Yarborough and I had seen in the parking area.

"Did he make a comment?" Ariana asked.

"Vince just said, 'Oh, dear' a couple of times. He seemed so uncomfortable about it, I thought it best to pretend I hadn't seen a thing."

* * *

At the end of the meeting I'd mentioned to Bob that someone had been talking about the Hollywood Forever Cemetery. Bob was immediately superenthusiastic, and promised to take me there one day soon. "You'll love it! Tinseltown's hallowed ground!"

He'd reeled off the names of some of the luminaries buried there: Jayne Mansfield, Rudolph Valentino, Cecil B. DeMille, Fay Wray of *King Kong* fame, mobster Bugsy Siegel…And, of course, Quintina Ladd, Wendell Yalty's famous mother.

Before Bob left my office he insisted on punching up the web-site of a Hollywood Forever historic cemetery tour. I was dutifully scrolling through this when Lonnie knocked on my door.

"I tried to trace the source of your stalker's e-mail again, but still got nowhere. What I do have is some of the info you wanted on the Evenstar staff and residents. Also, I have a favor to ask."

"What's the favor?"

"I've given up on that heap of junk out there, but I've got to have transport, so a friend of mine is lending me his motorcycle. It's a Harley."

The thought of Lonnie on two wheels was quite a daunting one—he was erratic enough on four. "You know how to ride a motorbike?"

"It's a motorcycle. Motorbikes are for wimps. And of course I can ride one—I was a regular Hell's Angel when I was young."

Somehow I doubted that. "So what's the favor?"

"Steve's going to drop the cycle off this evening, but he can't make it until after nine, so I was wondering if you'd mind if I came with you to Melodie's party. By the time we get back here, it'll be waiting for me."

"Right-oh?"

"And as a bonus, I'll be your own personal bodyguard. If your stalker shows his ugly face, I'll beat him up for you."

The thought of Lonnie beating anybody up was hilarious. "Don't you get woozy at the sight of blood?" I said.

He dismissed this with a wave of his pudgy hand. "A mere detail. Now, let me give you what I've got so far on the Evenstar people."

Because of the embezzlement, he'd checked to see if he could find any change in financial patterns, including large debts paid off or transfer of substantial sums, but there had been nothing of note. This was not surprising, as the whole point of embezzling was to hide the money trail.

In general the Evenstar people seemed a law-abiding lot, though often keen on litigation in civil matters. Lonnie was disappointed to find very little in the way of serious legal problems, though he perked up when I asked about Sir Rupert.

"You were right about the old goat," he said. "Arrested twice in the States for stalking, but never charged. Got up to the same tricks in London some years ago. He managed to wriggle out of charges there, too. I've printed out details, but could only get photos of the local victims. Pity your stalker messages started well before you met Sir Rupert, otherwise he'd be a prime suspect."

We discussed Sir Rupert for a few minutes, then I scanned through the rest of the names Lonnie had checked out. Over the years Oona Turner had sued, or been sued herself in various disputes, mostly to do with her behavior in her up-market neighborhood, where she seemed constantly at war with anyone owning property adjacent to hers. "Neighbor from hell," Lonnie remarked.

Emory Hastings had one DUI conviction six years ago, but nothing since. In a civil matter, last year he'd sued a builder who'd done alterations to his Brentwood home, but the issue had been settled out of court for an undisclosed sum.

Wendell Yalty, Quintina Ladd's son, had been apprehended in Hollywood Forever Cemetery defacing graves situated near his mother's with a spray can of black paint. In court he maintained he was fully justified in removing the names of those unworthy to be near the sacred ground that held Quintina's earthly remains. He was given a suspended sentence with the condition he voluntarily enter a mental health program.

Vanessa Banning, using her real name of Edith Smythe, was in the process of suing a well-known Beverly Hills plastic surgeon, claiming he'd botched her nipple lift. The matter was still pending, though as Lonnie said, "She's gambling the doc will cave and settle before it goes to court, and she's right. No way can he afford the bad publicity."

"There's nothing on Vincent Yarborough?" I asked. "He looks like a cautious accountant, but who knows? Maybe he has gambling problems and has been making up his losses from Evenstar's accounts."

"I'm still checking on divorces, bankruptcies, and the like. I'll get back to you."

"Emory Hastings is married to Zelda Webber."

Lonnie smacked his lips. "She's *hot*."

"There's a chance their marriage is in trouble. Without making waves, can you see if there's anything out there about it?"

"Researching the luscious Zelda? It'll be a pleasure?"

* * *

I went to Ariana's office with the details of Sir Rupert's stalking activities in my hand. "Something you should know about Sir Rupert," I said.

Ariana put down her pen and leaned back in her chair. She looked detached, ascetic—as Bob had described her, an ice princess. I was aware of a brittle unhappiness beneath her controlled façade. I ached to offer comfort, but was afraid that if I tried to get too close, Ariana would push me away even further.

"Lonnie's printed out photos of the two women Sir Rupert was accused of stalking." I leaned over the desk to place them in front of her. "One is a local TV news anchor, the other a Newport Beach socialite. Perhaps you notice something about them?"

Ariana Zellsteind at the photos and then looked up at me. "Both blue-eyed blonds," she said dryly, "as I am. So?"

"There's no photo available, but Lonnie's found out the woman Sir Rupert stalked in London—she was a nanny, by the way—was Norwegian and blond. I reckon she probably had blue eyes too."

When she didn't say anything, I added, "Crikey, Ariana, it's as plain as the nose on your face. You fit Sir Rupert's specifications."

"What if I do?"

I felt a surge of impatience. "I wish you'd take this to heart. He's not just an old bloke with a harmless fixation. He trespassed, he spied on these women, he followed them everywhere. Sent letters and flowers and gifts. Made a perfect pest of himself—a dangerous pest."

"I don't see it," said Ariana. "If Sir Rupert's such a menace, why wasn't he charged and convicted in at least one case?"

"Lonnie thinks the victims were bought off, or frightened off, because not one was willing to be a witness against him?"

"I've already told you and Bob I'll be careful. I can't do any more than that."

"I'm worried—"

"Kylie, don't be. I can look after myself."

"Are you sure you're not underestimating Sir Rupert?"

With a trace of a smile, she said, "You don't give up, do you? The man's a nuisance more than anything else." She paused, as if deciding whether to say something or not.

"What is it?" I said. "Tell me."

"Recently there's been someone who concerns me much more—" Ariana broke off as her phone rang. "This'll be the Phoenix case. I've got to take this call."

"Before you do, you said someone concerns you. Who is it?" She waved me off. "I'll get back to you later."

I wanted to ask exactly when later, to pin her down, but Ariana was already deep in a discussion about the deposition she'd given on Wednesday.

It seemed I'd have to wait to know the answer, because the call from Phoenix turned out to be an urgent request for Ariana to go to Bob Hope Airport to meet the private jet of the lead attorney for the insurance fraud case for which she'd been deposed.

"Please make my apologies to Melodie," she said when she looked into my office on her way out. "Tell her something vital has come up, and there's no way I can make it tonight."

She hesitated, then went on, "And Kylie, I must apologize to you too. It was wrong of me to present you with an ultimatum about our relationship and then refuse to discuss it." Her expression softened. "Brunch, on Sunday? My place? We can talk then."

"That would be bonzer. Ariana, before you go, about that other person—"

"I'll tell you all about it on Sunday."

Then she was gone.

CHAPTER TEN

Melodie's apartment was in rather exclusive Brentwood, just off San Vicente Boulevard. I expected the street parking to be difficult, but it turned out to be horrendous. San Vicente was a constant river of lights. Horns blared, vehicles darted from one lane to another, ran the red, and held up traffic as drivers shoehorned into rare parking spots.

The Friday evening traffic was bad enough, but adding to my woes was the complete personality change that came over Lonnie once he was in a vehicle. In the office he was a generally mild-mannered Clark Kent sort—except when Julia Roberts kicked his allergies into high gear—but once on the road a belligerent Lonnie surfaced. If he was as aggressive as this when only a passenger, what would he be like when he was behind the wheel? I made a mental note never to find out.

"Go around again, but quicker this time," Lonnie commanded, as I completed the umpteenth circuit of the streets surrounding our destination.

I jumped as he suddenly shrieked, "Down there!" He pointed urgently through the windscreen. "*There!* Someone's pulling out!"

I accelerated, but not fast enough for Lonnie. "Floor it! Floor it! Don't let anyone beat us to the spot!"

"Lonnie, stop yelling in my ear."

Lonnie didn't hear me. "Oh, no," he cried out in despair, "that Jaguar's just seen it, and he's closer."

"The Jag's on the other side of road," I said, "so he'll have to chuck a Uey. I can get there first. Hang on."

It was a near thing, but I rocketed into the spot a few seconds before the Jag arrived. He gave us the finger and roared off. "How's that?" I said, pleased with myself.

"Not too bad," Lonnie conceded.

Melodie's apartment was on the third floor of the building. If we'd been home in Australia, it would have been on the second floor, because what Americans called the first floor, we called the ground floor, so the first floor was the next one up. While we waited for the lift I explained this all to Lonnie, who'd reverted to his usual easygoing self now that we were out of the car.

"Very interesting," he said, not meaning it.

The party was in full swing. People were spilling out into the hallway, drinks in hand. We made our way through the front door into a jammed living room furnished in what I always thought of as undistinguished apartment style, where everything was functional but characterless.

I looked around for familiar faces. Bob had said he'd be there and Fran was bringing Quip. I spotted Bob and waved to him, then said G'day to Tiffany, Hunter, Caulfield, and Bron— all friends of Melodie's I'd met before.

"Which one's the new roommate?" Lonnie asked me.

"Yolanda's the tall one over there wearing the starry outfit."

"Boy, she makes quite an impression."

Yolanda certainly stood out in the crowd. Tonight she'd chosen a long black dress liberally festooned with scintillating silver stars. Her abundant honey-blond curls were threaded with silver ribbons. I couldn't see from where I was, but I reckoned she'd be wearing silver sandals and have silver nail polish on her toes.

"Kylie! Lonnie!" Melodie came rushing up to us. I noticed Lonnie check out her cleavage. She was wearing a brief scarlet top, tight black pants, and her signature high, high heels.

I relayed Ariana's apology, which Melodie took in her stride, as her attention was all on the evening's high point. "You're just in time!" she exclaimed. "The minireadings are about to start in the mystic nook."

"Mystic nook?" said Lonnie with a puzzled frown. "What's that?"

Melodie indicated with a wave of her hand the far corner of the room. "It's a special place where the vibrations are in tune with the deeper rhythms of the cosmos." She added in a tone much more her own, "Like, Cassandra says it's real important to get a clear link."

Lonnie looked even more confused. "Who's Cassandra?"

"Cassandra's Yolanda's *professional* name," said Melodie with a touch of impatience. "She's Cassandra when she's in touch with the Other Side, and Yolanda when she isn't."

Seeing that Lonnie was poised to ask what the Other Side might be, she added hastily, "Kylie will explain it all to you. I've got to get things organized."

As she zipped off, I said to Lonnie, "Didn't Melodie mention that her new roommate was a psychic when she asked you to the party?"

"She could've, but I wasn't paying that much attention. Since Pauline split with me, I've had trouble concentrating. And being here with everyone having a good time…"

He trailed off into silence, looking so wretched that I put my arm around his slumping shoulders and gave him a half hug. "Cheer up."

"Easy for you to say."

No, it's not, I thought. I was fighting a constant battle to hide the nagging misery I felt over Ariana, although at least I had Sunday to look forward to, when something might be resolved.

My mum was the queen of the cliché and the platitude. Lonnie's tragic expression reminded me of one of her favorites: "Laugh, and the world laughs with you. Cry, and you cry alone."

While I was considering whether or not it would help to repeat this advice to him, Fran and Quip turned up. They made an arresting couple. Recently Quip had had his nose broken in a fight, and the slight misalignment made his handsome face seem more intriguing than before. And Fran was actually smiling. Because her customary expression was usually a negative one, it was easy to forget how attractive she could be.

The smile didn't last for long. Fran assessed Lonnie's defeated, heartbroken demeanor with one Zellstein. Her face darkened. "Get a grip, Lonnie. Pauline Feeney's a total bitch and you're better off without her. You know it's true."

"That's rather harsh, sweetheart," said Quip.

Lonnie drew himself to his full height, which wasn't very much, but was still more than Fran's. "I'm not better off without Pauline," he said with dignity. "I happen to love her, totally, absolutely."

Fran's lip was already curling in a sneer, when with the most fortunate timing, Melodie yelled, "People! People! It's time for the minireadings, so please gather around the mystic nook."

There was a general move in that direction. I followed close behind Lonnie, who was showing an unsuspected talent for worming his way through a crowd. For that reason we ended up in the front row, right next to the mystic nook and an arm's length from the mystic sheila herself, Cassandra Smith-Jones, Full-Service Psychic Medium, standing serenely with her hands clasped and her eyes closed. Glancing behind us, I saw that Fran and Quip were close by.

There was a loud hum of conversation. I wasn't the only one giving the nook the once-over. The area was partly enclosed by a tall black lacquer screen and a small black bookcase, which held several ancient-looking leather-bound books and a series of unidentifiable items, one looking disturbingly like a dagger. Inside these boundaries was set a smallish circular table covered by a black cloth long enough to touch the floor. Two plain black chairs were placed opposite each other at the table, which held a silver candlestick with an unlit black candle. In the very center was what seemed to be a dinky-di crystal ball on a silver stand. The smell of incense filled the air.

Taking her place beside Yolanda/Cassandra, who still had her eyes shut, Melodie energetically tinkled a small silver bell for attention. "Quiet please, everyone."

When silence finally fell—the people at the back were slow to obey, and I heard Bob's braying laugh before he was shushed—Melodie continued in a deeply significant tone, "Cassandra requires absolute silence to allow the full strength of her powers to be manifested in this mystic nook, a nook which this afternoon she ceremonially cleansed of all negativity, so that the psychic pathway is fully open to other dimensions."

I hid a smile. Melodie had learned her lines for this performance, and was delivering them with relish. I Zellsteind at Lonnie, thinking he'd be amused too, but he was staring at Cassandra fixedly with an odd expression on his face. Abruptly, he turned to me and whispered, "I've got the strangest feeling we've met before."

"It's quite likely—we do work in the same office."

Lonnie shook his head. "Not *you*, Kylie. *Cassandra*." He paused, then murmured, "It sounds weird, but I believe we've met in another life."

"Shhh!" Melodie was glaring at us.

Cassandra's heavy-lidded eyes popped open. "Welcome, everyone. You are about to enter a world extraordinary to many, but totally familiar to sensitives such as myself." She put up one hand in a languid movement. "A word about the minireadings this evening. Those of you who wish to participate will have a taste of a psychic experience at no cost as, although I will be using the resources of my crystal ball, I will not be entering the full trance state."

"Psychic lite," I said in an aside to Lonnie, but his whole attention was focused on Cassandra.

She went on, "Should you find, as I anticipate, your minireading is a revelation to you, then may I suggest you consider making an appointment for a full, professional interpretation of your past, present, and future lives at my consulting rooms in Westwood. And you may have friends and family who would wish to avail themselves of this opportunity for psychic guidance too. Please check with Melodie for a schedule of my availabilities and fees. I do offer a senior-citizen discount."

She signaled to Melodie, who hurried to light the candle on the nook's table. This accomplished, Melodie raised her voice to call out, "Dim the lights, Tiff."

Obligingly, Tiffany dimmed the lights. Cassandra took her place at the little table, the flickering candlelight making her face seem almost satanic. There was a murmur of anticipation from the crowd. Someone behind me said, "Any idea how much she charges for a full reading?"

"I've heard six hundred dollars for thirty minutes."

"You're kidding! Phyllis Bleaker's psychic only asks for three, but mostly does it by phone, so I guess it's not the same."

Melodie tinkled her silver bell. "Absolute quiet, please. Who will volunteer for the first minireading?"

"Me," said Lonnie, thrusting himself forward. "I'll take it."

In a moment he was seated opposite Cassandra, who stretched her hands across the table to take both of his. She closed her eyes. A minute passed. People moved restlessly and whispered to each other. Melodie, standing to one side, tinkled her bell for quiet. I felt a giggle coming on.

Suddenly, Cassandra opened her eyes wide. Gazing into Lonnie's, she said, "People around you don't understand you fully, or realize how very sensitive, how very perceptive you really are."

Lonnie looked embarrassed and pleased at the same time. "I suppose that could be true."

"It is true," Cassandra stated with certainty. "And in your life certain circumstances at times have held you back, so you've never attained your full, splendid potential."

He nodded. "I have felt that, yes."

Fran, who with Quip had wriggled through the crush to the front, murmured to me, "Who wouldn't agree with what she's saying? Lonnie's a fool if he thinks it's some psychic flash."

"You've got that right," I said. "Pretty well everyone thinks they're misunderstood and haven't yet reached their full potential."

"Full, *splendid* potential," corrected Quip, grinning.

"Shhh!" said Melodie.

Cassandra released Lonnie's hands. "Concentrate upon your life as it is at the moment," she instructed him.

"Oh, okay?"

She bent her head to stare into the crystal ball. "I sense you are in a potent love-hate relationship, one that has brought you both great joy and searing pain. Wait, I see initials forming." She leaned closer to the ball. "Is that a D? Does a D mean something to you? Has a D, perhaps, a profound emotional connection?"

"Ummm," said Lonnie, obviously trying to be helpful. "Not that I can think of at the moment."

Cassandra squinted into the crystal. "Wait!" A long pause, then she declared, "I was mistaken. It's not a D, it's a P. Yes, definitely a P."

"Creepy!" said Melodic. "She must mean Pauline Feeney."

Fran snorted derisively. "I don't believe it."

Lonnie obviously did. "How did you know about Pauline?" he asked, his tone close to awe.

Cassandra didn't answer. Her eyes rolled up and she slumped back in her chair with a low moan. Lonnie sat frozen. He was never at his best with anything to do with illness.

"She's fainted," someone called out. "Let me through. I know first aid."

"I'm a nurse," said someone else. "Let me handle it."

"Stop!" Melodic put up her hand. "Medical help is not necessary. Cassandra warned me this might happen. A trance state has suddenly come upon her. It means she's in contact with the Other Side."

Cassandra groaned and stirred. She did her abrupt eye-opening routine. "You!" she said, pointing a trembling finger at

Lonnie. "I knew you as Leonardo. You knew me as Yvette. There was a third person, Portia. We were together"—she paused for a dramatic moment—"in a former life."

CHAPTER ELEVEN

Lonnie, looking rather like a stunned mullet, gave up his position at the psychic nook to the next person eager to partake of cosmic truths, and came over to where I was standing with Fran, Quip having left to find Bob.

Obviously shaken, Lonnie said, "I've always thought reincarnation was a great idea, but I've never really believed in it. Now I'm not so sure."

"Be sure," said Fran. "It's a crock."

"Leonardo, Yvette, and Portia." Lonnie mused for a moment. "Maybe the Portia is really Pauline," he said with a hopeful smile. "I've heard that the same people turn up again and again in successive lives."

Fran, who held a grudge against Pauline Feeney because she felt Quip had been dissed by her in the past, muttered something uncomplimentary under her breath about how one life was one too many for Pauline.

Lonnie didn't notice. "Do you think the name Leonardo means in another life I was Italian?"

"Leonardo da Vinci, maybe?"

Lonnie ignored Fran's mockery. "Don't laugh," he said earnestly, "but during my reading I really felt as though the unknown and I were somehow connected."

"The unknown!" she snorted. "This supernatural stuff is absolute rubbish."

"I'm not saying there aren't frauds. That doesn't mean genuine psychic powers don't exist?"

"Trust me," said Fran, "they don't exist."

Lonnie turned to me. "What do you think, Kylie?"

The concept of a hidden, supernatural realm wasn't foreign to me. Because my mum was part Aboriginal, I'd been brought up with knowledge of the Dreamtime, which explained the Earth and its creation with rich, mythic stories. There were three linked worlds—the physical, the human, and the sacred. To enter the last of these required an altered state of consciousness similar to a trance.

Although I accepted that mysterious forces did exist, I was pretty sure Yolanda/Cassandra's act wasn't true blue. Deciding to sit on the fence, I shrugged and said, "Who knows?"

Not one of the subsequent minireadings reached the level of drama Lonnie's had, but there was no shortage of volunteers keen to have a psychic take on their lives, and Melodie was kept busy booking full-length readings. Lonnie managed to grab one of the first available appointments on Monday evening.

After watching Cassandra in action for a while, I noticed there was a repetitive pattern to the comments she made. Although her insights in each case were worded differently, it was amazing how many people appeared to be misunderstood, undervalued, and unappreciated.

Melodie had given up tinkling her bell for silence because many of the guests had drifted away in search of food or drink, leaving only a small queue of people waiting for readings.

"Tiff goes to psychics all the time," she confided to Fran, Lonnie, and me as Melodie's friend Tiffany took her place at the nook's table. "She says she finds it real helpful."

"How is it helpful?" Lonnie asked in a serious tone.

"It's just an ego boost, being the center of attention," said Fran scathingly.

In the nook, Cassandra was poring over the crystal ball. "No one knows the *real* you," she said to Tiffany. "Life has not yet given you the opportunity to use your many talents to the full. Indeed, I sense you're considering a major career change?"

"Awesome! That's so totally true!" Tiffany squealed.

"Spooky!" Melodie cried. "It's as if Cassandra knows Tiff inside out, but they've only just met."

Fran had little patience with this. "But *you* know Tiffany well, and she's talked to you about changing her job."

"I don't get what you mean?"

"What I mean is that you know Tiffany, you know Lonnie, you know most of the people here tonight. You're a source of information for Cassandra, or whatever her name is. Face it, Melodie, it's a scam."

Frowning, Lonnie said, "It can't be a scam. Cassandra's totally sincere. I'm sure of it."

"I didn't tell her anything," Melodie protested.

Her skepticism plain, Fran said, "Oh, yeah? Did you happen to chat about Kendall & Creeling and who worked there?"

"Well, of course. She was interested."

"I guess she was said Fran with an air of triumph. "Perhaps you recall telling her about Lonnie's break-up with Pauline?"

"I don't remember doing that," said Melodie defiantly.

Lonnie emitted a little moan. "Have you been discussing me and Pauline?"

"Get a grip, Lonnie," Fran advised. She turned to Melodie again. "Even you should be able to see what's happening here. She gets you talking and stores up any little details she might be able to use in the future."

"Like, that's so unfair, Fran. When she was Yolanda she was telling me how non-believers always try to drag Cassandra down."

"Wait a minute," I said, "what do you mean *when* she was Yolanda? She's Yolanda all the time, isn't she? Cassandra's simply a stage name."

Melodie went quite pink. "I accidentally let that slip. Forget I said it."

Fran had no intention of forgetting. "A roommate with a split personality? Wow!"

"Hold on," said Lonnie, "that doesn't mean she has a split personality."

Melodie was horrified. Looking over her shoulder she hissed, "Shhh! She'll hear."

"Is Yolanda/ Cassandra in therapy?" asked Fran cheerily. She amused herself by adding, "And does she eat for two?"

"Yolanda *hasn't* got a split personality," Melodie said in a furious whisper. "It's just when she performs as medium, she allows Cassandra to take over."

"Cassandra takes over? Even better! So now you're telling us she's possessed." Fran cocked her head and cupped a hand behind one ear. "Is that the theme music from *The Exorcist* I hear?"

Quip arrived with Bob in tow as Fran was saying this. "*The Exorcist?*" Quip enthused. "Got to be one of my favorite movies. Love it when Linda Blair spews that green glop."

"The three-sixty rotating head always gets me," said Bob.

"Melodie's just been telling us that her roommate is possessed?" Fran announced.

"I have not!"

Bob waggled his eyebrows comically. "Quip and I have been discussing which one of us will volunteer for a reading, but if an evil spirit's involved I'm not so keen."

Melodie drew herself up with dignity. "Being a psychic medium isn't a joke," she said. "Cassandra has helped many people."

"I'm sure she has,"said Lonnie stoutly.

Fran was determined to be combative. "Name one person she's helped," she demanded.

Melodie did her shampoo-ad hair toss and actually stamped one high-heeled foot. "If you must know, *me.* She's helped me."

Hands on hips, Fran said, "How? And I want specifics."

Melodie mirrored her by putting her hands on her hips. They glowered at each other.

"Well?" said Fran.

"For one thing, Cassandra's illuminated Chilley Dorsal's deep, inner motivations."

"Who?" asked Bob. "Who's this Chilley?"

"Audition," I said, as if that one word would explain everything—which actually, it did.

"Oh, right?" Bob was obviously sorry he'd asked the question. We all knew that once Melodie got the audition bit between her teeth, she'd run with it until the last eyeball glazed over.

"Larry-my-agent says—"

"Sorry to interrupt," said Bob hurriedly, "but I'd better get over to the nook before the medium folds her tent and steals away."

"This should be good," said Quip. "Bob doesn't believe a word of it, so he's going to be a challenge to anyone peddling the supernatural."

The number of people waiting for a minireading had dwindled, so it was only a few minutes before Bob folded his angular height into the chair opposite Cassandra.

She was getting perfunctory in her routine. Bob had only a token hand-holding before she switched to the crystal ball. "You have depths," she announced. "Unsuspected depths."

"Really, I'm quite shallow," he said.

Her rosebud mouth quirked with irritation. "Even if you don't suspect the unsuspected depths you have, the unsuspected depths are still there."

"I have depths," Melodie remarked to no one in particular.

Bob leaned back in his chair. "Okaaay," he said. "What else?"

Cassandra gave him a sharp Zellstein. "Negative feelings can be destructive," she said. "If you allow doubts to fill your mind, it makes it difficult for me to give an accurate reading."

"I get the message," said Bob. "Positive feelings are now welling up from my unsuspected depths."

Cassandra returned to the crystal ball. "In the workplace you receive a measure of respect and esteem, but not as much as you deserve."

"Do you mean am I appreciated? I am. Too much, if you ask me. Frankly, everyone thinks I work harder than I do."

It was clear Cassandra was rapidly losing interest in Bob's reading. She peered into the crystal and announced, "I regret to say a mist seems to be forming. We may not be able to continue."

"A faulty extrasensory connection?" he inquired.

"Something like that."

"This is very disappointing. Can't you tell me at least one thing you've got for me from the Other Side?"

Cassandra repressed an impatient sigh. "Very well," she said, "I'll concentrate. But you must concentrate too?"

For several long moments she bent over the crystal while Bob watched her with a faint smile.

"Nothing?" he said.

She raised her head. There was an odd expression of surprise on her face. "Years ago you lost someone very close to you. A sister? She disappeared without a trace. There was a little dog who fretted."

Bob's smile vanished.

"What's the matter with him?" Fran said. "He's gone quite white."

Quip frowned. "I never knew Bob had a sister."

Bob sat forward. "Is there more?" he asked urgently.

"You will learn something soon."

"What will I learn? How soon?"

She shook her head, her face almost as pale as Bob's. "I don't know." Abruptly, she got to her feet. "That's all I can tell you."

"What's going on?" Melodie asked.

"Crikey, I think we may have seen a genuine psychic moment," I said.

CHAPTER TWELVE

Quite recently Bob had told me about his sister, Kerrie. The only other person at Kendall & Creeling who knew about this tragedy in Bob's life was Ariana. Fifteen years ago Kerrie Verritt, twenty-six, had left her workplace, climbed into her car, and vanished, never to be seen again. There'd been nothing to suggest she'd deliberately engineered her disappearance. Kerrie had been in excellent health, had had a promotion at work, and was engaged to marry her childhood sweetheart. Suicide seemed out of the question and no one could discover any pressing reason for her to run away and start a new life.

I could only imagine what Bob was feeling at this moment. I was pretty well gobsmacked myself, because I'd thought it close to a cert that Cassandra was a fake.

Bob and Cassandra both left the mystic nook at the same time, Cassandra hurrying towards the kitchen, Bob coming straight over to me. He put a hand on my shoulder and steered me away from the others. His homely face was drawn. "How could she possibly have known about Kerrie? You didn't say anything to her, did you? Or to Melodie?"

"Not a word. I've never told anyone about your sister."

"Ariana?"

"You know she wouldn't discuss it. Besides, she hasn't even met Melodie's roommate."

Bob shook his head. "I don't understand this. There's got to be some way she found out. Maybe Ariana mentioned it to Janette, and Janette told Fran…"

"That doesn't work, Bob. Ariana wouldn't have passed on to her sister anything she'd been told in confidence. Besides, Quip was really surprised to find you even had a sister, and Fran would have told him if she'd known."

His expression grim, Bob said, "The information came from somewhere." He craned his head to peer around. "Where did she go? I'm going to find her and shake the truth out of her."

"Bob, don't."

"Why not?"

"There are two possibilities you haven't considered."

"That she's a genuine medium is one option," said Bob, "and I can't swallow that."

"The other is she makes a lucky hit. She mentions a sister, sees you react, and builds on it."

"There's a third scenario," he said. "It's a shakedown. Someone who knows about my sister's disappearance has set this up. Cassandra will suck me into paying big bucks for psychic sessions, keeping me hooked with a series of convincing lies about what happened to Kerrie."

"But how could anyone be sure you'd volunteer for a reading tonight? It wouldn't work if you didn't."

Baffled rage filled his face. "Jesus! I don't know." He scanned the room again.

I put my hand on his arm. "Please, Bob. You're not going to get anywhere by being aggro."

The anger seemed to drain out of him like air out of a leaky balloon. "You're right, Kylie. I've got to think this through."

"As far as I know, her legal name is Yolanda Smith-Jones," I said. "Why don't you run a full background check this weekend? In the meantime, I'll have a friendly chat with her."

Quip joined us, his handsome face concerned. "Are you okay, Bob?"

"Fine. Thanks. Look, I've got to go." He turned on his heel and made a beeline for the front door.

"He never mentioned a sister before," Quip said. "I wonder why not."

Now that the news was out I wouldn't be betraying any secrets. "Why would he?" I said. "She's been a missing person for fifteen years."

* * *

As I suspected, Melodie's roommate had headed towards the kitchen because that was where the bar had been set up. Ignoring the people chatting and laughing around her, she was chugging down a glass of neat vodka when I found her.

"Are you Yolanda now?" I said.

She focused her pale blue eyes on me. "Yes, Yolanda," she said in a monotone. As if I didn't know, she added, "Cassandra is my professional name."

"We need to have a little heart-to-heart, Yolanda." I grabbed the half-full vodka bottle. "Come with me."

Clutching her glass she followed, unresisting, as I pushed through the crowd in the kitchen and made my way back to the nook area, which was deserted now that the minireadings were finished for the night. I sat her down in one chair and took the opposite one.

"A splash?" I asked, gesturing with the vodka bottle.

Wordlessly she extended her glass. Yolanda was looking wan. Even the silver stars on her long black dress seemed to have lost their sparkle.

Leaning my elbows on the table, I said, "It gave you the willies, did it?"

"What?"

"Bob's reading? The last one that you did?"

She took a big gulp of vodka. "Cassandra did the reading."

Stone the crows! Maybe Fran had been on the money, and this sheila *did* have a split personality. Or maybe it was the vodka talking…

"Cassandra and you are the same person, right?" When she looked at me blankly, I added, "Just asking for clarification."

"I like to keep a separation—Cassandra being the gifted psychic and Yolanda the talented businesswoman."

"Right-oh," I said, "let's start again. The reading gave Cassandra the willies. She acted like something really scary had happened."

Straightening in her chair, she said, "Scary? There was nothing like that. It was simply that Cassandra was tired, as I am. The level of concentration required takes its toll."

"Don't try to spin me a yarn."

She looked down her long nose at me. "I'm not trying to spin you anything. Now, as I was saying, I'm really tired, so if you don't mind…"

"I do mind," I said sharply. "Bob's a mate of mine, and what you told him upset him a lot. I want to know why you did that."

Perhaps Yolanda wouldn't have revealed anything if she hadn't been half stonkered from the vodka she'd been chug-a-lugging, but she sighed and said, "Cassandra wasn't expecting anything startling, it just happened."

"Exactly what happened?"

She was silent for a moment, then she said, "A sensitive's powers fluctuate. The connection to the Other Side can be sporadic and the crystal doesn't always show a clear picture. Sometimes the psychic medium is forced to improvise. But this time…" She trailed off, looking somber.

"How was this time different?"

"As the reading progressed, Cassandra felt that she was in touch with a higher power. She knew with absolute certainty that the young woman she saw in the depths of the crystal was missing, and had been for many years."

"How did you—how did Cassandra—know it was Bob's sister?"

For some reason her answer gave *me* the willies. "There were shadows all around and she looked so sad, but there was such a strong family resemblance I knew it had to be his sister."

* * *

Much later, driving Lonnie back to the office so he could pick up the motorbike, I found he'd gone from being bemused over Cassandra's revelations to giddy enthusiasm about the whole evening. It amazed me to see someone who was usually so analytical surrender to the lure of the inexplicable.

Lonnie was so buzzed he even neglected to backseat drive, which was a golden opportunity lost, since there was a lot to comment on. Being on the road late-night Friday was much more challenging than earlier, because added to the volume of cars was the volume of alcohol many drivers appeared to have consumed.

"I've never paid much attention to this extrasensory stuff," Lonnie confided, "but meeting Cassandra and having that reading has opened my eyes to the supernatural and the possibility of past lives. It's exciting. A new frontier."

"That's bonzer," I said, braking hard to avoid a black Escalade that had wandered out of its lane into mine.

"Did I tell you I'm booked on Monday for a full-trance reading?"

"You did mention it."

"Can I ask you something?"

I coasted to a stop at a red light, hoping the Mercedes driver who'd been tailgating us would stop in time. He did, barely. "Ask away," I said.

"I want you to be brutally frank with me."

"Right-oh."

"You know Fran insists the whole medium routine is a confidence trick? Well, I say there's no way Cassandra is making things up. F'instance, how could she know that someone with the initial P had broken up with me? Melodie swears she didn't mention Pauline to her."

The Merc driver blasted his horn when I didn't floor it immediately when the green light appeared. I changed lanes and he roared righteously past us.

"So, what do you think?" said Lonnie, oblivious to the near carnage outside our vehicle.

I was coming to the conclusion that there was a real possibility Yolanda/Cassandra was not a complete fake. I was willing to grant she might have authentic psychic moments, although I reckoned most of her patter was based on generalizations and information she'd picked up in casual conversation.

I said diplomatically, "Maybe Melodie mentioned Pauline in passing while she and Yolanda were getting to know each other, but Melodie has forgotten about it."

"But it's also possible Cassandra *did* see Pauline's initial in the crystal ball, isn't it?" he insisted.

"Could be," I said neutrally.

Lonnie was determined to prove to himself, as well as to me, that he'd undergone a fair dinkum psychic experience. "Another thing, Kylie, didn't I say to you before my reading I had a feeling she and I had known each other in a former life? There's no way Cassandra could have known that."

"Yes, there is, Lonnie."

"Well, tell me how," he said huffily.

"Remember, before the readings started, she was standing no more than a meter away from us with her eyes closed. It's possible she overheard you telling me you had a feeling the two of you had met before in another life."

"I was speaking softly. She couldn't have picked it up."

Recalling that my invaluable *Complete Handbook* described how a person with normal hearing could use a hearing aid to eavesdrop on conversations, I said, "Have you considered Cassandra could be using one of those miniature hearing aids?"

Silence from Lonnie. I Zellsteind across at him. From his expression, his naïve, credulous side was in the process of being replaced by his logical, technical side. "No, I didn't consider that," he said despondently. "I didn't consider a lot of things. For example, if Cassandra can get names in advance—Melodie wouldn't even notice she was being milked for information—and then Google them, she'd be likely to come up with lots of usable material."

Perversely, I found myself defending Cassandra. "She may not be using any technology at all. She could be relying on a combination of intuition and psychic ability."

Lonnie's gusto for the paranormal appeared to have suffered a death blow. When I stopped at a red light on Sunset, I looked over at him. He was slumped in his seat, all his earlier enthusiasm quite drained away.

Catching my eye, he grimaced. "Of all people, I should have been more cynical. After all, I deal with electronic trickery all the time. I feel such an idiot. I was sucked in because I wanted to believe it was true."

"Bob certainly acted like she'd hit the bull's-eye."

"Yeah, he did. Maybe you're right, and sometimes Cassandra does have a true psychic flash." Slightly cheered, he went on, "The problem is to tell what's genuinely paranormal and what's deception."

"Are you going to keep your Monday appointment for a full trance reading?" I asked, curious to know if he was still willing to spend the money.

Looking resolute, Lonnie declared, "I'll keep the appointment, but I'll be on full alert for any trickery."

"Crikey, Lonnie, isn't a full psychic reading six hundred dollars? That's a lot to blow on something you don't fully believe."

He shrugged. "I haven't decided not to believe, I've decided to be skeptical. Besides, if I catch her cheating, no way does she keep my six hundred dollars."

Lonnie sat silently for the rest of the journey, no doubt meditating on strategies to trap Cassandra. He perked up as I turned through Kendall & Creeling's gates and my headlights illuminated the gleaming red and chrome monster his mate had left for him. "Can't wait to get on a cycle again. It's been years."

"Are you sure you're up to riding that motorbike tonight?" I asked, thinking the traffic we'd just been in was bad enough on four wheels, but would be infinitely hairier on two. "You can spend the night here. I'll make up a bed for you on the sofa in Bob's office."

"Thanks, but I'd rather go home. And why do you keep calling it a motorbike? It's a *cycle*. A motorbike's a puny little thing."

"That's what we call all two-wheelers in Australia. Motorbikes."

While Lonnie went over to the motorbike, I checked out the parking area for intruders. Apart from Lonnie's terminally sick brown Nissan there were no other vehicles to hide behind and the new lighting just set up eliminated shadowy areas where a stalker could lurk.

Lonnie had found the bike's ignition key, which had been concealed on top of his car's front tire. "Want a quick spin?" he asked, grinning widely. "There are two helmets."

"Not on your nelly!"

That made him laugh. "I guess that means no."

"Too right it does."

"Okay, since I'm your bodyguard tonight, let's check around the building before I put my leathers on."

A quick dekko showed nothing amiss, so we went back to the parking area, where Lonnie opened up a compartment at the back of the bike and took out a worn leather jacket and black leather gloves.

Shrugging on the jacket, he said, "Sure you don't want to change your mind about a spin? Last chance."

I shook my head. "No, thanks."

"Okay, see you tomorrow. I'm coming in to work on the Evenstar backgrounds."

Fully attired as a biker, Lonnie was rather a comical sight. His friend Steve was obviously a much bigger man, because the leather jacket swam on Lonnie. And the gloves looked too large as well. When the bulbous silver helmet was in place, Lonnie reminded me irresistibly of a little boy playing with adult toys.

"Lonnie, you will be extra careful, won't you?"

He gave me the thumbs up, fiddled around for a while, and finally got the motorcycle to roar into very loud life. As he wobbled out of the parking area and onto Sunset I said a little prayer that he'd make it home in one piece.

Inside, Julia Roberts was waiting for me. If she'd worn a watch she'd have looked at it pointedly. She led the way to the kitchen, having correctly divined that I needed the restorative qualities of a good hot cup of tea.

"Jules, I know it's very late, but I've had a fascinating evening. What's your opinion of mediums?"

She gave me a flat stare. "I agree with you," I said, "they're to be taken with a grain of salt."

Still, I couldn't help feeling like Lonnie—that I'd like to believe in the paranormal. It certainly made life more interesting.

CHAPTER THIRTEEN

On Saturday mornings when the weather was good—which it was 90 percent of the time in Southern California—Julia Roberts and I had breakfast in the back yard. Well, more accurately, *I* had breakfast and Jules reclined in a patch of sun watching birds, squirrels, and an occasional lizard while daydreaming of being a savage predator. Fortunately for the wildlife, she wasn't even a predator's bootlace.

Shaded by a large green umbrella, I had the morning newspaper spread out on the redwood table I'd bought to spruce up the yard. Between sips of my second cuppa I was reading aloud to Jules an item about a heroic cat who had saved his humans from being burnt to a crisp by meowing so loudly that they woke up just in time to escape the flames consuming their house.

"Inspiring, eh, Jules?" I said. "Should the opportunity present itself, I know you'd leap at the chance to be a hero too."

She wasn't listening because her attention was glued on Rocky, who'd come trotting through the back door. He was closely followed by Bob, a mug of coffee in his hand.

Spotting her, Rocky halted with a muffled snuffle of alarm. Julia Roberts sat up in one graceful movement and regarded the little pug with narrowed eyes.

"Let the two of them work it out," said Bob, sliding onto the redwood bench beside me. Instead of his weekday dark suit white shirt and tie, faded blue jeans clung to his narrow hips and a tight T-shirt revealed the outlines of his boney chest.

Julia Roberts indulged in a huge pink yawn. Rocky, his wrinkled little velvety face intent, hesitantly advanced. He stopped a meter away from her and gave a tentative wag of his curly tail. Nothing bad happened, so he grew bolder. When they were almost nose-to-nose, Julia Roberts abruptly stood up. Rocky yelped and rushed back to Bob. Jules twitched her whiskers in a feline smile.

"They've got it worked out," I said. "Julia Roberts is at the very top of the pecking order and Rocky is at the very bottom. He'll be fine as long as he displays the appropriate obsequiousness."

"My," said Bob, "a vocabulary lesson, no less, but I don't think Rocky knows that word. He's very young."

"A good vocab's important. You'll have to start reading literature to him," I suggested facetiously. I stopped, astonished at the sudden change in Bob.

"Kerrie used to read poetry to her pug, Annabella," he said, sorrow washing over his face. "It was a family joke."

"I'm sorry, Bob. I didn't know."

"That's okay. How could you?"

Rocky had detected a squirrel foraging for food under the jacaranda tree. Julia Roberts watched impassively as he made a wide detour around her. He had the most adorable way of walking, with a rolling gait rather like a sailor who'd had one rum too many.

"Is that why you got Rocky?" I asked. "Because your sister had a pug?"

"Pugs were the dog of choice for our family. I grew up with a succession of them. My parents still have two, Helen and Troy."

Rocky barked at the squirrel, who streaked up the tree, did an athletic leap onto the garage roof and scampered out of sight. Rocky didn't let disappointment get him down, but immediately began to pursue a passing butterfly.

"Last night at the reading did you hear what she said to me about a little dog fretting?" Bob asked. "That was poor Annabella. When Kerrie disappeared she was inconsolable."

"It would have been more convincing if Cassandra had identified the little dog as a pug," I said, wishing I'd thought to ask her what sort of dog she saw in the crystal.

He nodded slowly. "I guess so, but the very fact that she mentioned a small dog fretting gets me."

"So you've come around to believing Cassandra is genuine?"

"I don't know what to believe, Kylie. I researched her as best I could, but Lonnie, of course, will do a much more thorough job. According to Cassandra's website she's given valuable advice to various small-town police departments on cases of missing or murdered children, usually at the urging of the victims' families. Her claims of success are hard to evaluate, as cops tend to be reluctant to admit allowing anything paranormal to be involved in their investigations."

"I suppose anyone can claim to be a medium," I remarked. "It's a pity there isn't some sort of exam they have to do to get a license."

With a flicker of amusement, Bob said, "Believe it or not, there is a trade association. Yolanda Smith-Jones a.k.a. Cassandra, happens to be the current president of The United Psychics of America. The UPA website even lists a code of ethics."

I hesitated before asking, but decided to go ahead. "Did your family consult with a psychic when your sister disappeared?"

He grimaced. "Yes, we did, after it became apparent the cops were getting nowhere. Kerrie had vanished from the face of the earth and there were no viable leads left to follow. Dad was reluctant, but my mom was particularly insistent, saying we should do anything and everything to find Kerrie, no matter how farfetched or expensive. In the end Mom employed three different mediums, who came up with three different stories about what had occurred. None of them panned out."

He added bitterly, "It was all a colossal waste of time and money."

"Is Cassandra any better? All she's done is tell you two things: your sister's been missing for years and a dog fretted. Couldn't this simply be a couple of lucky guesses?"

Bob lifted his shoulders in resignation. "I wish I knew. Part of me wants to believe, because just maybe this is someone who can truly say what happened to Kerrie all those years ago. The cynic in me says she's a fake and it's a scam."

"I got the impression the reading she did for you pretty well swept Cassandra off her tootsies, because when I went to look for her after you'd gone, she was in the kitchen tossing down vodka like it was water. She announced she was back being Yolanda, and spoke of Cassandra as if she were another person altogether. Like Melodie would say, 'Creepy!'"

"What drove her to drink?"

"As I see it, Cassandra was going through her standard routine with you when it got too real. For once she actually saw something in the crystal ball—your sister's face. And that brush with the supernatural gave her the willies."

"What are the willies?" said Lonnie indistinctly, as he stepped out into the yard. "Sounds obscene to me."

In one hand he held a half-eaten chocolate doughnut and in the other a huge carton of coffee. He was wearing an ancient sports shirt and a shapeless pair of blue shorts, which revealed his pale, dimpled knees.

"The willies is a feeling somewhere between uneasiness and downright fear," I said.

"Cassandra was spooked?"

"I reckon so."

Lonnie plunked himself down at the table. "Sorry about your sister, Bob."

"It was a long time ago."

Bob went off to rescue Rocky, who was making a commotion because he'd managed to jam himself in the narrow space between the garage and the fence. Julia Roberts stirred herself to go over and assess the situation.

Demolishing the remainder of the doughnut, Lonnie took a gulp of coffee to wash it down. He seemed much cheerier this morning. When I said so, he declared, "It's the Harley. Clears my head, puts things in perspective."

"So you didn't fall off on the way home?"

"Fall off? Of course not." He looked insulted at the very suggestion.

When Bob came back with Rocky tucked under one arm, Lonnie asked, "Are you booked for a full-trance reading with Cassandra?"

"Not yet. Maybe never." He put the wriggling puppy down. Rocky checked Julia Roberts' location, then set off in the opposite direction.

"I'm seeing her on Monday night," said Lonnie. "Anything you'd like me to ask?"

"Hold on," I said, "aren't you supposed to concentrate on your own personal problems?"

"For six hundred dollars I can concentrate on anything I damn well like," said Lonnie, grinning. "How about you, Kylie? Have you got a question?"

I shook my head. "Not one."

"Seems to me," said Lonnie to Bob, "that if there's any chance at all of finding out where your sister is, you should take it."

"You're talking about a paranormal growth industry, Lonnie," said Bob caustically. "So-called psychics prey on families who have lost someone in mysterious circumstances. They're easy marks because they're desperate to find the family member."

"How many people just up and disappear?" I asked.

"For obvious reasons I've become something of an expert in the area," said Bob. "Every year in California over forty thousand adults are reported missing."

"Fair dinkum? That many? But they don't all stay missing, do they?"

"Kendall & Creeling have traced quite a few," Lonnie said. "You'll find the majority deliberately walk away to escape a life they can't or won't put up with anymore. Eventually they turn up on their own account, or someone from their past life recognizes them and blows the whistle?"

"That wasn't Kerrie," Bob said. "She was one of the approximately fourteen thousand Californians each year who are never located. And nationwide well over a hundred thousand missing-person cases remain open."

"I've seen estimates," said Lonnie, "that morgues across the county are holding at least fifty thousand unidentified corpses, but records are so badly kept in different areas that this is just a guess at the numbers."

It was too horrible a thought to imagine someone close to me lying unclaimed in a refrigerated drawer. Then I realized this was an image I'd picked up from movies and television—the deceased person being rolled out for inspection from a wall of refrigerated drawers. Maybe in reality these bodies were stacked on shelves in cold storage rooms.

"What happens to all these thousands of dead bodies?" I asked, thinking of them piling up, year after year.

"The local authorities bury or cremate them as cheaply as possible," said Bob bleakly. "It haunts me to think of Kerrie in a pauper's grave with nothing to mark her passing."

"Couldn't DNA be used to identify at least some of these people?"

"The technology's not widely used with John and Jane Does," said Lonnie. "Local authorities don't budget to send DNA samples to a central clearinghouse. Corpses don't vote, so politicians don't care. The end result is there's no effective national data base."

Recalling a recent story in the news about two young kids who'd been kidnapped by their estranged father, I asked, "But there's some sort of registry for missing children, isn't there?"

"The National Center for Missing and Exploited Children is comparatively well-funded," said Bob, "because a young person's disappearance causes widespread alarm and so gets media attention. In contrast, the National Center for Missing Adults, doesn't attract the same interest, and has recently had its budget cut."

"Get away from me!"

Julia Roberts, who'd lost interest in Rocky's activities, had decided on the much more rewarding pastime of teasing Lonnie. She brushed against his bare legs with a pleased *berroww* sound.

Lonnie leaped to his feet. "I'm outta here," he announced, glaring at Jules, "before I start sneezing or, worse still, get a rash." Heading for the back door, he called over his shoulder, "Kylie, if you let that diabolical cat follow me to my office, I swear I won't be responsible for my actions."

Following Lonnie was precisely what Jules intended to do. She protested as I scooped her up into my arms.

With a wry grin, Bob said, "And what are the odds that at Lonnie's psychic reading tomorrow night, Cassandra slips in something about his allergies? I'd bet good money on it."

* * *

I spent an uneventful Saturday grocery shopping and pottering around. Lonnie worked in his office until lunchtime. Before he left, he popped into the kitchen to give me the fascinating information that TV personality Zelda Webber, Emory Hastings' wife, was strongly rumored to be hopelessly addicted to cocaine.

"Not your recreational user," he said. "Zelda has a *baaad* cocaine habit. Seems she's sniffed most of her considerable TV salary up her nose. Also, contrary to the tough-but-compassionate image she projects to her public, she can be a real piece of work. Zelda's gone through countless personal assistants, which is really saying something in this town. Looking after the affairs of insecure, difficult celebrities accustoms a PA to an incredible amount of verbal abuse, just as a matter of course."

After Lonnie left, I mused over why it was that the job of personal assistant in the entertainment industry was so sought after, considering there were so many horror stories about how they were treated by their impossibly demanding bosses.

I added it to my list of things about LA I might never understand, like why most drivers were allergic to indicating a turn or lane change or why, in the Southern California semidesert environment, householders insisted on having lush lawns kept green by garden sprinklers spraying water so copiously that it ran off into the gutters.

* * *

As I'd be spending Saturday evening alone, I'd lined up a couple of DVDs to watch and was just contemplating whether to throw a frozen meal into the microwave or go to the trouble of cooking from scratch, when the phone rang.

"Kylie? It's Janette. Is Ariana with you?"

"No, I haven't seen her today." The thread of worry in Ariana's sister's voice alarmed me. "Is something wrong?"

"I'm not sure. Ariana was supposed to come to dinner this evening. She called a couple of hours ago to ask if she could bring wine. Everything seemed okay. When she didn't arrive on schedule at seven, I waited for a while, thinking she'd been delayed. Then I called her cell but just got voicemail. Same with her house—no answer."

A cold dread swept over me. Ariana was the most punctual of individuals. If she said she would be at a certain place at a certain time, it was a sure thing she would be. Disturbing scenarios ricocheted through my mind. What if a humungous SUV had plowed into her car? Or Gussie had been hurt, and Ariana had rushed her to a vet? Or maybe Ariana had been on a stepladder reaching for something, and had overbalanced?

"Perhaps Ariana's had an accident at home and can't get to the phone."

"I'm calling from her place," said Janette. "Gussie was waiting inside but there's no sign of Ariana anywhere. Her keys and wallet are gone, and the BMW isn't here."

"A car accident?"

"I drove the route she'd take to get to my house. Nothing. She's so reliable. Even if there'd been an emergency, she would have contacted me."

"What can I do?" I said. My voice seemed to belong to somebody else.

"I'll start Fran and Quip checking the hospitals, in case Ariana has been brought in unconscious. I'll contact the local police. Would you call everyone in your office, just in case they know something? And the Phoenix law firm she's working for? I guess there'll be contact numbers in her files. I know it's the weekend, but try them, will you?"

I put down the phone with a sense of the terrible irony that Bob, Lonnie, and I had been discussing missing persons only this morning, and now Ariana could be one of their number.

CHAPTER FOURTEEN

Sunday was a blur of telephone calls and futile meetings. Ariana's friend, Detective Lark of the LAPD, immediately became involved, because even though she hadn't been missing long enough for official action, Ariana, being an ex-cop, was, as Ted Lark said, family.

Ariana had vanished, as the cliché went, without a trace. Her car had not been found, her cell phone wasn't working, her credit cards had not been used, and no one had tried to withdraw money from her bank accounts through an ATM. She was licensed to carry a concealed weapon, and as her handgun, a Glock automatic, was not in her home or office, it was presumed Ariana had had it with her when she disappeared.

Late Sunday afternoon we held a council of war to summarize what we knew and to plan our next moves. Melodie got coffee for everyone while Lonnie and I moved additional chairs into Anriana's office. I looked at her neat desk, her high-backed chair, and wished with all my heart that it was still Friday, and Ariana was sitting there, cool and contained. We'd been discussing Sir Rupert's infatuation. If I could rerun those few moments, I'd make her tell me who it was she referred to when she'd said, "Recently there's been someone who concerns me much more."

Ted Lark, chairing the meeting, took Ariana's seat. He was a rumpled, heavy-set man whose face reminded me of a bloodhound. Everything had a lugubrious cast: his mournful eyes, his long nose, his sagging jowls.

The rest of us—me, Bob, Lonnie, Fran, Quip, and Janette—arranged ourselves in a rough semicircle. Melodie passed around coffee mugs, then sat down herself. We were all worn down by fatigue and worry. Janette, who was a softer, pastel version of Ariana, looked particularly exhausted.

"Before we start, Ted," said Bob to Lark, "do you think there can be any link between Kylie's stalker and Ariana's disappearance?"

Lark shrugged his heavy shoulders. "There doesn't seem to be a connection, but I'm keeping the possibility in mind."

The thought that somehow, unwittingly, I was responsible had haunted me since last night. Could I have done more to find out who was leaving the notes? Should I have staked out my car in an effort to catch my stalker red-handed?

Lark cleared his throat for attention. "Okay," he said, "we all know the situation. Yesterday evening, at five o'clock, Ariana last spoke with Janette. We have the house security camera showing Ariana's BMW leaving her place at six-fifteen. We don't know who was behind the wheel, as the vehicle was accessed through an internal door into the garage, and the angle of the camera only shows the vehicle, once outside, from behind. This means there's no way to be sure Ariana was driving her own car. She failed to arrive at Janette's house at seven, when she was expected. There's an all-points on her vehicle, which hasn't yet been located. I have an alert out in case anyone tries to use her credit cards or gain access to her bank accounts. I've also listed her handgun as stolen."

"A thought," said Bob. "Have you accessed any surveillance cameras on the route Ariana was likely to have taken on her way to Janette's place?"

"I've got it covered, Bob."

"What are these cameras for?" I asked.

"You have no idea how many public places are under surveillance," said Bob. "Some cameras are for traffic flow, others for security. And that's not counting private systems. There's always a chance the BMW's route can be tracked."

Janette's face twisted. "Oh, God, I keep on thinking of Ariana trussed up in the trunk."

"I know the situation's upsetting," said Lark, "but it's best if we can approach this logically, so let's look at the possible scenarios. The first is that Ariana had some sort of accident in her car, either mechanical trouble or involving another vehicle. I think we can rule this out, as during the time in question there were only a couple of minor collisions in the general area, none involving her BMW. Also, no one answering her description has been admitted to any local hospital."

Quip leaned forward to say, "You hear of people in cars plunging off the road into a patch of vegetation and not being found for days, even though they're close to traffic. There was one on Mulholland Drive the other week."

"That does occasionally happen," Lark acknowledged, "but not in this case. I had patrol officers check out any likely spots."

Quip settled back in his chair, his expression drawn. I noticed he and Fran were holding hands and felt the familiar pang of something close to envy. They were an odd couple—Quip sunny-natured and almost certainly gay, Fran gloomy, cynical, and negative. Opposites they might be, but they clearly adored each other.

"The second scenario," said Lark, "has Ariana having some other sort of accident, or being the victim of an attack. As you know, her house has been searched thoroughly and the adjacent areas have been combed. None of her neighbors noticed anything amiss. I'm satisfied she hasn't fallen off a cliff or been struck by a vehicle while walking along those narrow Hollywood Hills roads."

He paused to take a mouthful of coffee. "Third, she's had a total mental or emotional breakdown."

"Amnesia?" said Bob. "It's very rare, even though it's a staple in popular entertainment."

"True," said Lark, "and someone with amnesia is essentially helpless. If that were the case with Ariana, I'd expect her to be found by now, unless she fell into the clutches of someone who took advantage of the situation."

Janette buried her face in her hands. "This is a nightmare."

"The fourth possibility," said Lark, frowning at Janette's bent head, "is kidnapping. I'd expect ransom demands by now, and there are none."

"What if she's been taken to stop her from giving evidence in that Phoenix million-dollar insurance scam?" Lonnie asked.

This morning I'd talked to the lead attorney for the insurance company. I already knew the broad outlines of Kendall & Creeling's involvement. We had been hired to gather evidence that several patients of the same orthopedic specialist were fraudulently claiming compensation for crippling back injuries. The videos showing claimants, apparently without a twinge of pain, bowling, gardening, and lifting heavy objects, plus Ariana's personal observations, were pivotal to the case. She had already given depositions covering the various claimants, but her testimony in open court was vital, and the attorney had taken the opportunity when flying into LA on Friday to meet with her to discuss in detail the questions he would ask her when she appeared in the witness box and what she might expect in vigorous cross-examination.

"Kidnapping's a much more serious crime than defrauding an insurance company," said Lark. "It wouldn't be worth the risk, especially as she's given sworn depositions and there's extensive video proof. It wouldn't be as persuasive as a personal appearance, but if Ariana's unavailable, the judge can direct that both be entered in evidence."

"Like, you hear of witnesses being murdered all the time," Melodie piped up. "I saw it on *Law and Order* the other night."

"Oh, for God's sake, Melodie, that's a television show!" Fran snapped.

Affronted, Melodie declared, "*Law and Order* is based on true stories. It says so at the beginning."

"If we can get on?" said Ted Lark with a world-weary sigh. "Possibility five is that Ariana has been murdered and her body concealed."

I felt sick. Ted Lark was talking about Ariana. *Ariana. Murdered.* Her living, breathing body stilled, her blue, blue eyes closed forever? I couldn't accept it. I loved her so much, wouldn't I somehow know if she were dead?

"If murder is the answer, it's important whether it was a premeditated crime or done on the spur of the moment. The first is planned, and often harder to crack, the second, a sudden violent outburst, usually provides more evidence to lead us to the perp."

Pale as paper, Janette protested, "No one could hate Ariana enough to murder her."

"Trust me, it doesn't have to be deep hatred that drives someone to murder. People kill each other for what seem to be the most trivial of reasons." Lark's melancholy expression deepened as he added, "No one can know what's going on in the murky depths of someone else's mind."

"Ariana was a former police officer," said Bob. "She put a lot of people away. I guess you're looking at that angle."

"That's precisely why I've got someone checking through the names of anyone released in recent months who could conceivably hold a grudge against her. It's already quite a list."

"So," said Lonnie, "since an accident can probably be ruled out, that leaves us with kidnapping or murder." He hung his head. "Not a happy choice."

"There is one other scenario," Lark said. "Ariana has engineered her own disappearance."

Fran glared at him. "No way! She wouldn't do that."

"Every year we investigate faked abductions. There was one last month that got a big exposure in the media. You might remember it—the 19-year-old woman who turned up naked, bruised, and handcuffed. She claimed to have been kidnapped and beaten by two men. There were holes in her story, and eventually she broke down and confessed it was a fabrication."

"Why would anyone go to that much trouble?" Quip asked.

"Sometimes it's to get a former partner, family member, or friend in hot water by accusing them of being behind the abduction," Lark said. "Often it's a pathetic attempt to draw attention to themselves. For those who disappear completely, it's the opportunity to create a new identity."

"Let's rule that one out right now," said Bob emphatically.

"The Ariana I know would never fabricate her own abduction," Lark spread his hands. "Just exploring all the possibilities."

"I can think of another one," said Melodie, very earnestly. "Like, it's real scary."

We all looked at her.

"What?" said Janette. "What is it?"

"Alien abduction."

Fran's eyes flashed fire. "A flying saucer swooped down and snatched Ariana? Is that what you're saying?"

Melodie bridled at Fran's tone. "It could happen."

"You're seriously suggesting as we sit here, little green men have got Ariana in a space ship?"

"Well…"

"Well, what?" Fran demanded. "They *haven't* got Ariana captive in a space ship."

"They're not green," said Melodie. "Cassandra says they're sort of a silvery gray."

* * *

Later, Janette, Fran, Quip, and I perched on tall stools in the kitchen. Quip was back with pizzas from the local Italian pizza parlor, and I'd made fresh coffee for everyone else and a pot of tea for myself.

"We've got to *do* something," said Janette, a note of hysteria in her voice. "God knows what's happening to Ariana while we just sit around waiting for—" She broke off as her eyes filled with tears.

Quip leaned over to put an arm around Janette's shoulders. "Maybe we can come up with an angle Ted Lark hasn't covered."

"We should be offering a reward—a substantial reward—right now. I don't understand why Detective Lark is so against it. I mean, money isn't the problem."

Janette was a very successful artist whose paintings sold for astonishing sums. I wasn't a fan—I found her work disturbing. She specialized in meticulously rendered scenes of ordinary life, but in the mundane images there was always some jarring element—a severed tongue resting on the edge of a sink, a glass jar full of eyeballs ripped from their sockets.

Fran, her expression softer than I'd ever seen, took her mother's hand. "Mom, he's the expert. He's saying to wait a few days before offering a reward because he knows that, along with genuine callers, the crazies will come out of the woodwork and swamp the cops with leads that won't pan out. He wants the investigation to start off without those distractions."

I swallowed a bite of pizza that tasted like sawdust in my mouth. I wasn't hungry, but I had to eat, so I forced myself to take another bite.

Quip gave his mother-in-law a gentle hug, then slid off his kitchen stool and went over to the whiteboard Fran had recently put up on the wall for listing supplies that were running low and, more importantly from her point of view, the schedule detailing disaster-preparedness sessions she was determined we would all attend.

"Honey, can I clean this off?" Quip asked. "I think it would help to list who might possibly kidnap Ariana."

Unspoken, the words "or murder" hung in the air.

"Let's start with her career as a cop," he said. In the next few minutes we all contributed, until the whiteboard was full of Quip's neat printing.

"A criminal Ariana jailed when she was a cop (Lark to check)"

"Someone bearing a grudge about a case handled by Kendall & Creeling (Bob and Lonnie to check)"

"Sir Rupert—stalker? Heidi Brandstett? (cops to interview)"

"A person not named by Ariana—at Evenstar? (Kylie)"

"Someone from Ariana's past/Natalie's past (Janette)"

"A random kidnapper"

The last was the most chilling of the kidnap scenarios. Ted Lark had pointed out that although rare, there were opportunistic individuals, often sociopaths, who committed serious crimes simply because the opportunity to do so presented itself. Because the victim was chosen at random, the crime was difficult to solve.

With the whiteboard pen, Quip bracketed the first two items. "I think the most likely perp would be someone bearing a grudge against Ariana. Lark can handle the LAPD angle, and I'll help Bob and Lonnie at the Kendall & Creeling end."

"Evenstar's the key," I said. "I'm sure of it." I couldn't logically explain my conviction, but I felt it strongly.

Quip stood back to look at the board. "You could be right, but we need a lot more information before we can make even an educated guess."

Janette and Quip went off to go through Ariana's desk once more, on the off-chance that she'd left a name or some other information that might provide a lead. Ariana kept her appointment diary on an electronic organizer, and it was missing, so it presumably had been with her when she disappeared.

Fran helped me clean up the kitchen. She was pensive, not at all the customary confrontational Fran for whom every obstacle, real or imaginary, was worthy of a fast frontal assault.

She looked at me somberly. "Mom asked me if I thought Ariana was still alive. Of course I said she was, but I don't know…What do you think, Kylie?"

"I can't imagine a world without Ariana in it." My voice cracked on her name.

Fran gave my shoulder a gentle squeeze. "Hang in there," she said.

"Be your usual tough self with me, Fran, or I'll start bawling."

"Do that, and I'll join you," she said.

* * *

When Janette, Fran, and Quip left, Julia Roberts followed me around as I double-checked every window and door. Before this weekend I'd felt faintly ridiculous keeping a handgun within easy reach when I was safely locked in, but now its lethal black weight at my waist was a comfort.

"Should I practice a quick draw from the holster?" I asked Jules. From her expression, she thought it unwise. "You're right, as always," I said. "I'm likely to shoot myself in the foot—or, worse still, shoot *you* in the foot."

I was so emotionally spent, picturing this made me giggle hysterically. Rattled by my odd behavior, Julia Roberts stared at me, her ears out sideways. "Pull yourself together," she was clearly saying.

So I pulled myself together, wiped my eyes, and blew my nose. "I'll make myself another cup of tea," I said to Jules, "and then I have to ring Mum. I'd rather not, but I do have to tell her what's happened."

Last time we spoke, I hadn't told her I had a stalker, as it would be ammunition for demands that I come home. And now I wouldn't mention Evenstar to my mum, although I was now absolutely convinced that someone there held the key to Ariana's disappearance. I'd let Mum think I was leaving everything to the cops, which was far from the truth.

"I'll do anything to find Ariana," I told Jules, "no matter what's involved."

She looked approving, though this may have been because I'd just put tuna treats into her bowl.

I was just filling the kettle when it struck me that I'd better not delay giving the news to my mother. If she hadn't already, Melodie would be calling Lexus, traveling cross-country with my cousin, to tell her Ariana had been abducted. Lexus would naturally tell Brucie, who would contact his mother, my Aunt Millie, back in the 'Gudge. Then Aunt Millie would rush to Mum with who knows what sensationalized version of the story.

I abandoned the idea of tea. I had to get to my mother before Aunt Millie did. Julia Roberts came to keep me company as I sat cross-legged on my bed and dialed the Wombat's number.

"Mum? It's me, Kylie?"

"Kylie! I was about to ring you." She let out a long, dramatic sigh worthy of Melodie. "We've been cursed with more success, worse luck. The Platypus Posse's excursion to Dead Man's Creek was a triumph. The whole lot of them have come back totally gaga over platypuses. 'So cute! So darling!' they keep shrieking. Now everyone wants to see a blasted platypus—not just the Yanks, the Germans too. In fact, pretty well every tourist in town."

"Crikey," I said.

"It's no use pointing out that the Posse was lucky to see a platypus at all, them being so retiring. And they didn't want to know when I said their cute, darling platypus had a hidden poison spur. Looks can be deceiving, I said. It's an old saying, but a good one, but no one listened."

Mum gusted another sigh. "So out of the blue here I am with a wildlife hit on my hands. It's just too much, especially now that Uncle Ernie has gone completely troppo and wants to build a Wollegudgerie platypus exhibition complete with a Big Platypus."

"You mean like the Big Pineapple?"

"Uncle Ernie claims the Big Pineapple was his inspiration. Have you ever heard of anything so harebrained?"

As a kid I recalled being taken to a tropical fruit plantation that featured a gigantic yellow fiberglass pineapple as a tourist attraction. Inside there were pineapple milkshakes and pineapple ice-cream and pineapple jam and so on. And there were souvenirs for sale—pineapple pens and pineapple notebooks and pineapple magnets and pineapple purses, etc. I also remembered climbing up a central spiral staircase for the view from the lookout set in the fiberglass crown of the Big Pineapple.

"I can't quite visualize a Big Platypus," I said. "Where was Uncle Ernie thinking of putting it?"

"Right in front of The Wombat's Retreat." My mum's tone showed the deep disgust with which she viewed this suggestion. "And you know what a boothead Ernie can be. He actually expected me to change the name of the pub to The Platypus's Retreat. I put a flea in his ear over that, and he dropped the idea quick smart."

Before she could build up another head of steam and launch into why, under these trying circumstances, she urgently needed me by her side, I said, "Mum, I'm calling because something's happened here, something bad."

"What? You're not sick, are you?"

"No, I'm fine. It's Ariana Creeling. She's disappeared."

I gave her an edited version of the situation, again not mentioning the threats I'd received. It was touching how concerned Mum was. "Darl,' that's terrible. Poor woman—I pray that she's okay. You must be beside yourself with worry."

"It is pretty awful."

"So don't even think of coming home until Ariana has been found."

"Mum, I wasn't thinking of coming home."

"We'll discuss all that later. In the meantime, Kylie, I want you to promise that you'll eat well and get enough sleep. You'll be no use to anybody if you drop your bundle."

I promised to try to follow Mum's advice and to contact her the minute there were new developments.

After I'd hung up, I sat absently stroking Julia Roberts's sleek, tawny fur until she purred. It wasn't surprising that seeing a platypus in the wild had created such a stir with Mum's tourists. Platypuses were the most fascinating creatures, one of only two egg-laying mammals on earth—the other was the echidna—and unique to Australia.

And a platypus *was* terribly cute, with a streamlined, furry body, broad tail, webbed feet, and, most amazing of all, a soft, pliable duck bill.

They lived in burrows dug into the banks of rivers or streams and were very shy, usually venturing out only in early morning and evening, so it took patience and luck to see one. It had taken me many hours to get the photograph of a swimming platypus I had displayed on the wall of my office with my other wildlife shots.

I thought of what Mum had said about the Platypus Posse members not wanting to know that the gorgeous little animal they were so taken with had a hidden poison spur on the inner side of each hind limb. Used as a defense against natural enemies, the poison was capable of inflicting a very painful injury to humans.

"A platypus is so adorable people think it must be harmless," I said to Jules, "but they're mistaken. Like Mum says, looks can be deceiving."

Her green eyes slowly closed and her purr wound down. Obviously egg-laying mammals were of little interest to an American cat.

"Jules!" Rudely jolted awake, she glared at me. "I've got it! The platypus ploy! When I'm at Evenstar I'll be incredibly sweet and appealing—endearing if I can manage it."

Julia Roberts fixed me with a perplexed stare. "Don't you see, Jules? It's the platypus ploy in action. Whoever's responsible for Ariana's disappearance won't think of me as any threat. But they'll be wrong. And when they're totally disarmed, I'll strike!"

CHAPTER FIFTEEN

I expected to lie awake, but I was so exhausted that I had several hours of deep, dreamless sleep before I woke very early on Monday morning. Horrible images of what Ariana might be enduring began teeming in my mind, so to marshall my thoughts I got up and went for a run through the neighborhood, sticking to the back streets. I'd shoved a can of pepper spray in my pocket, being fully aware my stalker could be watching. The way I felt I'd almost welcome a confrontation, because it would mean I could *do* something, rather than passively wait for news.

Back home, showered and dressed in jeans and a denim shirt, I sat in the kitchen with, naturally, Julia Roberts for breakfast company, and, in between forcing myself to eat spoonfuls of porridge, made a list of Evenstar people I'd concentrate upon at the committee meeting this evening.

In the light of day the Platypus Ploy—it had capitals now that it was the name of the new file I would start after breakfast—still seemed a workable strategy. Of course, if I were wrong and Ariana's disappearance had nothing to do with Evenstar, I'd be wasting valuable time. Ariana hadn't specifically indicated whether the person was male or female, nor if he or she was associated with Evenstar, but I was going to follow my instincts and focus my efforts there.

The morning newspaper had a short piece about Ariana's presumed abduction. When I flipped around the TV newscasts there were similarly brief items. It was a jolt to see Ariana's face on the screen and to hear applied to her the familiar call for anyone with information about this missing person to contact the police.

Without warning, feelings of dread and despair would sweep over me. I felt as though I could fly apart at any moment. I gave myself a savage talking to, pointing out that indulging in self-centered responses wouldn't help Ariana. I had to be tough-minded, directed towards one thing—finding her. I could be as emotional as I liked later, when she was safe.

* * *

Later in the morning, I had a call from Oona Turner. She didn't waste time with pleasantries. "I see in the news that Ariana Creeling's missing," she said in her gravel voice. "I must know how this will affect your investigation at the Evenstar Home. If you're unable to continue at a fully professional level, I'll be expecting a full refund of Kendall & Creeling's exorbitant retainer."

"The investigation won't be affected at all, Ms. Turner," I said with calm assurance. "Everything will proceed exactly as before." It was imperative I persuade Oona to keep Kendall & Creeling involved, otherwise I'd have no excuse to continue my undercover role.

"So I gather it doesn't worry you that your partner has been kidnapped or whatever?"

I gritted my teeth. *Platypus Ploy* I reminded myself.

"It's so nice of you to be concerned," I said. "We're all worried, of course, but have absolute confidence that the police are following leads that will shortly solve the mystery."

Oona grunted. I could picture her stocky body and truculent expression. I said reassuringly, "I unconditionally guarantee that our investigation of the embezzlement is going ahead as planned."

"Oh, yes? What progress have you made so far?"

"We're still running extensive background checks and tracing financial records. I'll be able to give you a comprehensive report later this week."

"Do that," Oona said, and slammed down the phone.

I was contemplating what a charmless twerp the woman was, when it occurred to me I should add her to my list of possible suspects. I hadn't thought of it before, but for all I knew, underneath her toadlike exterior, Oona Turner's heart burned with a passion to possess Ariana.

Yerks! There were some things it was too awful to even try to imagine.

To put these revolting images out of my mind, I headed for the front desk to ask Melodie why the receptionists' network had unaccountably missed what seemed to be an affair between Emory Hastings and Evenstar employee Nancy McDuff.

Normally, unless it was relevant to the case of embezzlement I was investigating, I wouldn't consider this relationship as being anything more than fuel for idle gossip, and certainly none of my business. But times weren't normal, and finding Ariana was more important than having scruples about ethical standards.

I found Melodie pleading with Lonnie, whom she had backed up against her black faux-Spanish reception desk. In her super high heels, she towered over him. I could tell he didn't altogether mind the invasion of his personal space, as Melodie was a bit of all right, and her noticeably heaving bosom was mere centimeters from his nose.

"*Please*, Lonnie, I'm beseeching you," she half-whispered in a trembling voice. "I didn't know until this morning I was scheduled for today, or I wouldn't ask at this short notice."

Lonnie screwed up his face in an attempt to look tough. "You can beseech as much as you like, but the answer's still no."

"But Larry-my-agent swears this audition for *Paranormality Incorporated* is my one big chance to make it big-time in a hit TV show. Lonnie, think of it—my one big chance."

"How many times have I heard it's your one big chance? Maybe a million? It's getting old, Melodie."

"I'm better prepared to play the character of Chilley Dorsal than any other actor could possibly be. Like, who else has a genuine psychic medium guiding them the way I do?"

"What part of no don't you understand?"

"Thanks to Cassandra, I'm so into the essential self of Chilley Dorsal that I *am* her! I actually feel the cold finger of premonition down my spine." Melodie clasped her hands in entreaty. "This means so much to me. I'll never ask you another favor, Lonnie, I promise."

"How many times have you promised me you'll never ask another favor? And of course, you always do. So no way am I answering the phone for you."

Melodie gave a strangled sob. Deep grief showed in every line. "This means so very, very much to me."

Tears always melted Lonnie's defenses. "Well…"

"Oh, Lonnie, thank you!" Melodie kissed his cheek, grabbed her bulky makeup bag, and headed rapidly for the door. "Be back as soon as I can," she called out as she exited.

"What just happened?" Lonnie asked me. "For a moment there everything went black."

"You did what you always say you'll never do again," I said without much sympathy. It really was pathetic the way Melodie could wind people around her little finger—not that she hadn't wound me successfully a couple of times.

He groaned. "I'm such a sap."

"You fell for the audition maneuver," I said. "Again."

He nodded gloomily. The phone rang. Lonnie flung himself into Melodie's chair. "Good morning. Kendall & Creeling Investigative Services. How may I help you?" he asked in a monotone.

Once he'd put the call through to Bob, he looked up at me and said, "About Ariana's disappearance—I'm going to ask

Cassandra tonight if she can tell me anything at all about it. Do you want to come along and see what she says?"

"I can't. I've got a meeting at the Evenstar Home for the Swan Song committee. Tomorrow we actively start canvassing for funds, so we're having a practice run of how to approach potential donors."

Lonnie answered another call and, after putting it through to Fran, said to me, "Did you catch the news this morning? Weird, wasn't it? I had to keep on reminding myself this was our Ariana they were talking about. Not that they gave many details, just that she was presumed abducted and the detectives were looking into the LAPD angle, since she'd been a cop herself."

Knowing Lonnie and Bob had been going through our files, I asked, "Have you and Bob turned up anyone with a serious grudge against Ariana?"

"No one stands out so far. There're certainly cases where threats were made by individuals who bitterly resented what Ariana had uncovered, particularly in the area of industrial espionage, but it's common for things to be said in the heat of the moment. Very few people follow through."

Lonnie ran a hand through his floppy brown hair. "About the trance session tonight with Cassandra, you'll be pleased to know she's not going to fool me again. I know she'll have seen the news and talked with Melodie, so if she just repeats those details, it won't mean a thing. In my heart I don't really believe she can do anything to help find Ariana. But what if she *can* and we ignore it?"

Fishing in his shirt pocket, he came up with a creased piece of paper. "I've jotted down some questions. The first one would be to ask if Ariana is still alive." He saw my expression, and grimaced. "I'm sorry, Kylie, but it's a logical question."

"What about her BMW?" I said.

"Where the hell is the car? Good question, and it'd be great if Cassandra could clue us in. It's common in missing person cases to find the vehicle in an airport parking structure. Or it can be left on the street with keys in the ignition, the hope being that someone will steal it, and if they're caught, muddy the waters with a false lead."

I thought of Ariana's beloved dark blue BMW. It wasn't a new car, but she looked after it so well it could have just been driven off a showroom floor.

"If you were the kidnapper," I said, "what would you do with the BMW?"

"Like I said, let it be stolen, or leave it in public parking where people are coming and going all the time, although increased surveillance because of terrorism might be a problem. Another alternative would be to drive it off the road and hide it in some remote area, maybe in the Angeles National Forest. You'd need an accomplice though, to pick you up after you'd disposed of the vehicle."

"Not necessarily. You could bring a bicycle or one of those little motor scooters in the car."

Lonnie's dimples showed in a momentary grin. "Thinking like a criminal—that's a great help to a PI."

"Why take risks driving around?" I said. "You could park it in the garage of a suburban house and lock the door, and who would know?"

Lonnie shook his head. "I can think of a lot of people—a wife, a husband, kids, friends, neighbors, workmen. Basically, anyone who has access to the home."

A call came in. "Good morning, Kendall & Creeling—Lexus, hi! How are you and Bruce getting along? Really? That well? Melodie? Sorry, she's not here. An audition. Yeah, her 'one big chance.' She'll get back to you as soon as she comes in. Okay, take care."

Hanging up, he said to me, "I couldn't face telling Lexus about Ariana. I'll leave that to Melodie."

Obviously I'd got to Mum in the nick of time.

The next call was a wrong number. When he finally got rid of the woman, who apparently refused to believe she'd made a mistake dialing, I said to him, "Let's say for the moment Cassandra does have genuine psychic powers at least some of the time. She claims she saw Bob's sister's face clearly in her crystal ball. Why not ask her if she sees the face of whoever it is who has Ariana?"

"Okay," said Lonnie, looking doubtful.

"And where Ariana's being held. Is it a room? A cabin in the mountains?" I didn't put into words the possibility I most dreaded—a coffin-sized, covered pit dug into the floor of a basement, or gouged out of the ground in some remote location.

"How about an old bomb shelter from the fifties?" said Lonnie. "Some are still around."

The phone rang. "It's for you," said Lonnie. "Heidi Brandstett calling."

"I'll take it in my office."

There was no mystery to her having my telephone number, as I'd filled in all the relevant personal details when I'd applied to join the fundraising committee. But why was Heidi calling me? I feared the worst. Perhaps my strategy of playing enthusiastic fan of Vanessa Banning had failed to permanently discourage Heidi. Was she again offering a nightcap after the meeting tonight? I'd have to find some graceful way to wriggle out of the invitation.

I picked up the phone and said politely, "Ms Brandstett?"

"Heidi, *please!*" she replied in a throaty growl.

"Sorry. G'day, Heidi."

"The place is buzzing with the news that Ariana Creeling, your business partner, has been abducted. I'm calling to give you my deepest, most sincere sympathy."

"Thank you."

"Of course, I knew her quite well."

"You did?" I said, with a pang that Heidi was using the past tense as though Ariana no longer existed.

Heidi gave a roguish laugh. "She was somewhat of a rival, if I may call her that."

"A rival?"

"Certain of the men folk here at the Evenstar Home found Ariana most attractive." Another roguish laugh. "Frankly, I did myself."

Although I already knew this because Ariana had named Heidi as a would-be suitor, I said, "I beg your pardon?"

"Young women of your generation are so much more open minded about sexual matters, don't you agree?"

"I don't know what to say," I said, truthfully.

"Say nothing, my dear," she purred. "Actions speak louder than words."

Crikey!

Heidi went on, "You'll be at the meeting tonight?"

Belatedly recalling I was supposed to be playing the part of a cooperative, sweet, harmless individual, I said enthusiastically, "Wouldn't miss it for the world."

"Excellent. I so look forward to seeing you again. So until then, au revoir."

"Hooroo."

"Too cute," she said, and rang off.

* * *

I opened my copy of *Private Investigation: The Complete Handbook* and turned to the chapter on kidnapping and abduction. There was a section on captivity written by a psychologist specializing in stress and mental health issues.

The section began with the series of questions victims invariably ask themselves when first captured: *What happened? Where am I? Why me? Who is at fault? Could I have done something? Could I have done more?*

The psychologist went to say that when victims realize they cannot escape and may be captive for some time, they then make a conscious decision to do whatever it takes to survive.

"That's you, Ariana," I said to the empty air. "You're a survivor."

I imagined her taking the itemized steps:

- develop a relationship with the captor
- establish a personal mission to escape

- if escape seems impossible, gather as much data about the person and the place as possible
- take care of self by making specific requests for water, food, blankets, and any other necessities
- keep one's mind occupied
- have faith that the ordeal will end

There was a separate section briefly describing the Stockholm Syndrome. Occurring over time and under tremendous emotional and often physical duress, and in a situation where normal perspectives are impossible, captives begin to identify with their captors as a defense mechanism.

I already knew that the name came from a hostage situation in a bank in Stockholm, Sweden, where after six days several kidnap victims resisted rescue attempts and later refused to testify against their captors. And of course the most famous example was heiress Patty Hearst, who was kidnapped by a radical political group and eventually became an accomplice in several bank robberies.

It seemed impossible to imagine Ariana falling prey to the Stockholm Syndrome, but I had no idea of the extent of the psychological and physical pressure she was enduring while I was sitting in the comfort of my office.

I got up and began to pace around. I had to do something—but what? Every nerve I had seemed to be standing on end and shrieking. By tonight, Ariana would have been missing for 48 hours. I recalled reading that that the optimum time to solve a murder was within the first two days. After that period of time an arrest became less likely. Did the same general rule apply to abductions? I was sure it did.

To streamline communications, Bob had been designated to liaise with Ted Lark and then pass on any information to the rest of us. Although I knew he would tell me the moment there was any news, I went along to his office anyway.

"Anything?" I said to him.

Bob shook his head. "Nothing yet."

The movie posters of fictional dramas looked down from the walls. Tidy stories, with beginnings and ends, everything resolved in some way, for good or evil.

"What if we never know?" I said. "What if it's like your sister?" I choked up. "Sorry, Bob, I'm a bit of a crybaby today."

"Kylie, we'll find Ariana."

I took a deep breath. "I've been reading about the psychology of captivity."

"She's a survivor. She'll do everything necessary. Believe that." I imagined myself in her situation. She had to be in a state of constant anxiety, not knowing what to expect next. I wasn't sure how I would cope with that unrelenting tension. "How could anyone come through such an experience unscathed?"

"They don't," said Bob. "Rescue isn't the end of the ordeal. Captivity creates extreme stress, and victims must be guided through a recovery process."

"Talking about this is good," I said, "because it makes me feel it's going to happen with Ariana."

"Okay, here's the sequence." Ticking off the points on his fingers, Bob went on, "First is assurance—you're rescued, it's over, you're not to blame, everything's all right. Second, is a comprehensive medical exam and initial treatment of any problems."

"Some could show up later," I pointed out, "like trouble sleeping or anxiety attacks."

"Debriefing, done correctly, is a help there. Steps three and four are the two kinds of debriefing, tactical, which basically asks, 'What did you observe?' and stress debriefing, which requires the victim to describe how he or she felt about every experience of captivity."

"But haven't they already gone through this with people close to them?"

"No," said Bob, "because a rescued captive hasn't been allowed to see friends or family yet. Reunification, as it's called, can't take place until the first four items in the sequence have been covered."

"Will Ariana really have to go through all of this?"

"She will, but she'll probably not need the final step. Especially if it's a high-profile case, guidance in dealing with possible media frenzy is provided."

"I reckon I could handle media frenzy," I said. "After this, I reckon I could handle anything."

* * *

Before getting changed to leave for the Evenstar meeting, I went online to check my e-mail messages. One caught my eye immediately with the two-word subject line "Boo Hoo." When I opened it the message was three words: "Who's crying now?"

CHAPTER SIXTEEN

I came through the door of the Evenstar meeting room to find I was one of the last to arrive. Most of my fellow committee members were milling about, talking animatedly. An exception was Wendell Yalty, who stood by himself, jiggling from foot to foot. Carrie Wentworth, still clutching her autograph book, was moving from group to group, no doubt obtaining entries she'd missed the other night.

Heidi Brandstett, her womanly curves swathed in turquoise silk and her hair teased into a tall blond helmet that increased her height by inches, came over to greet me. I reminded myself that I was in platypus mode, so I flashed her a shy smile. "G'day, Heidi."

Before she could respond, Sir Rupert Martindale rushed up. "Reputation, reputation, reputation!" he declared in sonorous tones, his snowy eyebrows shooting up and down. "Oh! I have lost my reputation. I have lost the immortal part of myself, and what remains is bestial."

"*Othello?*"

"Excellent, Miss Kendall. Act Two, to be precise."

"The police interviewed Sir Rupert this afternoon," said Heidi with a malicious smile. "As you see, he's all shook up."

"It was a shockingly demeaning experience," he said. "My warm feelings for Ariana Creeling were virtually trampled in the dust by insensitive boors. Apparently I am—totally astounding though the concept is—a suspect in her disappearance. Outrageous!"

"Outrageous?" Heidi arched one perfectly drawn eyebrow. "What's outrageous is that we now learn that Sir Rupert has been involved in several unsavory stalking incidents."

"Blimey," I said, "is it true, Sir Rupert?"

He burned with righteous indignation. "The very suggestion is contemptible! They were misunderstandings, unfortunate misunderstandings. Poor gels allowed themselves to be influenced by troublemakers and made baseless accusations." He struck a pose. "As the Bard so presciently wrote, 'Frailty, thy name is woman!'"

"You old goat," said Heidi with a sneer, "everyone knows stalking is the mark of a desperate creature, unable to form normal, healthy relationships."

Mortally offended, his face scarlet, Sir Rupert snarled, "Normal? You speak of normal, healthy relationships? No one would call your rapacious, indiscriminate sexual appetites anything close to normal!"

They glared daggers at each other. Strewth, there was going to be a nasty blue any minute now. With relief I saw Emory Hastings approaching at a fast clip.

"Heidi, a private word," Emory said, taking her arm and trying to guide her away. She went unwillingly, hissing to Sir Rupert over her shoulder, "You're toast, Martindale. Toast!"

"Poor, pathetic nymphomaniac," Sir Rupert said, when Heidi was safely out of earshot. "I caution you to be ever vigilant where that woman is concerned."

"It must have been awful being questioned by the detectives," I said with solemn sympathy.

He inclined his head in assent. "Most unpleasant. Detective Lark's attitude in particular was unconscionable. His partner, a Detective Philips, was far more circumspect."

After a pause to smooth his mustache and adjust his cravat, he continued, "The very suggestion that I, Sir Rupert Martindale, could ever be involved in anything as heinous as a kidnapping is preposterous. However, I fancy I comported myself well in the circumstances, certainly better than other recipients of the excessively abrasive interrogation techniques."

"Who else did the detectives interview?"

Sir Rupert made a vague gesture. "Practically everyone, I gather."

He gestured towards Cory Grainger, who was deep in urgent conversation with Glenys Clarkson, and said with evident pleasure, "I did hear that Grainger handled things rather badly. Made quite a hash of things and aroused the detectives' suspicions."

"Crikey," I said, "do you think Cory Grainger has anything to do with Ariana's abduction?"

"I'd like to think not, but, as Sir Walter Scott says so tellingly, 'Oh, what a tangled web we weave, when first we practice to deceive!'"

"Are you saying Cory Grainger was lying to the cops?"

"He was somewhat careless with the truth, telling them that he barely knew Ariana, although I've observed them speaking to each other on several occasions. During my interview, when I was pointing out I was no means the prime suspect in the case, I happened to mention, just in passing, Grainger's obsessive interest in Ariana."

Cory Grainger looked over our way and his pleasant expression changed to a scowl. "It looks like he knows you dobbed him in," I said.

"Attention!" Heidi Brandstett smashed down her gavel with extraordinary force. "I'm calling the Swan Song fundraising committee to order. Tonight there are no designated seats, so please take any place for the formal part of the meeting, after which we will split into small groups to roleplay strategies tailored to encourage potential donors to give generously in support of *Swan Song for the Luminaries*."

We all obediently moved to sit down. "I didn't realize you owned a private-eye company," said Frank Franklin as he settled his huge bulk into the chair next to mine. "Why didn't you mention it before?"

"Didn't seem relevant," I said.

"Glenys told me there are no new developments in your partner's disappearance."

"Do you know Ariana Creeling?"

"As I told the cops this afternoon, I've seen her around," he said vaguely. A flicker of enthusiasm crossed his face. "So great to see some of the SOBs squirm," he said, folding his arms over his protruding stomach. "I especially enjoyed Vince's expression after his interrogation. Looked as though he'd swallowed something very nasty."

All innocence, I asked, "But why would Vincent Yarborough be upset by a few questions?"

He lifted his massive shoulders in a shrug that strained the seams of the light gray jacket he was wearing. "Who knows?" His smile was sly. "Could have something to do with me spilling the beans."

"The beans?" I echoed.

"Looking out for Glenys as I do, and her being the vital center of administration, there's not much gets by me at Evenstar."

His chair creaked as he leaned over to murmur confidentially, "I told the cop in charge—Lark, I think his name is—a few valuable tidbits about our accountant, our administrator, and incidentally"—he jerked his head in Sir Rupert's direction— "that overacting English piece of shit."

"Stone the crows," I said admiringly, "the police must have been impressed."

His jowls wobbled as he nodded vigorously. "I think they were."

Whack! went Heidi's gavel. "Order!" When silence fell, she gestured to Emory Hastings. "Emory will now speak about your mission."

"Boring," said someone.

I looked around the table. Everyone who'd been at the first meeting seemed to be present, with the exception of Oona Turner, Nancy McDuff, and Vince Yarborough.

Emory rose to speak, but before he could open his mouth Wendell Yalty leapt to his feet. "I have a statement to make!"

"Oh, God, not his mother again," Frank Franklin muttered.

"Last meeting I made a formal request that my mother, Quintina Ladd, radiant star of Hollywood musicals—"

"Yada, yada, yada," came from down the other end of the table. "Just get on with it!"

Heidi pounded her gavel. "I second that motion."

"It wasn't a motion," someone pointed out.

"Last meeting," said Wendell Yalty, "I made a formal request that the Evenstar extravaganza be named *Quintina Ladds Swan Song for the Luminaries* in recognition of her incalculable contributions to *Swan Song* over the years. Cruelly, and without even a pretence that my request was given due consideration, it was denied."

He paused for the enormity of this rejection to sink in. No one looked impressed. Jutting his jaw, he went on, "Therefore it is with regret, deep regret, that I must resign from the fundraising committee, effective immediately."

"Done," said Heidi with a whack of her gavel.

Yalty cast her a look of burning anger, then, head held high, stalked from the room.

Beside me, Frank gave a throaty chuckle. "How unwise of Heidi to make an enemy of Wendell Yalty," he said. "Over the years he's made it his business to know where all the bodies are buried."

"You know Mr. Yalty? I thought like me he was just a volunteer for the committee."

"From the time his mother, the moderately talented songstress with, incidentally, a monstrous ego, became a resident of Evenstar Home, Wendell has had an obsessive interest in the place. Since she died, he's proposed his mother's name be immortalized in various places—The Quintina Ladd Dining Hall, The Quintina Ladd Auditorium, even The Quintina Ladd Grove of Native Trees."

"No success?" I said.

"Turned down every time. He never had any chance because Oona Turner loathes him. Of course, Oona Turner loathes everyone."

Emory cleared his throat for attention. Heidi took the opportunity to pound her gavel a couple of times. He began with, "Our mission, your mission, the mission each one of us has…"

Although good-looking and possessing an attractive baritone voice, Emory Hastings was an incredibly boring public speaker. I tuned out as he droned on. Looking around the table, I saw I wasn't the only one. It was glazed eyes galore. Vanessa Banning, resting her head against her brother's shoulder, actually seemed to be dozing.

"…and in conclusion, may I say we all go proudly forth, our mission in our hearts and minds, cognizant of the proud tradition of *Swan Song for the Luminaries* and its influence down the ages." Emory made a half bow to the table. "On behalf of The Clarice Turner Evenstar Home, thank you, all of you, thank you."

"Thank God that's over," someone murmured.

With undiminished zeal, Heidi pounded her gavel. Fair dinkum, I was thinking that giving her anything resembling a hammer could be dangerous. "Order, please! Before we split into our roleplaying groups, I'll announce the pairings."

"Oh, sex games! Fun!" exclaimed Vanessa Banning to general laughter.

Heidi didn't smile. "The pairings of less-experienced members of the committee with Evenstar luminaries is for the purpose of effective fundraising," she said severely. She consulted a page in front of her, then bestowed a warm smile on me. "First pairing is Kylie Kendall with Cory Grainger."

"Oh, I say," said Sir Rupert, "that's not at all fair. You know I made a specific request for Miss Kendall."

"The second pairing," said Heidi, ignoring the interruption, "is Carrie Wentworth with Sir Rupert Martindale."

"Oh, I say!" exclaimed Sir Rupert, far from delighted. From the expression on her face, Carrie shared his displeasure.

Heidi finished the pairings, then organized us into our role-playing groups. Cory and I ended up with Frank Franklin and an anorexic woman whose name I'd never caught. Glenys Clarkson was there as designated leader, to guide us through our roleplays.

"G'day," I said to the woman. "I'm Kylie Kendall."

She murmured something.

"I beg your pardon?"

"Rita. Her name's Rita," Frank said, looming over her like a huge beach ball. He added in an undertone, "Rita never-eater." She didn't seem to hear.

"G'day, Rita."

"Hello," she breathed. Her neck was pencil-thin, her eyes enormous in a skeletal face. I reckoned it wouldn't take all that much effort to snap her in two.

"You're new to the committee, like me," I said conversationally.

She whispered, "Not exactly. I've been involved in several extravaganzas. I'm a friend of Vince's."

"Vince Yarborough?" I said, wondering if Rita knew the bloke she was paired with had enjoyed getting Vince into trouble with the cops.

I strained to hear her say softly, "He's a wonderful friend."

"I met him for the first time the other night. He did seem awfully nice," I gushed. Frank Franklin rolled his eyes, but luckily didn't comment.

I was all set to cultivate Rita as a source of information about Vince Yarborough, but I didn't have to make the effort.

"Could we meet for coffee, perhaps?" she murmured. "Vince has been so good to me, I'd love to share with someone who appreciates him. Do you have a business card? I'll call."

Crikey! Rita had suddenly become my second best friend. I didn't flatter myself it was my Aussie charm. So why?

* * *

The roleplaying exercises that followed made it delightfully clear that I was on a fundraising winner with Cory Grainger by my side. Glenys instructed Frank Franklin to play a hard-nosed businessman who had reluctantly agreed to see us as a favor for a friend. I had little to do but admire Cory's skills at extracting money from potential donors. Even Frank, who played his character as a loud-mouthed yobbo, was won over.

The team of Frank and Rita was not nearly as successful trying to persuade husband-and-wife fashion entrepreneurs— Cory and me—to fork over a substantial donation. Rita whispered her way through her role and Frank blustered through his. Even succinct advice from Glenys Clarkson, the woman Frank so admired, failed to achieve a positive result.

"Perhaps, Glenys, some private sessions with you might help," said Frank hopefully. Glenys was polite but firm. Private sessions were out of the question.

Later everyone descended on the refreshments in the same plague-of-locusts manner as after the first meeting. The spread was not nearly as lavish, but roleplaying was hard work, so sandwiches and coffee were more than welcome.

I found myself next to Carrie Wentworth's sturdy form. Her wispy blond hair and pink, perspiring face made her seem like an overheated baby. Not wishing to waste an opportunity to take advantage of her interest in celebrities, I said with warm enthusiasm, "What an absolutely fascinating pastime collecting autographs is. Do you have Zelda Webber's?"

I'd struck the right note. Carrie smiled broadly. "I do! She was so gracious, sending me an autographed photograph too. I'm one of her keenest fans."

"She's married to Emory Hastings, isn't she?"

Carrie made a dismissive gesture. "Not for long."

"Not for long? What do you mean?"

"It's not generally known," Carrie said, obviously taking pleasure in being the bearer of bad tidings, "but their marriage is totally on the rocks. Zelda moved out of the house in Brentwood months ago."

"I hadn't heard. Are you sure?" I was in full celebrity-gossip mode. "I don't think there's been any mention of a breakup on her television talk show."

Carrie gave me a pitying look. "You haven't read my blog, have you?" She produced a card. "Check it out."

"'Carrie's Hot Scandalmania'?" I said. "Bonzer name." When a frown creased her damp brow, I hastened to add, "I'm saying it's a terrific name for your blog."

She glowed with pride. "It's getting more hits every day. I'm making quite a name for myself in show-biz circles for breaking news. *Variety* has even picked up material from my blog." She added smugly, "Like, I was the first to out Jasper Guerney. That was the end of his career as a romantic lead."

"So about the marriage," I said, "do you think there is there any chance Emory and Zelda will get back together again?"

"No way! Zelda's not going to put up with Emory one second more.

"Affairs?"

Carrie shrugged. "Uh! Affairs? They mean nothing."

"What, then?"

"He's a control freak. Had to know where Zelda was and who she was with every moment of every day. It was too much for a free spirit like Zelda, so she left."

"I've heard she's into cocaine in a big way."

Carrie lifted her shoulders again. "Uh! Cocaine? It means nothing."

"So has Emory got a new love interest in his life?"

"Who cares?" she said. "It's not as if he's a *star*. I mean, while he was with Zelda Webber at least he was someone. Now..." She threw up her hands. "Uh!"

"He's nobody?"

"Nobody."

"I hate to interrupt," said Heidi, "but I need Kylie rather badly." Her inviting smile sent a chill down my spine worthy of Chilley Dorsal. "I was just leaving," I said.

She took my arm and looked up at me suggestively. "Nonsense. We have a great deal to discuss."

"Actually, we do," I said, thinking that, as well as having some romantic interest in Ariana, Heidi seemed to be at the center of things at Evenstar. "We need to discuss Ariana Creeling."

Heidi frowned. "I've made it clear how sorry I am she's been abducted. What more is there to say?"

I drew her aside as I looked around furtively. "What I'm about to tell you is deeply confidential, Heidi."

Keen interest flooded her face. "You can rely on me to keep a secret."

I knew I was probably bending the client's privileged information rules, but Ariana's safety trumped everything. Deliberately leaving out my undercover role, I said, "Under any other circumstances, I wouldn't mention this, but Ariana's disappearance may be related to a case of embezzlement she's been investigating here at the Evenstar Home."

Heidi's astonishment had to be genuine. "Embezzlement? Here at Evenstar? I haven't heard a word about this."

I was flying on a wing and a prayer, making up things as I went along. "That's because you're a suspect," I declared.

Her jaw dropped. "What!"

I looked around again. "Shhh!"

All thoughts of seduction gone, she stared at me, "I'm totally bewildered by all of this. How could I possibly have embezzled any money?"

"Heidi, I truly believe you have nothing to do with it," I said sincerely, "but the problem is that the Swan Song accounts are the ones where shortfalls have been discovered."

"Are you sure it isn't a mistake? Frankly, Vince Yarborough is a lovely man, but a very slapdash accountant. If it wasn't for Rita, he wouldn't have the job."

"Rita? I think I met her this evening. She speaks very softly?"

"That's Rita Foyle. She's known as Murmur. Friend of Oona Turner's."

I blinked at this. The thought that Oona had even one friend was startling.

Amused by my reaction, Heidi said, "Hard to believe, I know, but Oona and Murmur went to school together, and somehow have remained friends. Murmur has been Vince's champion. She got him the position at Evenstar and kept him in it through Oona's influence, even though, as I said, he's mediocre at his job, at best."

"He was on the ball enough to discover at least one misappropriation in the Swan Song figures."

Heidi's perfectly made-up face was thoughtful. "Are you sure Oona didn't put Vince up to it? Oona's been trying to get rid of Emory Hastings for ages, but the Evenstar Home board won't cooperate."

A credible accusation of embezzlement would do the trick?

"Emory'd be out on his ear in a New York minute."

CHAPTER SEVENTEEN

"You left for an audition yesterday and never came back," I said pointedly.

Melodie, who'd just come rushing through the front door ten minutes late for work, had the grace to blush. "I'm real sorry, Kylie, but there were so many bees the auditions went on, like, forever."

"Bees," was the disparaging term Melodie used for those she dismissed as would-be actors.

She deposited her things behind the reception desk and took her seat. "I called Lonnie as soon as I realized. Didn't he tell you?"

"He told me you'd have a snowball's chance in hell of having him fill in for you again."

Melodie bit her lip with her cosmetically enhanced teeth. "Was Lonnie real mad?"

"Mad as a cut snake. And so was Fran. She didn't appreciate having to fill in when Lonnie had urgent work to do."

Wilting with remorse, she said with a catch in her voice, "I hope they can find it in their hearts to forgive me. I'll do anything to make it up to them."

"Good luck with that." Thinking I'd better ask, I added, "How did the audition go?"

In a flash Melodie had switched from remorse to effervescent joy. "Oh, Kylie! I aced it, I really did. It was as if Chilley Dorsal possessed the very essence of my soul! Larry-my-agent said he'd never seen anything like it. And so did Yolanda/Cassandra."

"She was there at the audition?"

"As my paranormal coach. Isn't it awesome? No one else had one."

Simultaneously, the phone rang and Lonnie flung open the front door and stomped in.

"Oh, she's actually here," he said, glaring resentfully at Melodie as she answered the call. "What a big surprise."

"Lexus, hi!" Melodie exclaimed. "No, I didn't get the message you'd called. You've heard about Ariana? Omigod, it's awful, isn't it?"

Lonnie jabbed savagely at a pile of message slips on the desk. "These all came in yesterday for her," he said to me. "Gives you some idea of how many personal calls Melodie gets."

On the phone, Melodie had finished with the subject of Ariana and was onto her audition. "Like, it was just the best audition I've ever done in my life. As Larry-my-agent says…"

Lonnie rolled his eyes. "I can only hope she's right—the audition was a roaring success and Melodie gets the part. The sooner we can hire someone dependable for the front desk, the happier I'll be."

My attention was caught by Melodie, who, white-faced, sat bolt upright in her seat. "Say that again, Lexus." There was a tremor in her voice.

"It must be bad news," said Lonnie, concerned.

Finishing the call, Melodie swung around to us. Her expression tragic, she said, "That was Lexus."

"Is something wrong?" I asked.

"No, nothing's wrong," said Melodie unconvincingly. "It's great. Really." She took a shuddering breath. "Lexus and Bruce, they're…"

"Spit it out," said Lonnie.

Melodie sniffed, straightened her shoulders, and said valiantly, "Lexus and Bruce are announcing their engagement."

* * *

I left Melodie with the task of finding out why the receptionist network had failed to report an affair between Emory Hastings and Evenstar's receptionist, Nancy McDuff, and went to my office to call Wendell Yalty. Heidi had given me his number.

Lonnie came in as I was putting down the receiver. "That last e-mail you got isn't traceable either." he said. "I've passed it on to Lark, but his technicians won't have any better luck."

"It's from the same person who has Ariana."

"Kylie, you don't know that for sure. It could simply be that your stalker heard the news about her and took advantage of the situation to needle you."

"But in this one he says, 'Who's crying now?' and in the first email, which was sent before Ariana disappeared, he wrote, 'You're forcing me to take action. Crying time coming.' It's the same person."

We both looked up as Fran and Bob came in. "How's Janette?" I asked.

Fran looked somber. "I'm very worried about Mom. She isn't coping at all well. Quip's staying with her today and Harriet's offered to come tomorrow if she can bring the baby. Mom's doctor's given her something to help her sleep, but she'll scarcely take a bite of food. Ask Bob, he had no luck getting her to eat breakfast this morning."

"I called by to give a progress report," said Bob, folding his long body into a chair. "Not that there's been much progress."

"How did you go last night with your fake psychic?" Fran asked Lonnie. "Does Yolanda/Cassandra see you getting back with Pauline?"

"As a matter of fact she does see that happening."

"And you actually believed her?" Fran jeered.

"I'm keeping an open mind. And she had something to say about Ariana. Do you want to hear it or not?"

"I'd like a blow-by-blow," said Bob. "Start at the beginning."

"I've already told Kylie all this, but I'll go through it again. Cassandra shares a rather dumpy little office building on Westwood Boulevard with an acupuncturist, a chiropractor, and a direct-mail service."

"Low woo-woo factor," said Bob with a grin.

"She's gone to a lot of trouble setting up her room to create the right atmosphere," said Lonnie. "Incense burning, dim, flickering light from candles, dark drapery everywhere, and soft, barely audible music, which sounded to me vaguely Asian. And, of course, the table and the crystal ball. Oh, and she was wearing a long purple robe affair, the color carefully chosen, she informed me, to enhance the out-of-this-world connection."

With a sour smile, Fran remarked, "I guarantee she made you pay those six hundred dollars up front. Am I right?"

Lonnie nodded. "She did." He added sardonically, "Cassandra made it clear it was important to get crass commercial transactions out of the way before entering the spiritual dimension."

Fran snorted her derision. "Surely you can't still have a shred of belief that this con artist's in touch with another reality."

"Maybe she is...sometimes."

"For six hundred dollars, 'sometimes' doesn't cut it."

Lonnie shrugged. "Anyway, Cassandra went through her whole trance routine, eyeballs rolling up, collapsing unconscious in the chair, etc. Then her eyes snapped open and she stared into the crystal ball. Kylie and I had worked out some questions about Ariana, but before I could start Cassandra announced Pauline and I had been together in several past lives. I said, 'What about *this* life?' and Cassandra said we would be getting back together again. When? She wasn't sure, but soon. And would it all work out? She said she saw children, a boy and girl."

"Pauline Feeney with children?" hooted Fran. "The woman's got the mother instinct of a cuckoo bird."

Lonnie winced at Fran's take on the woman he loved. "Pauline's not like that, Fran. You don't know her like I do?"

"Let's get to Ariana," said Bob. "What did Cassandra have to say?"

"Overall, I wasn't all that impressed. She came up with general stuff she could have learned through news reports or pumping Melodie. She did assure me Ariana was still alive and in good health. I asked her some specific questions, and here are her answers: Who snatched her? It's a white male, well-educated, and Ariana knew him before she was kidnapped. Location of her BMW? It's in an enclosed space. Where is Ariana being kept? Cassandra can't say for sure, but feels it's within a radius of thirty miles."

"And that was it?" said Bob scornfully.

With obvious reluctance, Lonnie said, "Cassandra did ask me to pass on something to you, Bob. I'm to tell you she has a message from Kerrie that you need to hear, but it must be given to you in person.

I thought Bob might be upset by this, but he gave a cynical smile. "That's a classic move for a sham psychic—claim to have a message from the missing person that can only be delivered via a supernatural link, which will—big surprise!—take the payment of money to open."

"I said all along she was a fake," snapped Fran, "but nobody listened."

"Um, one more thing." Lonnie hesitated, then said in a rush, "Cassandra said to tell you Kerrie's little dog was a pug."

For a moment Bob seemed taken aback, but then he made an impatient gesture. "We've wasted enough time on the woman. Let's get to something concrete. I had a long conversation with Ted Lark about the interviews he conducted yesterday afternoon at the Evenstar Home."

Flipping open a notebook, he went on, "Heidi Brandstett went first and she turned on the charm big time, but that was all she did. As a source of information she was a bust. Some of the men, however, were keen to pass on gossip. Sir Rupert Martindale stated he was sure Cory Grainger was involved in Ariana's disappearance, although he had no evidence to back this up, other than to say he noticed them talking together at times and Grainger had been very attentive."

"There's a history of animosity between them," I pointed out.

"You're right about that. When he was interviewed, Grainger announced Sir Rupert was capable of anything, including kidnapping."

"Sir Rupert Martindale?" said Fran. "He's a wonderful actor."

"Not everybody appreciates him," I said. "For example, Frank Franklin, who seems to be a nasty piece of work, boasted to me last night that he'd dobbed in Sir Rupert to the cops, along with Emory Hastings and Vince Yarborough."

"The fat man did shaft them," Bob agreed. "Franklin mentioned Sir Rupert's stalking episodes with some relish, implying he'd paid good money to have the victims drop the charges."

"Did Sir Rupert pay hush money?" Lonnie wanted to know.

"It sure looks that way. Ted Lark has someone going back over Sir Rupert's life to see if there are other similar incidents that he's managed to keep quiet."

"What did Franklin have on Vince Yarborough and Emory Hastings?" I asked.

"Yarborough's gay, which Franklin sniggered about until Lark made it clear it was a nonissue. Yarborough's never made a big thing of it, but equally he hasn't hidden his sexual orientation. In fact he was living openly in a long-term relationship until his partner died a couple of years ago."

"Crikey, to know Frank Franklin is to love him," I said sarcastically.

"As for Emory Hastings," Bob continued, "Franklin announced he was almost certainly mentally ill. Paranoid schizophrenia was his layman's diagnosis, apparently based on the way Hastings treats his assistant, Glenys."

"Franklin has a crush on Glenys. I don't think he's rational when she's concerned."

"Bad news for Glenys," Lonnie said.

"During her interview she complained to Lark that Franklin dogged her like a shadow, but he's never done or said anything that could be construed as a threat. Glenys said her boss had instructed her to be pleasant to Franklin, because Hastings believes, given an excuse, Franklin will sue, claiming he's discriminated against because he's grossly overweight."

"Jesus," said Fran, "what if this fat guy's got Ariana?"

Up until now, I'd dismissed him as a rather unpleasant, but pretty well harmless bloke. Now I felt a visceral alarm. To be Frank Franklin's captive would be skin-crawlingly dreadful. "Has he got an alibi for Saturday evening?"

"Ah, alibis said Bob, shaking his narrow head. "Beloved in crime fiction, in real life they're as slippery as hell. The fact is, unless there's a specific reason to remember, most people are very vague about time. They even confuse which day something happened. This group is no exception."

It seemed the alibis covering early Saturday evening were inconclusive. It was a time of day when people were often making preparations to go out later. Sir Rupert claimed to be dressing for a concert by a string quartet, which he may or may not have attended—he went solo and said he hadn't spoken to anyone. Vince Yarborough was in Studio City, walking his dogs—two golden retrievers—in the streets near his home. Emory Hastings was catching up on urgent work in his office. Glenys had been assisting him some of the time. Frank Franklin was watching television alone in his Evenstar apartment. Cory Grainger was with his sister, Vanessa Banning, although as I pointed out, brother and sister were so close that providing an alibi for each other would be automatic, whether it was true or not.

I told everyone about Wendell Yalty, and how Franklin had said Yalty knew where the bodies were buried. "He sounds like a good source of information about Evenstar. Heidi gave me his address and phone number. I called him earlier, and he's agreed to see me this afternoon."

"You're not going alone," said Bob. "This guy sounds like a nut. I'm coming with you."

When I told them about Rita "Murmur" Foyle's pending invitation to coffee so she could discuss her friend Vince, Fran frowned darkly. "Whisperers—I don't like 'em. While you're distracted, trying to catch what they're saying, they get away with murder."

"It's clear I've got to start whispering around here," announced Lonnie, smirking.

Fran rolled her eyes. "Very funny, Lonnie. You're the life of the party."

"One more thing about last night," I said. "Carrie Wentworth, another of the volunteers, writes a celebrity blog. She told me Zelda Webber walked out on Emory Hastings months ago."

"Can't be," said Lonnie. "They were together at a movie launch Glowing Bodies organized the other night."

"Glowing Bodies?" said Fran, eyes narrowing. "You've broken up with Pauline, so why have you anything to do with her company?"

Lonnie went rather pink. "If you must know, I just happened to be in Hollywood and saw the limos pulling up and all the guests going in."

"Just *happened* to be in Hollywood?"

"Well, yes."

"Come clean, Lonnie. You were there to catch a glimpse of Pauline Feeney, weren't you?"

Lonnie went a shade pinker. "Maybe."

"There's a name for what you're doing, Lonnie," Fran declared righteously. "It's stalking."

CHAPTER EIGHTEEN

Wendell Yalty had a West Hollywood address. His apartment was one of six in a yellow stucco building just off Santa Monica Boulevard.

"I thought you were coming alone. Who is this?" he asked when he opened the door. His face dark with suspicion, he sized up Bob. They were both thin, but Bob was considerably taller and definitely less intense.

"My colleague at Kendall & Creeling, Bob Verritt," I said. "Bob, this is Wendell Yalty. Wendell's mother was Quintina Ladd."

"Your mother was a consummate entertainer," said Bob, whose devotion to old movies was paying off in spades. "My favorite musical of Quintina's would be, I think, *Dapple Dawn Chorus*. Who could forget the scene where she sings along with the birds at daybreak? Pure magic!"

Wendell's scowl had been replaced with a welcoming smile. He ushered us into his apartment saying, "It's wonderful to hear you say that, Bob. *Dapple* would be one of my favorites too, although what about Quintina's fantasy musical, *Song of the Hive?*"

Bob shook his head admiringly. "I can't think of another star who could sing the role with such accomplished skill while wearing a bee outfit."

"No one could have ever guessed how much my mother hated wearing that queen-bee costume. Singing was bad enough, but dancing was torture."

Bob shook his head again. "They don't make artists like Quintina Ladd anymore."

There was silence while they communed over Wendell's mother, Bob standing quietly reflective, Wendell twitching and jiggling. It was tiring just to look at him, so I took the opportunity to give the place a quick once-over.

I wasn't surprised to find the room was a shrine to Quintina Ladd. Her face beamed down from every wall. Publicity photographs, framed movie posters, even an oil portrait in a heavy gilt frame, perhaps by the artist who had painted the portrait of Clarice Turner that hung in the entrance of Emory Hastings' office. It had the same turgid style.

The furniture was very old-fashioned, dark wood and overstuffed, uncomfortable-looking sofas with faded floral patterns. There were many little tables scattered around, each crowded with knickknacks and more framed photographs, mainly family shots. In them a smiling Quintina Ladd was seen with various men, all handsome. Often included in the snaps was a small, solemn boy, who I reckoned had to be Wendell when young.

Bob, who collected old movie posters, was quite genuinely admiring Wendell's collection. "I have a poster you seem to be missing," he said.

Wendell was galvanized. "Really? Which one?"

"*Stolen Nights on the Nile.*"

"Ah, yes! My mother made a stunning Cleopatra, did she not? So much more definitive an interpretation than Elizabeth Taylor's blowsy Egyptian broad."

"Quintina's Cleopatra was every shapely inch a queen Bob declared.

I thought he was laying it on a bit too thick, but Wendell lapped it up. "Every inch," he agreed. "The poster's in good condition?"

"Pristine."

Avarice filled Wendell's face. "How much?"

"I'm sorry, it's not for sale."

"Please! I must have it! It's one of the few missing from my collection."

"We'll talk later," said Bob smoothly, obviously realizing the poster was an excellent bargaining chip. He Zellsteind my way to indicate I should take over.

"It's bonzer that you've agreed to see us, Wendell," I began. "You know, of course, it's about the disappearance of Ariana Creeling, my business partner. We believe she's been abducted and is being held against her will. As I said on the phone, your special knowledge of the Evenstar Home and the people there may help us find her."

"Sit down," he said, indicating one of the floral sofas. "I'll get coffee."

The sofa was rather dusty and just as unyielding as I'd thought it would be.

"I'm guessing this furniture belonged to Quintina Ladd," said Bob, grimacing as he tried to find a comfortable spot. He shot me a quick grin. "I'm willing to make the ultimate sacrifice and give up the *Stolen Nights on the Nile* poster, if that's what it takes."

Wendell returned with a tray bearing three mugs, each of which had a likeness of Quintina Ladd and the name of one of her movies.

"You must feel very close to your mother," I said, stating the glaringly obvious.

"Oh, I do. And the séances, of course, let me draw even closer to her dear presence." He Zellsteind around the apartment. "For me, she's always here."

"Séances?" said Bob. "You use a psychic?"

I knew Bob must have the same thought as me—it couldn't possibly be Yolanda/Cassandra, could it?

"Patrick Orlando," said Wendell. "Perhaps you've heard of him. He's the paramount celebrity channeler. Marilyn Monroe speaks with him almost every day."

He handed us our mugs of coffee—mine showed Quintina starring in *Dancing During the Deluge*—offered sugar and cream, then took a seat on the sofa opposite us. He crossed, then recrossed his legs. "About that poster…" he began.

"I'd be happy to discuss that later," said Bob, "but in the meantime, we're here about Ariana Creeling."

"Yes, I know Ariana. Not well, but we've met several times at Evenstar. I recall she was good enough to sign a petition for the proposed Quintina Ladd Nature Walk. Her sudden disappearance was a shock. In fact, I asked Patrick Orlando about her at the séance last night."

Bob and I looked at each other. Bob spoke first. "What did he say?"

Wendell shook his head. "It was disappointing. Patrick tried to contact her via telepathy, but had no success."

I didn't want to believe a celebrity psychic who claimed to regularly chat with Marilyn Monroe was anything but a fake, but my skin prickled with apprehension. "Why couldn't he make contact with Ariana? Does that mean she's dead?"

This elicited a bark of laughter from Wendell. "My dear young lady, if Ariana Creeling were dead, Patrick would have no trouble at all speaking with her. It's his specialty to have conversations with those on the Other Side. No, in her case she's throwing up psychic barriers. Patrick says someone's messing with her mind, and she's resisting with all her power."

"We believe that someone is associated with Evenstar," said Bob. "That's why we've come to you. You know the place and all the people in it."

I added, "Frank Franklin told me you knew where all the bodies were buried."

"Franklin? He's a gross pig. A mountain of lard with a vicious tongue."

"Can you see him carrying out a kidnapping?" I asked.

Wendell sneezed. He took out a handkerchief and blew his nose. "Excuse me. Allergies," he said. "My mother was a martyr to them also." Tucking the handkerchief neatly away in his pocket, he continued, "Mercifully, on the Other Side Quintina no longer suffers from such maladies."

I was seized with a totally inappropriate desire to giggle. Visualizing Ariana in Franklin's power sobered me up fast. I repeated my question: "Can you see Frank Franklin carrying out a kidnapping?"

He cracked his knuckles, twitched a bit, then said, "Franklin's capable of anything. Have you seen the way he harasses Glenys Clarkson? It's disgusting. Anyone but Emory Hastings would have given the guy the bum's rush long ago."

"What's stopping Hastings from doing just that?" Bob inquired. "He's the administrator of the Evenstar Home. He must have a say in who the residents are. If Franklin's so unpleasant, why hasn't he been asked to leave?"

Picking up his mug, Wendell took a sip. He put the mug down, picked it up again. "I can think of two reasons. One, Franklin's got something on Emory Hastings. A little blackmail would be right up Franklin's alley. If that's the case, whatever it is keeps Franklin secure at Evenstar, no matter how he behaves."

He put down the coffee mug and yanked his ear. "Two, Oona Turner's on Franklin's side, maybe not for any other reason than to annoy Hastings."

"Do you get on with Oona?" I asked, recalling that Heidi had said Oona loathed Wendell and took pleasure in blocking any attempt of his to memorialize Quintina Ladd's name.

Wendell smiled bitterly. "I used to, as well as anybody did. Then I made the big mistake of mentioning the séances with Patrick Orlando in casual conversation one day. Oona was immediately mad to attend a séance herself, saying she was keen to contact her grandmother, Clarice Turner, the founder of the Evenstar Home."

"Something went wrong?" said Bob. "She didn't get to have a chat with her grandmother?"

"Clarice Turner came through loud and clear," said Wendell, now so agitated that his feet were beating a tap dance on the floor. "That was the problem. Clarice told Oona she was a disgrace to the Turner name, that Evenstar Home was doomed to mediocrity as long as Oona was associated with it."

"I imagine she wasn't all that happy to hear this," said Bob, grinning.

"Oona stormed out, but not before slapping Patrick across the face—*so* dangerous when one's a medium in a trance. Unreasonably, Oona totally blamed me for the outcome of the séance, insisting I'd set Patrick up to embarrass and upset her. From that day she's been determined to thwart me at every turn."

"Oona supports Vincent Yarborough," I remarked.

"That's because of Murmur Foyle. Oona listens to her"—he chuckled—"that is, if she can catch what Murmur's saying."

"Can you see Vince Yarborough as a kidnapper?"

"Never!" said Wendell warmly. "He wouldn't hurt a fly. I count him as a friend. And by the way, if you want someone who really knows where the bodies are buried at Evenstar, talk to Murmur. She's a good listener and so quiet, people hardly notice she's there."

"How about Cory Grainger as a suspect?" I said.

Wendell startled us both by throwing back his head and laughing immoderately. Wiping his eyes, he said, "Surely you realize that Grainger loves himself exclusively. Self-adoration takes all his time and energy. Oh, maybe he has a little affection to spare for his sister, Vanessa, but otherwise it's Grainger, Grainger, Grainger all the way. Have you seen how he checks himself out in every reflecting surface? I caught him admiring himself in a spoon the other day."

Bob said, "Sir Rupert Martindale?"

"Incapable of organizing a yard sale, let alone an abduction."

"He's stalked three women," I pointed out. Ted Lark had reported that this seemed to be the sum total of Sir Rupert's offences.

"Not very expertly," said Wendell scornfully. "I gather there was no problem in identifying him every time."

Although I didn't believe Heidi could be involved, Ariana had mentioned her as being a problem, so I said, "What about Heidi Brandstett? I know she's been paying a lot of attention to Ariana."

"Oh, *Heidi*," said Wendell derisively. "Give her a little authority and she becomes a mini tyrant. Did you see the ludicrous way she pounds that gavel at the meetings? Obviously power mad. But as for abducting anyone? No way. She wouldn't put her wig and makeup at risk."

"Emory Hastings? How about him?"

Wendell frowned at Bob's question. "I'd like to say it's likely, because he's a miserable excuse for a human being. He's cold, obsessive, wants to control every detail. But I don't think he cares enough to abduct anybody. He's certainly not brave enough, since a scumbag like Franklin can intimidate him so easily."

"And how about *you?*" I said.

Wendell gave me a sly smile. "How can you ask that, when my mother fills my nights and days? Besides, she'd never countenance another woman, particularly one as attractive as Ariana Creeling."

* * *

As we were leaving Wendell Yalty's apartment, he brought up the subject of Bob's movie poster for *Stolen Nights on the Nile*. "It's yours," said Bob, "if you can meet my price. I'll call you tomorrow and we'll discuss it."

Wendell was almost pathetically grateful. "You can't know what this means to me!"

On our way back to the office in Bob's silver Lexus, Bob remarked, "I don't know about you, but when Wendell Yalty mentioned contacting his mother through a spirit medium, for one wild moment I was sure it'd be Yolanda/Cassandra running a celestial switchboard service."

"I had the same ghastly thought."

"I've got Lonnie on Cassandra's trail," said Bob, a grim note in his voice. "I've told him to keep digging until he finds something."

"Lonnie half-believes Cassandra's seeing the future when she says he and Pauline will get back together again."

Bob gave a contemptuous snort. "It cost him enough to have her tell him exactly what he wanted to hear."

"I'm going to pay Lonnie back the money," I said. "After all, most of the reading was about Ariana."

Bob looked sideways at me. "Kylie, you don't have to do that. Didn't Lonnie himself suggest devoting the time to questions about Ariana?"

"That's why I'm paying him back."

By LA standards, the traffic was reasonably light, and as Wendell's apartment was not far from our building, within a few minutes we were turning into Kendall & Creeling's parking area.

As Bob drew up in his spot, I said, "I wanted to believe that Wendell's psychic, Patrick Orlando, was right when he said Ariana was alive and in some way able to resist."

"Hold that thought, Kylie. I intend to."

"I've got Rocky up here with me," said Melodie as we came through the front door. "Poor little guy was crying, left alone in his pen in your office." She leaned over to speak to Rocky, who was sleepily blinking in his sheepskin basket. "Widdle man was lonely, wasn't he?"

"Thank you, Melodie," said Bob, picking up the basket and Rocky. "Any messages?"

"Not for you. There's one for Kylie." Melodie gave me the oddest look—a combination of defiance and guilt. "Your Aunt Millie. You're to call her." She paused, then added, "It's real urgent."

I was immediately concerned. "Is something wrong?"

Melodie looked shifty. "Um…sort of."

Bob scowled. "Fess up, Melodie. I know you've done something you shouldn't have. What is it?"

"Is it wrong to congratulate someone?" asked Melodie self-righteously. "I don't think so!"

Bob looked puzzled; I didn't.

"Melodie! You called Aunt Millie yourself and told her about Brucie's engagement to Lexus, didn't you?"

All injured innocence, Melodie said, "How was I to know Bruce hadn't told his mother?"

"Whoa," said Bob, who along with everyone else at Kendall & Creeling, had met my aunt. "I see storm clouds gathering on the horizon."

My heart sank. "She's on the warpath, isn't she?"

Melodie unsuccessfully tried to suppress her evident pleasure at this state of affairs. "She's never liked Lexus, your Aunt Millie said. And she might have to come back to the States to straighten Bruce out."

"Oh, no!"

Aunt Millie, whose dark view of life made Fran in comparison seem like Pollyanna? Aunt Millie, who was never backward in coming forward with unwelcome advice? I was only now getting over her last visit to Los Angeles.

"Thank you so much, Melodie," I said with deepest sarcasm.

"Don't blame me. Bruce should have told her himself. His mom was going to find out sooner or later, anyway."

"She's got a point," said Bob.

True though this was, it didn't stop me from bitterly resenting the fact that I had to deal with an enraged aunt at a time when I should be concentrating on one thing, and one thing only—finding Ariana.

This must have showed on my face, because Melodie said apologetically, "I'm sorry, Kylie. Like, I didn't think." She brightened as she went on, "I have got some info for you about the receptionist at Evenstar. It's real interesting."

My mum always said that if there was something you dreaded, it was best to get it over and done with straight away, so you had no chance to brood about it. "I'll ring Aunt Millie first," I said.

Melodie looked ready to protest, as it was nearly time to close the office. I pointed an admonishing finger at her. "And don't you dare leave before you tell me about Nancy McDuff."

"But Kylie, I'll be late for trance protocol."

Bob, who had started for his office with Rocky and his basket under one arm, turned around and came back. "I know I'm going to be sorry I asked, but what is trance protocol?"

"Cassandra's running a class for beginning psychics. She says there's a right way and a wrong way to accomplish trancing."

"Trancing? God help us all," said Bob. "There's a sucker born every minute."

Slighted, Melodie snapped, "I'm taking the class to enrich my interpretation of Chilley Dorsal."

"You've actually got the part?" Bob asked.

"Well, no, not yet, but Larry-my-agent says it's the surest thing he's ever seen." She cast an imploring look my way. "That's why I desperately need Cassandra's class. I'm aiming to be the most authentic TV psychic actor ever."

"Believe me," I said dourly, "the last thing I want is a long conversation with Aunt Millie."

CHAPTER NINETEEN

"Hello, Aunt Millie, it's Kylie."

"I suppose you already know Brucie's up and got himself engaged to that Lexus. I warned him not to have anything to do with someone named after a vehicle, but did he listen? No!"

"Aunt—"

"And who did I learn this from? That blond flibbertigibbet Melodie!"

"Aunt—"

"You could have warned me this was coming. My boy's head's always been turned by a pretty face. You should have stepped in and stopped it quick smart."

"Bruce is an adult, Aunt. I can't tell him what to do."

"Bruce? Since when has he been Bruce? He'll always be Brucie to me."

I sighed. Having a conversation with Aunt Millie was always draining and this one was particularly wearing.

"And don't sigh at me, my girl. If anyone's sighing, it should be me. Your betrayal is a sharp knife in my heart. To think I trusted you to keep an eye on your cousin and basically save him from himself. Did you? No!"

This was too much. I had to put my foot down before the conversation got entirely out of hand. "Did Mum tell you that Ariana Creeling has disappeared?"

"Yes, she did."

"So you understand that next to Ariana's kidnapping or"—I took a breath—"possible murder, Brucie's engagement to Lexus doesn't rate highly on my list of things to worry about."

Silence. Then, "I was going to get around to asking you what was happening with Ariana. She's a nice woman. I like her."

"There's no news yet. Now, if there's nothing else, Aunt..."

"If you speak to Brucie," she said, sounding astonishingly meek, "would you ask him to call me? I've tried to get him several times, but he refuses to talk to me." With a trace of her usual spirit, she added, "His own mother!"

"Right-oh," I said. "If I speak with him, I will. Bye, now."

Whoo-ee! I was going to get through a conversation with Aunt Millie without a single mention of my mother's desperate need for me to return to the 'Gudge.

"One last thing," said Aunt Millie, "your mum's in a shocking bad way, what with the Platypus people and all..."

* * *

Back at the front desk, Melodie was packed and ready to go. "I'm still here," she announced with a virtuous smile.

"Good thing too," I snapped, "or you'd be looking for another job."

Clearly astonished, Melodie stared at me. "Kylie?"

Immediately I felt contrite. "I'm sorry, Melodie. Aunt Millie brings out the worst in me."

"And there's Ariana too," said Melodie soberly. "I keep wondering where she is and if she's okay. It's so horrible, because I guess you always think the worst."

"The worst is that she's dead."

At my bleak words, Melodie's eyes filled with tears. They were genuine ones—she wasn't acting. "Don't say that, Kylie, *please*."

In a moment, I'd be crying too. I said, "I don't want you to be late for your class, so tell me about Nancy McDuff."

"Well, I got back to Crystal at Heavenly Shores Cemetery, who's known Nancy for ages. And Emma at Shoot for the Stars Crematoria Rockets—they launch people's ashes into space— who's known Nancy even longer, and asked how they could possibly have missed a fellow receptionist's affair with her boss. I mean, that's heavy stuff."

She paused to consider. "We don't encourage relationships like this because of the danger of pillow talk. A receptionist worth her salt is aware of just about everything that goes on in a place, but that's not what you want someone at the top to know."

"Crikey, why not?"

Melodie gave me a sorry-you-don't-get-it look. "They can't handle it, that's why."

"Someone running an organization can't handle what the receptionist knows?"

Melodie nodded. "Trust me, it's true. Information overload and no receptionist skills to process it."

Fascinating though this byway was, I had to stick to the main road. "So what about Nancy McDuff? Did she pillow talk?"

"No, she didn't. This is *real* interesting, Kylie. Nancy told Crystal and Emma in *absolute* confidence. They had to vow not to repeat it to another living person."

"How come they've repeated it to you, then?"

"I pointed out to Crystal and Emma that in a life-and-death situation the receptionist code of ethics allows them to break their vow to Nancy. So they did. Not that it came easy to them. I mean, a vow's a vow."

With an effort I resisted shaking the story out of her. "Go on," I said.

"Like, it seems Nancy started flirting with Emory Hastings, not really meaning anything, but he got real serious about it and said he loved Nancy and couldn't live without her. And she said to him that he was going to have to live without her because she was in a meaningful relationship with someone else, and he said…"

Melodie trailed off in one of her dramatic pauses. I'd learned not to try hurrying her up because that made her huffy, which delayed things further, so I waited patiently until she started up again.

"And he said, 'Don't make me kill this guy of yours.' And Nancy freaked, because she told Crystal and Emma her blood literally ran cold when she realized he really meant what he was saying."

"Stone the crows! What happened then?"

Gratified at my response, Melodie dropped her voice to a confidential purr. "So Nancy told Emory Hastings she was resigning as Evenstar Home receptionist and she was going to the cops about his threat of murdering her rocket-scientist lover. And she was considering a sexual-harassment lawsuit."

A stray question floated across my mind. Did Nancy's retired rocket scientist once work at Shoot for the Stars preparing rockets to dispatch deceased people's ashes into orbit?

As though she'd heard my query, Melodie said, "Emma was just so upset, because she'd known Barry—that's Nancy's rocket scientist—when he worked in the launch department of Shoot for the Stars. Emma even set up the blind date where Barry and Nancy met."

"There's no record Nancy ever went to the cops. And she's still got her job."

"That's because Emory Hastings totally begged her, practically groveling on his knees, not to tell the cops and not to resign as Evenstar's receptionist. He said he'd had a sort of nervous breakdown because of terrible tension over his wife's cocaine addiction…Kylie, did you know Zelda Webber was an addict?"

"I've heard rumors. Go on about Nancy."

"Like, he actually cried while he was imploring her to forget what had happened and to promise not to tell, anyone. Nancy said okay, she'd do it as long as he never came on to her again and he swore he wouldn't."

"Until the other night."

Melodie looked at me with new respect. "You know about that?"

"Vince Yarborough was walking me to my car after the introductory committee meeting at Evenstar, when we saw Hastings and Nancy together in a corner of the parking area. It was pretty dark, but it looked like they were kissing."

"He was trying to kiss her, but she wasn't having any of it. Nancy told Crystal and Emma it was real frightening. She was just unlocking her car when Hastings appeared out of the blue and said his marriage was over and he was getting a divorce. And wasn't it wonderful that he and Nancy could now be together? Before she could tell him to get lost, he grabbed her and tried to kiss her. She told him Barry was furious and just itching to teach him a lesson he wouldn't forget. Then people turned up— must have been you, Kylie—and Hastings let her go and Nancy jumped in her car and got out of there."

"Hell's bells," I said.

"*And*," said Melodie meaningfully, "you'll never guess what happened next."

"Right-oh, I won't even try guessing. What happened next?"

Typically, Melodie was milking the story for every bit of possible drama. Her green eyes wide, she breathed, "Like, the very next morning, when Nancy was getting ready to march into Hastings office and resign—which she totally hated to do because she loves working at Evenstar, and it wasn't fair anyway because she hadn't done anything wrong—he came rushing up to her and apologized."

"What excuse did he make this time?"

"Hastings said he'd had too much to drink because he was so broken-hearted about his marriage to Zelda Webber falling apart. He'd lost control and said things to Nancy he only dimly remembered and didn't mean. He swore it would never happen again, and pleaded with her not to resign."

Melodie paused to do her patented hair toss. "Men!"

"Nancy's planning to stay at Evenstar?"

"Unless he does it again and it doesn't look like he's going to because Nancy says he's been a perfect gentleman and increased her salary, too."

I didn't often sneer, but I did now. "Buying silence. What a class act."

Melodie checked her watch. "Um…Kylie?"

"Go," I said. "And give my regards to Cassandra."

"She'll be real pleased. She thinks you don't like her."

"Stone the crows, I wonder where she got that idea."

"Cassandra's real sensitive, Kylie."

"Hah!" said Fran, stopping by the front desk on her way out. "Sensitive the way a killer shark is sensitive? Or a vulture? Or a—"

"Stop!" Melodie's eyes flashed with righteous indignation. "No way will I stay here and listen to you insult my friend."

"Hah!" said Fran. "A friend the way a killer shark is a friend? Or a vulture? Or a—"

The door slammed behind Melodie as she exited.

"I'm dying to know what your third example is," I said to Fran. "Killer shark, vulture, and…?"

"I was thinking a certain Lexus."

I had to smile at how apt it was. Melodie had taken Lexus' engagement to Bruce as an unexpected and vicious stab in the back from a longtime friend.

My smile died as Fran said, "What do I tell Mom tonight? She's going out of her mind with worry. We're minding Gussie until Ariana gets back and just about every time Mom looks at her she dissolves in tears."

I felt like dissolving in tears myself. "Poor Gussie. Everyone around her is upset and Ariana hasn't come to take her home. She must be wondering why."

"Gussie's fretting, like we all are. If I could just find something to say to Mom to give her even the slightest ray of hope. When Bob talked with Ted Lark this afternoon the message was essentially the same—no progress. There's nothing of note in Ariana's phone records, so that's a dead end. And the traffic cams didn't pick up Ariana's BMW, so it looks like she was abducted in the Hollywood Hills close to home, but no one in the area has come forward to say they saw anything odd."

"Do you want me to call around this evening?"

"No, Kylie, it's hard enough on you as it is."

This new, considerate Fran was taking some getting used to. And now that we had a genuine disaster to face, all mention of disaster-preparedness drills had gone out the window, as well as any reference to her catastrophe-survival book.

I said, "If there's anything I can do, just ask."

Fran sank down on Melodie's chair. "Ditto. I'd so much rather be involved instead of sitting on the sidelines watching my mother go slowly mad."

"Are you still working on your survival book?"

Fran sighed. "I'm trying to, but it's hard to concentrate on disaster scenarios when you're living one yourself."

"If you're still looking for a title, I've just thought of one that might work."

This got a suspicious look from Fran, but when she realized I was quite serious, she said, "None of the ones I've come up with feel right, if you know what I mean."

"I'm thinking something really simple, like *Catastrophe Survival*."

Fran cocked her head. "*Catastrophe Survival*. I like it."

"It's yours."

Lonnie, his chubby face exhausted, came slowly down the hall. "I'm beat," he said. "I've almost finished compiling dossiers on Frank Franklin, Emory Hastings, and Vince Yarborough. I'll work at home tonight, and be in early tomorrow."

"I'll bring doughnuts," said Fran.

Lonnie favored her with a sweet smile. "Where's the real Fran? This one's too nice to be anything but an imposter."

"Watch it!" she snapped.

"Ah, there she is—the Fran I know and love."

"Lonnie, before you go," I said, "I need to see Zelda Webber. Any ideas on how I might swing a meeting?"

"You can't."

"Fair dinkum, there must be some way."

Lonnie shook his head. "No way. I picked up the breaking news online—Zelda Webber's just had the obligatory teary media conference to bravely announce she's checking herself into an exclusive rehab joint in Malibu to fight her addiction to prescription drugs."

"Isn't she addicted to cocaine?" I said.

"Of course, but being hooked on drugs prescribed by your doctor for a mythical back injury is so much more public-relations friendly."

"I know she's married to Emory Hastings," said Fran, "but why in particular did you want to see her?"

I shrugged. I wasn't altogether sure why I needed to speak with Emory's estranged wife, especially as she had walked out on him months ago, so presumably would know nothing to explain his odd behavior with Evenstar's receptionist. But then, Lonnie had said Emory and Zelda were together at an entertainment event within the last few days…

"Lonnie, you said you saw Zelda with her husband the other night."

Lonnie looked sideways at Fran, obviously thinking she'd take another dig at him for trying to catch a glimpse of Pauline Feeney at the function, but Fran didn't respond.

"I know a bit more about it, for what it's worth," he said. He glared at Fran. "And I'm not expecting you to make a comment."

"As if I would," said Fran, all innocence.

"Okay, then. I've been talking with Tuesday, one of Pauline's assistants—"

"Tuesday?" Fran snickered. "Pauline Feeney has an assistant called Tuesday? What are the rest of her assistants called? Monday? Wednesday? Saturday Morning, perhaps?"

Highly irritated, Lonnie said, "Tuesday's named after Tuesday Weld, the actress. It's a perfectly good name."

"Or maybe Friday Afternoon? Thursday Lunch?"

He ostentatiously turned his back to Fran and said to me, "As I was saying before being so very rudely interrupted, Tuesday told me that Hastings virtually crashed the party. No one questioned him while he was waiting on the red carpet because the security guards knew him as Zelda's husband. When Zelda's limo pulled up he opened the door for her, then accompanied her inside. Tuesday said Zelda didn't want to cause a scene, so she went along with it."

"Crikey, rather a roundabout way to get to see her, wasn't it?"

"Hastings didn't have much choice," said Lonnie. "Zelda had cut him off completely. She even had her bodyguard forcibly remove him when he turned up at her Beverly Hills mansion. So I guess he decided the only chance he'd have to talk with her would be in a public place where she'd be unlikely to make a commotion."

"It must have been something mighty important to him," said Fran, intrigued enough to stop her teasing.

"Just about the most important thing there is," said Lonnie. "Money."

CHAPTER TWENTY

Wednesday morning dawned as a typical Southern California day, with perfect weather, smog in the air, and traffic reports that not only detailed the customary clotted conditions on the freeways but also helpfully included cheerful advice of alternate routes to take to avoid particularly horrific holdups.

I'd had another night of fragmentary dreams interspersed with long periods of wakefulness where I stared at the shadows on the ceiling and despaired of ever seeing Ariana again. Julia Roberts had responded to my bleak mood with quite touching concern, eschewing her usual demanding ways and spending time quietly curled up beside me on the bed.

"First Fran, now you, Jules," I'd said to her in the middle of the night. "I can't cope with all this kindness." Of course that made me sniffle and have to cuddle Jules for comfort. And she didn't even protest, which upset me even more.

This morning I had my first Swan Song fundraising appointment. I was to accompany Cory Grainger to the office of a captain of industry famous enough for even me to recognize his name. I chose my clothes carefully, not wanting to earn a disapproving look from Cory, who I was sure would be impeccably dressed.

It seemed I'd picked the right outfit—a classic dark blue suit that had cost an eyebrow-raising sum—because when I met Cory in reception at the appointed Wilshire Boulevard address, he gave me an appreciative smile and said gallantly, "A beautiful day and a beautiful woman. What a wonderful combination."

"You're not so bad yourself," I said. This was an understatement, as I reckoned he represented the true meaning of the old-fashioned term "fashion plate," Cory really was perfection, from the crown of his steel-gray hair to the tips of his polished-to-a-mirror-shine shoes.

The roleplay at Evenstar had prepared me for my part, which was basically to look enthusiastically supportive while Cory charmed the receptionist on the ground floor, the receptionist on the tenth floor, the captain of industry's personal assistant, and ultimately the captain of industry himself.

We left with a pledge of what to me was an astonishing sum, although in the lift on the way down Cory said with a dissatisfied frown, "He could have given more."

"You were magnificent," I said, meaning it.

Cory inclined his head graciously. "Thank you. I do try to give of my best."

"Let me buy you a coffee," I said, not wanting to lose the opportunity to pump him for information.

Another gracious nod. "I believe I can spare the time."

There was the ubiquitous Starbucks nearby. Cory chose to sit at a table outside, probably, I thought uncharitably, so he could be admired by people passing by.

When I brought the coffees out, a middle-aged woman was twittering over him. "I just took one look and knew it was you! I've *so* enjoyed your wonderful movies."

A modest smile from Cory. "Thank you, dear lady."

She clasped her hands in ecstasy. "Oh, I can't wait to tell the girls that I've met Sir Rupert Martindale in person!"

Cory's smile vanished.

"Your autograph, Sir Rupert, please," she cried, grabbing a paper serviette and thrusting it in front of him.

Stone-faced, Cory said coldly, "I don't give autographs to intrusive fans. Please leave."

He made a shooing motion. "Can I be more plain? Go away. Pester someone else."

"Oh!" She snatched back the paper serviette. "How rude! I'll never watch a movie of yours again."

Watching her retreating back, Cory said with a hint of satisfaction, "Such a shame. Martindale has lost yet another fan. Soon he'll have none left."

* * *

Driving back to the office, I reviewed our conversation at Starbucks. As a source of useful information, Cory Grainger had been a wash-out. Wendell Yalty's assessment of him had been all too true. It *was* Grainger, Grainger, Grainger all the way. Cory wasn't really interested in anything that didn't relate directly to him. When I'd raised the subject of Ariana's abduction, he'd expressed concern, but it was clear his heart wasn't in it.

I'd asked Cory whether he was aware that Emory Hastings was, as Lonnie had found out yesterday, in serious financial trouble. Cory had shrugged and said, "Really? I hadn't heard."

He had shown a little more animation at the mention of Frank Franklin. One side of his mustache had lifted in a sneer as he'd remarked, "Disgusting how he's let himself go. Did you know that he was a Tarzan once? Now he's just a fat man with absolutely no dress sense."

I'd come right out and said, "If you had to pick someone at Evenstar who'd be capable of kidnapping Ariana, who would you choose?"

"My dear young lady, I'm at a loss to say. The very concept of abduction is utterly foreign to me, as I've never lacked willing female companionship." He'd paused to muse for a moment. "If I had to choose, it'd be someone pathetic and needy, rather like Frank Franklin."

I was stopped at a red light when my phone rang. I fished around and got it out of my handbag. I didn't recognize the number. "G'day. Kylie Kendall here."

A whispery voice tickled my ear. I hit the volume switch on the phone. "Rita? Is that you? Rita Foyle?"

An affirmative murmur.

"Hold on," I said, "won't be a mo'."

When the light turned green, I took the first side street and pulled up at the curb. It was quieter here, and straining, I could just make out what Rita Foyle was murmuring. "Your place? Of course. This afternoon? I'll be there."

I hardly noticed the rest of the drive back to Kendall & Creeling as I was preoccupied with the questions I'd like to put to Rita Foyle when I saw her.

The moment I came through the door I said to Melodie, who had no pressing audition, since she was at her post, "This is a bit of a stab in the dark, but I'm interested in a woman on the Evenstar committee called Rita Foyle. She has the nickname of Murmur. Maybe you can ask Crystal or Emma to sound out Nancy McDuff."

"Nancy's not at work today. She called in sick."

Gobsmacked, I said, "How could you know that?"

Melodie looked mysterious. "Trade secret, so I can't say."

"I reckon you had some reason to speak with Crystal and/or Emma." These two names were now indelibly imprinted on my consciousness as an inseparable duo, like fish 'n' chips.

"Lucky guess," said Melodie, somewhat aggravated that I'd come up with the answer. "What was the name again? Mumbles?"

"Rita Foyle, a.k.a. Murmur Foyle."

"I'll see what I can do."

As I headed off in the direction of the kitchen for a restorative cuppa and to scope out the doughnut situation—Fran had come good with her promise to provide some—Melodie called after me, "Lonnie wants to see you."

Lonnie's office, if possible, was in even greater chaos than usual. With a pang of disappointment I spied the obviously empty doughnut box on the floor beside his chair. "Crikey," I said, "everything's all over the place like a madwoman's breakfast."

"Politically incorrect," said Lonnie severely, looking up from his computer screen. "You're denigrating an insane person's attempt to eat the first meal of the day."

"Oh, Lonnie, it's only a saying. It means to be in a total mess, like you are."

This aroused Lonnie's ire. "I'm working night and day for you, compiling dossiers on suspects." He shuffled folders on his overflowing desk and came up with two. "Here, take these. Franklin and Hastings are as complete as I can make them in the time. I haven't finished with Vincent Yarborough, but I don't think there's anything there. He seems very average at his job, but otherwise he's a nice guy."

As I took the folders, he went on, "So on top of that, I've got Bob wanting the skinny on Yolanda/Cassandra, like yesterday. Plus in my spare time I'm trying to come up with a strategy to win Pauline back. And any minute now Melodie's liable to be off on another audition and I'll be expected to answer the phone. Under the circumstances, you've got to agree I haven't got time for housekeeping."

I felt embarrassed to have been so critical. "Fair dinkum, Lonnie, I'm terribly sorry. Of course you're right."

"Okay, then," he said, slightly mollified.

"Have you spoken with Pauline?"

He shook his head. Then after what plainly was an internal struggle, he said, "I haven't told anyone else—and don't you— but I've written Pauline a poem."

I blinked. "An original poem?"

"Of course it's original. It took me ages to compose. I snail-mailed it to her yesterday. It seemed more personal handwritten."

From his expression, he was having second thoughts about telling me about his poetic efforts. "Kylie, I'm telling you this is absolute confidence."

"My lips are sealed."

In an obvious attempt to change the subject, he said, "What's happened to your stalker? He's gone quiet."

I'd been thinking about that very question. "I believe he saw me as a rival to be scared off. Now he's got Ariana, I'm of no further interest."

"What if you're wrong?" Lonnie asked. "He could still be stalking you, but not leaving notes. Because you don't feel threatened any longer, you let your guard down. And that's when you get snatched."

"Just let him try."

Lonnie looked grim. "I would have said no one would have any luck abducting Ariana, but someone accomplished it. My advice is to take the gun Bob gave you every time you step out the door."

"I'm not licensed to carry a concealed weapon."

"So what? When your life is on the line, that doesn't seem quite so important, does it?"

Somewhere on his desk, a phone hiccupped energetically. A standard ring was too boring for Lonnie, so he'd used his technical skills to come up with a series of different sounds. Recently I'd heard his phone belch as if the handset had severe indigestion, and Lonnie was threatening to unleash a farting phone in the future.

After much rustling he located it under a pile of electronic magazines. "Melodie? If you're calling to ask me to mind the front desk for you, the answer is never, never, *never* again. What? Oh, okay." He put the receiver down. "Melodie says to tell you she's got the information you wanted."

When I hot-footed it to reception, Melodie was looking very pleased with herself. "I know, like, just about all there is to know about Murmur Foyle."

"Let her rip."

"Well, first, she's a receptionist's nightmare. It's the bane of our lives, dealing with people who won't speak up. And Murmur Foyle's the worst of the worst—a whispering mumbler."

"I don't think she can help it."

"True, in her case the reason she whispers is real tragic. Elaine at Paranoia Pet Adoptions knows all about it because Murmur Foyle has been a volunteer there for years. She volunteers at lots of animal shelters."

"Hold on," I said, *"Paranoia* Pet Adoptions?"

"Like, if you're paranoid about intruders, you want a big-sounding, noisy pet to scare them off. The Paranoia shelter specializes in dogs with deep voices that can also do an awesome snarl on command. And of course, there's the trained barking parrots. They're awesome, too."

"I'm dinky-di sorry I asked," I said with perfect truth. "Let's get back to Murmur Foyle."

"It's real sad." Melodie drooped in sympathy. "Until she was twenty-five, Rita Foyle spoke like anyone else. Then the love of her life was killed just before they were to be married in London. *So* romantic." She hastened to add, "Not that the love of her life was killed, but that the marriage was in London. Have you been to London, Kylie? I've always wanted to go there."

Melodie's expression suddenly grew cold. "Lexus and I were making plans to vacation in England next year. Of course, that's totally fallen through now that Lexus is"—her eyes narrowed to slits—"engaged."

"Stiff cheese," I said, "but let's get back to the fiancé. What happened to him?"

Melodie's perfectly plucked eyebrows descended in a puzzled frown. "He died at breakfast. Choked on a kipper—whatever a kipper is."

"It's a salted fish."

"If you say so. Anyway, Elaine says from that awful moment on, Rita Foyle couldn't raise her voice above a whisper. And she never took up with anyone else, but devoted the rest of her life to animal charities."

Melodie clasped her hands and looked soulfully ceilingward. "It's, like, cosmic, to love someone that much, don't you think?"

I was skeptical. "Is this story dinkum?"

Obviously offended, Melodie switched her attention from the ceiling to me. "Look, Kylie, if Elaine says that it's true—it's true."

"Why? Because she can never tell a lie?"

"Because," said Melodie with dignity, "Elaine is a professional receptionist."

* * *

Rita Foyle's house was a tasteful white semi-Spanish number in the Hoimby Hills area of Westwood. It had the most gorgeous rose garden in the front, cleverly arranged so that the rose colors went from white at the beginning of the pathway through deepening shades of pink and coral until, at the front entrance, the roses were deep, deep red.

I parked right in front of the house, checked that Bob's gun was safely concealed under the driver's seat, and reminded myself I was in Platypus Ploy mode, so my task was to be unassumingly pleasant. This meant I'd have to keep under strict control my tendency to shoot from the lip before my mind was engaged.

"G'day, Rita," I said when her anorexic figure, clad in a tailored white jumpsuit, appeared at the front door in response to my ring. With her were two nondescript, cheerful dogs, who waved their tails heartily when I said, "G'day, dogs."

"Call me Murmur," Rita whispered. "Almost everybody does."

"You sure?" It seemed to me to be an unkind dig at her inability to speak at a normal volume.

She flashed a smile, revealing the standard perfect dental work. "I've been called Murmur for many years. As you might imagine, I'm used to it."

Could it be that decades ago an errant kipper in London had permanently turned down this woman's volume control? Intriguing though it was, it was impossible to ask the question, so I said, "Right-oh, Murmur it is."

"And this is Terri," she said, indicating the taller and hairier of the two dogs. "Beside her is Pirate."

I let each of them sniff the back of my hand, and only then did I pat them. Murmur looked at me approvingly. "You know dogs."

Terri and Pirate led the way down a cool, shadowy hall. "I hope you don't mind," Murmur said as she and I brought up the rear, "but I've convened a little council of war to save Vince."

"Save Mr. Yarborough? From what?"

"Prison, mainly."

The house had a central courtyard, airy and bright and filled with tree ferns. A sleek black cat snoozed near the fountain, which had water cascading over many levels and was much more elaborate than the one in Kendall & Creeling's little courtyard. The dogs disappeared under a large, olive-green cast-iron table and flung themselves down.

Seated at the table, tall glasses of some sort of juice in front of them, were Oona Turner and Nancy McDuff. Nancy was casual in jeans and a T-shirt. Clearly, she was very fit. Maybe doing the tango regularly truly was good for you. In contrast, Oona Turner's pudgy body was covered by a shapeless salmon dress that made her look like a swollen, pink amphibian.

Nancy said, "Hi." Oona grunted.

"G'day."

"Is there any news about Ariana Creeling?" Nancy asked.

"Not yet. We're hoping there'll be a break in the case soon." Everyone looked grave—even Oona seemed solemn. "What a dreadful situation, not knowing," said Nancy.

"I'm so sorry," said Murmur.

Oona grunted.

I said, "I'm convinced that someone at the Evenstar Home knows what happened to her."

"Who?" said Oona leaning forward, keen interest on her face. "It'd make my day if it's that son of a bitch, Emory Hastings."

Not wanting to direct their thinking towards anyone in particular, because it could skew any useful information they might have, I said, "I'd rather not name any names yet."

Oona sank back, clearly disappointed. "Devious little swine," she snarled, "he's capable of anything."

"Kylie, let me get you a glass of fruit punch," said Murmur. "It's entirely nonalcoholic, I'm afraid, but this afternoon it's important we all keep our wits about us."

I was hoping she wouldn't seat me next to Oona, but of course, because I was silently willing her not to, Murmur did. "Nice to see you again, Ms. Turner," I said inaccurately.

"Try Oona," she said in her grating gravel voice. "And where the hell's your report? It was promised for today, I believe? She saw me Zellstein at the others. "They know about your investigation."

"There've been recent developments," I said to her. "I'm happy to discuss them with you."

This got the patented Oona grunt.

Murmur placed a beaded glass of punch in front of me. Nudging Oona, she said, "Now, be gracious."

"I *am* gracious," she said. I kept a straight face, but Nancy and Murmur laughed out loud—Murmur very quietly. With the slightest of smiles, Oona admitted, "I never said gracious came easy to me."

"You're taking a sickie," I said to Nancy.

"Pardon me?"

"A sick day. Shouldn't you be at work?"

"Oh, I get what you mean. When Murmur decided we needed this urgent meeting, I got Barry to call Evenstar and say I'd come down with the flu."

"Okay, girls," whispered Murmur, putting a couple of manila folders in the center of the table, then taking her seat, "let me bring Kylie up to speed."

"I'll do it, Murmur," Oona announced. "She needs to hear every word, and with you, it's unlikely." She fixed me with her gimlet stare. "Listen up, I don't intend to repeat myself."

"Crikey, I'm all ears."

Without ceremony, Oona started, "You've met Glenys Clarkson, so you'll be aware that normally she hasn't got the backbone of a worm. Well, for once she showed some spirit.

Knowing Nancy was a close friend of Murmur's, Glenys went to her with the news that Emory Hastings was busy planting evidence to show it was Vince Yarborough who'd embezzled the Swan Song funds."

I wanted to know how Glenys knew this, as I couldn't imagine her boss letting her in on the scheme.

"Hastings is convinced he's smarter than every single person on the planet," Oona ground out with an impressive curl to her lip, "and most definitely much smarter than any mere woman. This explains why it would never occur to him that Glenys would understand how he was using the forensic accountant's report to identify areas where he could most easily incriminate Vince Yarborough."

"I requested to see that detailed report at my first meeting with Emory Hastings," I said. "I reckon that's why he stalled. He didn't want anyone else to see it, since he was using it as a template to fix the blame on someone else."

Murmur handed me one of the folders. "Thanks to Glenys, we now have a couple of copies."

"When did Vince find out the extent of the embezzlement?" I asked. "Emory Hastings assured me that he knew nothing, apart from the relatively small discrepancy Vince himself uncovered."

"Vince was totally clueless until a few days ago, when I set him straight," Oona announced. "And Murmur, everyone knows he's your friend, but don't rush to defend the man. Even you have to admit Vince Yarborough is not up there shining brightly in the accounting firmament. He's more a dim bulb."

"He's a sweet, kind man," Murmur protested. "You've no idea how much he does in volunteer work for animal charities."

"One can only hope he doesn't volunteer to do the books," said Oona with a sardonic smile.

Nancy drummed her fingers on the table. "Can we get back to the reason we're here?"

"Which is saving Vince," said Murmur.

"Getting Hastings," Oona snarled.

"Both," said Nancy. "Obviously Emory's setting up Vince because Emory himself is the embezzler."

"That bastard!" Oona's face and thick neck turned brick red. "He's guilty as sin, but proving it will be a major problem. As administrator, he has every right to examine all financial records, so it'll be a case of Glenys Clarkson's word against his. I'm afraid Glenys is too soft to stand up and be counted. Hastings will steamroll her. And then, as he's planned, Vince will be the fall guy."

"Emory's smart, Oona. Admit it," Murmur said.

Grudgingly, Oona nodded. "Hastings has a certain rat cunning. He insisted to the Evenstar board that Kendall & Creeling independently investigate the situation, which made him seem blameless. Of course, in Hastings' world view, a company run by two women would never get to the bottom of his brilliant scheme."

"Not so brilliant," I said. "Whatever funds he's embezzled, it's not enough. He's been reduced to frantically begging for money from his estranged wife."

Nancy looked thoughtful. "Maybe Emory's cracking up. Lately, his behavior towards me has been bizarre. You wouldn't know about this, Kylie, but one minute Emory's swearing he's madly in love with me, and the next minute he's apologizing and saying it's all a big mistake."

To save time, I said, "Actually, Nancy, I know all about it."

"You do?"

"Receptionist network."

Being a receptionist herself, she wasn't surprised, but she was angry. "I told Crystal and Emma in confidence."

I gave Melodie's explanation of a greater good trumping Nancy's right to privacy. "Any behavior so out of character could indicate something is very wrong."

Still annoyed, she nodded reluctantly. "I suppose."

Scowling, Oona said, "Bizarre behavior's not enough to persuade the idiots on the Evenstar board to get rid of Hastings. God knows why, but he's got supporters who'll take his side no matter what."

"I've got a favor to ask," I said, "that may help discredit Hastings. I need to speak with Glenys Clarkson without anyone else knowing about it. To Glenys, I'm just a sheila on the Swan Song committee, so she'll see no reason to meet with me in private to discuss any confidential stuff, unless one of you sets it up for me."

"This meeting," said Nancy, "will it be about Vince or Ariana Creeling?"

"Both."

Oona grunted. "Two birds with one stone, eh? Leave Glenys to me. I'll make sure she cooperates."

"No, Oona," whispered Murmur, "let Nancy do it. You frighten Glenys, you know you do. There's no point in alarming her. She's having enough trouble coping with Frank Franklin, without having to deal with you too."

Nancy grimaced. "That guy creeps me out. The moment I hear his voice on the phone my skin crawls. If you asked me who was capable of a kidnapping, he'd be top of my list."

"Then why didn't he kidnap Glenys? She's the object of his obsession," Murmur pointed out.

"Too obvious," Oona declared in her usual forthright manner. "If she disappeared, he'd be suspect number one."

"I'd hate to be a captive of Frank Franklin's," said Nancy feelingly. "Glenys says he's always wanting to discuss horror movies he's seen. His favorites are the ones where half-naked women are horribly tortured and scream a lot."

"Nancy!" Murmur said.

Nancy Zellsteind at me aghast. "Oh, God, I'm terribly sorry. I should never have said that in front of you. Forgive me."

"It's okay," I said. But it wasn't. Hideous images I'd managed to tamp down came bursting back into my mind.

Now was not the time to be platypus-shy. I said harshly, "I need some action here. I must see Glenys as soon as possible. Please arrange it right now."

CHAPTER TWENTY-ONE

I didn't expect anyone to still be at work when I got back to Kendall & Creeling, but the motorbike was in Lonnie's spot—he'd had his dead car towed away—and Bob's Lexus was in the parking area too.

Even before I opened the front door, my ears were assailed by a series of squeaks punctuated by high-pitched barks. Inside I found little Rocky attacking his squeaky toy, a yellow duck, with manic fervor. He alternately barked, pounced, seized it in his jaws, and shook it to death. Then he started the cycle all over again.

Her expression deeply pained, Julia Roberts looked down from the reception desk at Rocky's activities. She brightened when she saw me. She'd obviously been waiting for my arrival, as meal time was approaching.

"Before I get your dinner, Jules, where are Bob and Lonnie?" I didn't bother asking Rocky, who was playing so hard he was oblivious to everything else, including Julia Roberts. He hadn't even noticed me coming through the door.

Jules twitched her whiskers, leapt gracefully to the floor, completely ignoring the pug puppy, who had reached a crescendo of squeaks, and set off for the kitchen. I locked the front door and followed on behind.

I'd misjudged Julia Roberts, thinking her stomach alone had made the kitchen our destination, because Bob and Lonnie, each holding a can of beer, were there.

"We're celebrating nailing Cassandra," Bob said, saluting me with his can. "Want one?"

I declined. Compared to the robust Aussie beers I was used to, American brews seemed rather insipid.

"How did you nail her?"

"Hidden in plain sight," said Lonnie, chortling. "I'd hit a wall with Yolanda/Cassandra, so I went back to the United Psychics of America website to see if I could have possibly missed anything."

"We all missed it," said Bob. "I'd scanned the website too, and not noticed."

Lonnie picked up the story. "Cassandra, because she's the president, has a flattering biography on the UPA site. I was glancing through it again when something struck me right between the eyes. She claims to come from a psychic family, at least on the female side. Apparently her mother, aunts, grandmother, and great-grandmother are now, or were in the past, successful mediums."

"One of the psychics your mother employed after Kerrie disappeared was a relative of Cassandra's?" I asked Bob.

"Right on, Kylie. Lonnie did further research and came up with Phoebe X. Jones, a professional medium specializing in lost children and missing adults, who also happens to be Cassandra's aunt. I checked with my mom, who's getting on, but still sharp as a tack, and Mom confirmed she was one of the three psychics consulted when Kerrie vanished." He added wryly, "And to think I was sucked in by Cassandra's performance, even for a millisecond."

"Crikey," I said, "you weren't the only one fooled. I really believed she'd had a genuine psychic flash when she did your reading, because she seemed so shaken afterwards, to the point that she was hitting the bottle. Now I realize it was all an elaborate act to convince me she was fair dinkum. I feel a bit of a galah."

Bob patted my shoulder consolingly. "Don't be too hard on yourself. Deception is the name of the game she was playing. Besides, Cassandra may have actually seen something in the crystal ball, only it didn't come from the Other Side, it came from her own subconscious."

"But how would she know to ask her aunt about your missing sister in the first place?"

"My guess is when Cassandra pumped Melodie about Kendall & Creeling, she picked up on our family name of Verritt, which is very unusual. I wouldn't be at all surprised to find she maintains a cross-referenced data base which includes people who have consulted with other members of her family."

Downcast, Lonnie said, "Jeez, I was hoping Cassandra was really seeing the future when she said I'd get back with Pauline." He sneezed three times in quick succession, then glared at Julia Roberts. "Thank you so much, cat, for making it necessary for me to OD on allergy pills."

Julia Roberts ignored Lonnie's sarcasm and directed her full attention in my direction. She made a noise halfway between a moan and a meow, then pointedly Zellsteind at her empty dish.

"Sorry, Jules, for the delay. It's salmon tonight. One of your favorites." She watched critically as I opened the tin and deposited the contents in her dish.

"They're *all* her favorites," Bob remarked. "I've never met an animal with a better appetite."

"That's true," I conceded, "Jules does like her tucker."

The three of us stood and contemplated Julia Roberts eating until she stopped to give us all a *Please! Do you mind?* glower. It amused me to see how we then obediently turned our attention elsewhere.

"By the way," said Bob, "After a lot of haggling, I sold the Quintina Ladd movie poster to Wendell Yalty. He was ecstatic."

"Did you get a good price?" I asked.

Bob named a sum, and Lonnie whistled. "That much for an old movie poster? I'm in the wrong business."

A squeaking sound, growing louder, came down the hall. "That must be Rocky," said Bob. "I wondered where he'd got to."

"You'd better watch out," said Lonnie to Julia Roberts. From his gleeful expression he was anticipating a Rocky-Jules confrontation. "Where food's involved, all bets are off. Get ready to run for one of your nine lives."

Rocky wobbled through the doorway, still chomping on his squeaky toy. Jules continued eating. Seeing her on ground level and no doubt recalling his earlier unfortunate experience in the kitchen, Rocky halted and dropped his yellow duck. He scoped out the situation, then sidled over to Bob and indicated he'd like to be lifted out of the danger zone.

"Not much of a dog, is he?" said Lonnie disparagingly.

Obviously provoked by the unwarranted criticism of his pug, Bob retorted, "Rocky's too inexperienced to know how to deal with a strong woman. You should know how it feels."

Lonnie jutted his jaw. "What's that supposed to mean?"

"Let's just say that in personality Julia Roberts strongly reminds me of Pauline Feeney."

Before Lonnie, who'd gone bright pink, could splutter out a response, I stepped in. "Look, you lot, get your priorities in order. While you're sparring over cats and dogs, Ariana's being held captive somewhere. She could be thirsty and hungry. She could be hurt."

Both looked ashamed. "You're right," said Bob. "Sorry, Lonnie. I was out of line mentioning Pauline."

"And I was wrong to pick on Rocky. He's only a baby and can't be expected to take on a formidable cat like Julia Roberts."

Safely tucked under Bob's arm, Rocky looked down at his nemesis and barked a cheeky challenge.

* * *

Glenys Clarkson had agreed to see me that evening at her home in Inglewood. She and her husband lived in a neat white cottage on a quiet, tree-lined suburban street filled with similar well-kept dwellings.

"We're alone," she said as she let me into the house. "It's Dave's poker night with the boys. Do you mind if we sit in the kitchen? I'm baking tonight, and need to keep an eye on things."

The white-and-blue kitchen was filled with delicious cooking smells and bathed in eye-squintingly bright light. The refrigerator, stove and dishwasher were gleaming polished metal. The overall effect almost made me wish for sunglasses.

I was momentarily disconcerted to realize that the pinkish-beige sweats Glenys wore on her ample figure were extraordinarily close in color to her pinkish-beige hair.

"Something wrong?" she asked.

"Unusual color," I remarked, indicating her sweats.

"You won't find it anywhere else," she said with satisfaction. "I mixed dyes to get this precise shade. I enjoy doing things with my hands—sewing, embroidery, French polishing, a little woodwork, minor plumbing. Dave jokes that I'm the handyman around the house."

She indicated a breakfast nook. "Take a seat. I'll get coffee, or would you prefer a soda?"

"Coffee'd be bonzer," I said, thinking the caffeine would keep me firing on all cylinders.

"I've got some chocolate chip cookies cooling. Yes?"

"I never say no to chocolate anything."

When we were seated with mugs of coffee and a plate of warm cookies between us, Glenys began with, "Nancy said you wanted to talk with me about Frank and Emory, and that it's something to do with Ariana Creeling's disappearance."

"I'll lay my cards on the table, Glenys. I believe that someone at Evenstar abducted her, and right now those two blokes are the most likely suspects."

"Do the police agree with you?"

In fact, Ted Lark had no idea I was so actively involved. I shook my head and delivered the appropriate cliché. "They're pursuing other leads."

"Ariana was a constant visitor to our special-needs unit, as you must know. I knew her well enough to say hello. She was always very reserved but pleasant. Since she's been missing, I've included her in my prayers."

This kindness brought a lump to my throat. I gave myself a hard mental slap. Going all gooey wasn't going to help find Ariana. "May I be direct, Glenys?"

"Of course."

"What do you know of Emory Hastings' financial situation?" I asked.

I'd just read through Lonnie's report, so possibly I was as well-informed as Glenys, though as his personal assistant she might have information about Hastings that Lonnie couldn't access.

"It's not good." She sighed. "Please forgive me for saying this, but it doesn't feel right talking about Emory's private affairs."

Before I could respond, she put up a hand. "I know what you're going to say. Nancy told me this could be a life-and-death situation, otherwise we wouldn't be having this conversation."

She paused to collect her thoughts. "I know a lot more about his finances than Emory realizes. His house in Brentwood is mortgaged to the hilt. Emory's been struggling to make the payments. Then there's his wife—she's cost him a bundle so far, and the divorce will only make it worse. And trying desperately to get out of the financial hole he's in, Emory's made a series of risky investments, most of which have failed. What's keeping him afloat at the moment is the couple which did pay off."

"He could sell the Brentwood house."

"Unless he's absolutely forced to, Emory will never sell. Zelda was rarely there—she's always preferred her place in Beverly Hills—but Emory has made the Brentwood house his refuge from the world. He took out a second mortgage to pay for extensive alterations to turn it into his dream home."

"So he's living there alone?"

"Quite alone. Emory doesn't even have pets. I really think he prefers the solitary life."

"Needing money to cover his debts and to keep the Brentwood house provides an excellent motive for embezzlement."

Glenys shook her head ruefully. "If you'd asked me before this, I'd have said Emory would never do such a thing, but now that he's working to fix the blame on poor Vince Yarborough, it sure looks to me like he's guilty."

"I'd like to ask you about Frank Franklin."

A look of loathing crossed her face. "My shadow, as people have taken to calling Frank these days."

"Why does he think he has a chance with you?"

"I wish I knew! I suppose it started when Frank first came to Evenstar. He seemed so unhappy and friendless. I felt sorry for him, so spent time trying to introduce him to people and get him involved in various activities. Soon Frank became my shadow. Now everywhere I go, there he is." She made a face. "No good deed, as they say, goes unpunished."

"As administrator, couldn't Emory Hastings have a stern word with him and tell him to rack off?"

Glenys gave an exasperated sigh. "You'd think so, wouldn't you? Frank is in the office half the time. Emory obviously doesn't like it, but he also doesn't seem to be able to do anything about it."

"Why is that?"

Glenys gave a helpless shrug. "I don't know. It's really very unpleasant. Frank sees himself as an authority where movies are concerned, particularly horror movies. He enjoys discussing every gruesome detail with Emory, even though Emory seems uncomfortable. It's sick, really. And Frank's always dropping in DVDs of movies he recommends, mostly ones where women are tortured. I won't look at them, of course. I don't know whether Emory does or not. And the other day it was some book Frank insisted Emory should read. I heard him say, 'You'll get a charge out of this.' I didn't see the title."

She moodily chomped a piece of chocolate chip cookie. "Honestly, if the pay and benefits weren't so good, and I didn't have so many friends at Evenstar, I'd be out looking for another job just to get away from Frank."

"Blimey, looks like he's really got the upper hand. Could he be blackmailing your boss?"

"Over the embezzlement, you mean? I don't know how Frank could have known anything about it. I didn't, until recently, when Oona mentioned there was an investigation going on. She wanted me to keep an eye on Emory for her. I suppose you know they hate each other? Oona's relentless in her drive to get rid of him, and he feels the same way about her?"

"Maybe Frank knows something scandalous about Emory's wife?"

"Zelda?" Glenys pursed her lips disapprovingly. "Her whole life's an open scandal. Emory should never have married her. She was a disaster from the beginning. Money flows through Zelda's fingers like water. One day she's flush, the next she's broke. And she runs with a fast crowd. That's not Emory. He's much quieter and more devious. He likes to control things and people. That's why it's so odd about Frank. I would never have believed that someone like him could get Emory to do anything."

"Did you ever overhear anything that might indicate Frank was pressuring Emory for money?" I asked.

Glenys pondered for a moment, then said, "I recall there was something about a collector. Or maybe it was collecting. I suppose that could be a reference to money. The only reason I remember it at all is that when Emory realized I'd come into his office, he said, 'Yes, Glenys?' very loudly, and Frank broke off what he was saying."

"Lately, Emory's shown interest in Nancy, hasn't he?"

"That's a polite way to put it. Nancy is the latest in a long line of women Emory's been obsessed with. Usually it lasts a few weeks and then his attention switches to somebody else."

Thinking there'd been no sexual-harassment charges ever laid against Hastings, I said, "Have any of these women ever complained?"

"Not really. Mostly Emory doesn't do anything except delve into their lives and keep track of their movements. And the funny thing is, Emory doesn't think I know anything about these fixations of his. Take Nancy, for example. Last week, when I was looking for something else, I came across her personnel file hidden under papers in his desk drawer. I'd already noticed he was calling Nancy over unimportant things I'd normally handle for him." Glenys gave a little shudder. "Thank heavens he's never shown the slightest interest in me."

"You didn't say anything to Nancy about this?"

"I didn't need to. It was one of Emory's more fleeting obsessions. I knew it was over when I found the diary he'd been keeping of Nancy's movements torn up in the trash."

"When was this?"

"Last Friday, when I was putting papers in the recycling bin."

"That was the day before Ariana was abducted."

She stared at me, shocked. "I know you suspect him, but Emory would never do anything like that. He's not an aggressive person." She gave me a twisted smile. "Is he creepy? Yes, he can be. But violent? Never."

"What about Ariana? Was he obsessed with her?"

"Not in the same way as the others. His attitude towards Ariana has always been different, more respectful. I think she fascinated him from the beginning because she was so cool and unapproachable. Then, over time they became quite friendly, because Emory was so supportive when Professor Ives began that awful, inevitable decline into the final stages of Alzheimer's."

"Does Emory own a gun?"

I thought this abrupt question might throw her, but Glenys merely shrugged and said, "I imagine he does. Heavens, *I* own a gun. And I know how to use it."

Suddenly her soft face became militant. "You, being a foreigner, may not realize it's in our Constitution, the right to bear arms. Do you have a problem with that?"

Yerks! I had a vision of Glenys whipping out a pistol and blazing away. Then I had a vision of myself whipping out Bob's automatic and blazing away at Emory Hastings.

"No prob," I said. "No prob at all."

CHAPTER TWENTY-TWO

It was well after nine, but the Harley was still in the parking area, so I knew Lonnie hadn't yet left. I checked out the parking area and courtyard, mindful of Lonnie's point that although I was no longer receiving messages from my stalker, this didn't mean he wasn't lurking somewhere close.

Bob's Smith & Wesson 9 mm was a heavy weight in my bag. If I were suddenly attacked, I wasn't sure if I'd be able to use it effectively. It was a double-action semiautomatic, which meant, as Bob had explained to me at the shooting range, that the weapon had no safety catch. Instead, in the initial firing, the trigger had to be pulled harder and further—to first cock the hammer, and then release it to strike the firing pin and send the bullet on its way.

I recalled Bob had said, "For safety reasons, this isn't recommended, but if you're expecting a threatening situation where any delay could be fatal, you can prepare beforehand by chambering a cartridge, so the weapon is ready to fire."

For the moment, no threats were apparent, so I headed for the front door. Before I could put my key in the lock, Lonnie swung it open. His face flushed with joy, he burbled, "Kylie! Pauline called. She's meeting me here. Isn't that absolutely great? It was my poem, I think. I put my heart and soul into every word. It must have showed."

"Lonnie, I think Emory Hastings has got Ariana."

The elation faded from his face. "What have you found out that makes you think that?"

I quickly ran through the high points of my conversation with Glenys Clarkson.

"So he has these short-term infatuations with various women," said Lonnie. "And he's living alone in a big, luxurious house in Brentwood. That doesn't make him Ariana's abductor."

Impatience flooded me. "Lonnie, Frank Franklin is blackmailing Hastings over *something*."

"Hastings doesn't appear to have enough money to interest a blackmailer," Lonnie observed.

"I reckon Franklin isn't after money—he gets off on the power he has to push Emory Hastings around."

Lonnie patted my arm sympathetically. "I know you want Hastings to be the kidnapper, but this is awfully thin. Franklin could be holding any number of things over Hastings' head. If it did happen to be Ariana's abduction, Franklin would be running an awful risk of being charged as an accomplice. Would he take that chance?"

"I believe he would?"

"Believing isn't enough. Ted Lark would roll his eyes if asked to get a search warrant on such flimsy evidence."

"Then we need more," I said. "I have to make a call. The number's in my office."

"I'll stay here at the front. Pauline should be here any minute."

A few moments later, seated behind Dad's gray metal desk—how I wished he were here to guide me—I leafed quickly through the information Lonnie had collected on Emory Hastings. Last year a builder had sued him over payments for alterations done to the Brentwood house, but there were no details of the dispute as it had been settled before the case came up in civil court. Lonnie, bless him, had included the builder's name and contact information. E-mail would be too slow. I snatched up the phone and dialed the after-hours number.

* * *

Lonnie was pacing nervously around the reception area. "She's not here yet," he said unnecessarily.

"I've just spoken to the builder who did the alterations to the house in Brentwood. Hastings had him convert the basement area into a self-contained apartment."

"So? That's not unusual."

"Hastings specified the apartment have sound-proofing at the level of a professional recording studio. He was very insistent that no noise from the apartment would be able to seep into the house above. And the only entrance door was, the builder said, substantial enough to withstand a battering ram?"

"Now, that *is* interesting," said Lonnie, "but I'm guessing still not enough to get a warrant."

I sat down at Melodie's faux Spanish desk. "Do you know if Bob's at home this evening?"

"He was taking Rocky to his first puppy-obedience class, but that would be over by now."

I dialed Bob's number and put the call on speaker phone. He answered after two rings. "Bob Verritt."

"It's Kylie. I'm here with Lonnie at the office."

"What's up?"

I gave him a rapid rundown of the situation.

"Lonnie's right—it's not enough for a search warrant. But it is mighty suspicious."

"Hastings' personal assistant, Glenys, overheard a conversation where 'collecting' or 'collector' was mentioned. Because Franklin's a movie buff, I'm wondering if it could be the name of a movie."

"*Collecting?* No, but *Collector* strikes a bell. You might be on to something, Kylie. Hang on while I look it up."

There was a pause filled with the sound of flipping pages, then, "Here it is. *The Collector.* Released 1965. Starred Samantha Eggar and Terence Stamp. Directed by William Wyler. Based on a novel by John Fowles. Chilling story of a man who abducts a woman and keeps her captive in his basement for the pleasure of having her company and in the hope that she will eventually fall in love with him."

Lonnie and I looked at each other. There was silence on the other end of the line, then Bob exclaimed, "Hell! That son of a bitch!"

"I'm going there," I said.

"No, you're not," said Bob. "You stay put. I'll get hold of Ted Lark and see if I can persuade him to apply for a warrant on what we've got. At the very least he should agree to put Hastings' Brentwood house under surveillance."

He rang off. I leapt to my feet, tripped over Julia Roberts, who'd suddenly materialized, and was saved from pitching on my nose by Lonnie, who grabbed my arm to steady me. Jules only bothered to mime mortally-wounded-cat for a few seconds, then began to wash the area of her coat my feet had touched.

"I'll only be a mo I said to Lonnie. I rushed to my bedroom, where I rapidly changed into dark jeans, sneakers, and a dark-blue, loose top that would pretty well conceal the holster and gun I'd be wearing.

Back at the front desk, while Lonnie watched with a worried frown, I strapped on my weapon, feeling rather like someone in *High Noon* or any number of other cowboy epics.

As I was clipping on my phone, Lonnie pleaded, "Kylie, don't do this. Let the cops handle it."

"I'm not going to wait while they fiddle around deciding whether to act or not. I know Ariana's there."

"So what do you intend to do? Stick a gun in Emory Hastings' ribs and hold him up? You'll never get to be a private eye if you have a felony firearm conviction."

"Too bad. I'm off."

"Just wait one minute." Lonnie's face reflected his terrible conflict. "I'd go with you, but…"

"Pauline? I understand, Lonnie."

"If I'm not here when she arrives, Pauline will think I've stood her up, and that will be the end of us getting back together. But there's no way I can let you go alone…" He bit his lip. "Could you wait until Pauline arrives so I can explain it to her?"

"She's late already, isn't she?"

He nodded miserably. I headed for the door.

"Kylie, stop. I'll call Pauline's cell and tell her why I can't meet her tonight. And we'll take the Harley. A cycle will get us there faster, and it's easier to park off the road."

My phone vibrated against my hip. It was Oona Turner.

"I've always said Glenys Clarkson was a weak, spineless, pathetic creature," she snarled, "and she's proved me right yet again."

"I've just come from her place. What's happened?"

"Frank Franklin barged in after you left and terrorized that inadequate, faint-hearted excuse for a woman. As soon as he left, she called Nancy and sobbed her way through the whole sorry story. Then Nancy called me. I must say Nancy was a damn sight more sympathetic than I would have been. I've never been able to abide lily-livered whiners."

The last I'd seen of Glenys, she'd been emphatically defending the right for citizens to bear arms. I wondered why she hadn't grabbed one of those arms and threatened to put a bullet in Franklin's hide.

"I'm sorry Glenys has been terrorized, but I can't talk now. I've got something urgent I must do."

Ignoring this, Oona went on, "The bastard said he'd been constantly watching over Glenys like a guardian angel." Oona made an indescribable noise to indicate her profound disgust. "Frank Franklin describing himself as a bloody guardian angel!"

"Oona, I've really have to go."

"Hear me out. You need to know she babbled everything to that fat blimp."

A chill touched me. "What do you mean?"

"Apparently everything you discussed with Glenys she repeated to Franklin. She told him your questions made it plain you suspected Hastings had abducted Ariana and that Franklin had been blackmailing him over it. Glenys sniveled to Nancy she'd been afraid of what Franklin might do if she didn't spill the beans. Feeble excuse for craven cowardice!"

"Crikey, this isn't good."

"It may be worse than you imagine. After a few sharp questions about what you'd actually said, Franklin told Glenys to keep her mouth shut, then rushed out of there like the very devil was after him."

"To warn Hastings?"

"And to save his own skin," she scoffed.

"Thank you for letting me know."

Oona grunted. "Think on this," she said, "if you were Emory Hastings, wouldn't you be making damn sure there'd be no trace of Ariana to be found when the cops came calling?"

CHAPTER TWENTY-THREE

Perched behind Lonnie, I held on to him for dear life. In other circumstances I might have felt a panicky exhilaration—tonight I was totally focused on getting to Brentwood as fast as possible. The Harley sped through the streets like a red bullet, the slipstream pasting the loose top against me. The helmet I was wearing protected my eyes and face, but the rest of me was freezing cold.

In my pocket of my jeans I had the address of Emory Hastings' house and the plate number for his Cadillac Escalade SUV. I also had the plate for Frank Franklin's Jeep. I wasn't going to need to check them—they were burnt into my memory.

When our progress was finally halted by a red traffic signal—Lonnie had accelerated through all the yellow lights we'd hit—he swiveled his head to say, "Try Bob again."

I'd attempted to call Bob before we'd left the office, but had got his voice mail when I'd dialed his cell, and he hadn't answered the phone in his apartment. Although Bob didn't yet know there was a new and pressing urgency, I reckoned he was on the same mission as us—to rescue Ariana. I fervently hoped the cops were with him.

"I can't use the phone with this helmet on," I said.

"Then take it off."

Before I could comply, with a rush of power we were off again. I clung to Lonnie like a limpet, any idea of using the phone on hold.

Melodie's apartment was in the high-density area of Brentwood, where traffic was a constant and parking a nightmare. In contrast, Emory Hastings' luxurious house was situated in the rarified atmosphere of the upscale megamansion sector of Brentwood.

Lonnie knew exactly where we were going, having checked the location on Mapquest. We left the glare of San Vicente Boulevard for the muted lighting of quiet streets, where the roar of the motorcycle sounded intrusively loud. Most houses were hidden by hedges and high fences or were situated at the end of long drives. Only two cars passed us, both going the opposite way—one a Rolls, the other a top-of-the-line Mercedes.

Lonnie throttled down until the Harley was puttering along. Muffled by the helmet, I heard him say, "It's at a T-junction, just around this next corner. We'll drive past, and then walk back and reconnoiter."

"Maybe the cops are already here."

"Maybe," he said. "I don't hear any sirens."

We swept around the corner and dawdled through the T-junction, turning to the left. "It's the one with the sandstone wall," said Lonnie.

Tall, wrought-iron gates were fully open. The stone gateposts were topped with lamps casting a diffuse amber glow. The driveway leading directly to the house was dark, but the front of the building itself was brightly illuminated. I caught a glimpse of a parked vehicle that could be Franklin's Jeep.

Lonnie went only a few meters past the gates, then ran the Harley up onto the grass verge. The silence rushed in when he killed the engine. I leapt off the cycle and jammed my helmet in the storage compartment. Lonnie already had his helmet off and his phone out.

"Bob? Thank God I got you! We're outside Hastings' place in Brentwood. Where the hell are *you*? What? We're here because something's happened. Wait up." Lonnie shoved the phone at me. "You tell him."

Shaking with impatience, I had to force myself to speak calmly. As briefly as possible, I outlined the situation with Frank Franklin.

Bob was as terse as I had been. "I get it. I'm with Ted Lark. We're on our way. Don't do anything until we get there. Just stay out of sight."

"Hold it," said Lonnie, as I went to walk back to the entrance. "There could be a surveillance camera. Let me check." From the Harley's storage he whipped out binoculars. "Night vision," he said, peering through them at the gates.

I was burning with an anxiety to be doing something. Ariana was so close—I was sure of it—and we were wasting time. "Hurry up, Lonnie!"

"I think it's clear?"

As we moved towards the entrance, I made a sudden decision. "I'm not waiting."

He grabbed my arm. "Don't do anything stupid."

I shook myself free. "Lonnie, you stay here as my back-up. I'm going to get as close to the house as I can."

"Why? We can both watch from outside the gates?"

"What would you do in Emory Hastings' position? Wait around until the cops turn up and discover Ariana locked in his basement? Or move her somewhere else?"

"Jesus," said Lonnie, his face bleak. "Or kill her."

"Don't try and stop me. I'll get as close as I can to the house, and if it looks like they're leaving, I'll do something."

"Like what?" said Lonnie, his skepticism plain.

"Like this." I took the Smith & Wesson out of the holster and primed it to fire at the first pull of the trigger. "I'll do anything, Lonnie, if it means saving Ariana."

He let his breath out in a long sigh. "Kylie, I don't like it."

"I don't like it much, either. Let's hope the police arrive soon and take over."

Lonnie squeezed my hand. "Good luck."

I slipped through the gates and, keeping to one side and close to the bushes lining the drive, made my way towards the house. It was a huge, ugly stone building designed with a triple garage in the front. The three doors were closed, but I could see light seeping through, which could mean there was some activity behind them.

I halted where Frank Franklin's dark green Jeep was parked crookedly in the gravel turning area in front of the house. The windows of the Jeep were down and the key was still in the ignition. On impulse, I leaned through the driver's side window and removed it. Then I retreated behind the vehicle, praying no one had seen me.

Nothing happened. Crickets sounded, the breeze sighed in the bushes, a lone car drove past on the road. There were no sirens, no sudden appearance of grim-faced special teams. Waiting was torture. I imagined Ariana, so close to me, yet still a captive. Loving her as I did, I almost believed I could project my thoughts to let her know I was here, that help was at hand.

Abruptly, the garage doors swung open, spilling more light into the area. There was only one vehicle, Emory Hastings' bulky Cadillac Escalade. He was behind the wheel.

Frank Franklin, his ungainly body stretched awkwardly, was in the process of slamming the SUV's rear door. As it closed with a flat slapping sound, Hastings revved the engine.

I had no doubt Ariana, dead or alive, was in the back of the Escalade. Knowing I had to stop him driving off with her, I snatched the handgun and ran out into the light.

"Fuck!" screamed Franklin. "Go! Go! Go!"

It was hopeless to aim for the tires. I swung the gun up and aimed for the Escalade's windscreen. Simultaneously, Hastings stamped on the accelerator. The huge bulk of the SUV surged towards me. The bullet hit metal and went whining off into the night.

I desperately flung myself out of the way, but still suffered a glancing blow that spun me around and dumped me hard. Even so, I'd managed to hang on to the gun, but another shot was impossible, as the Escalade was already through the gates and turning onto the road.

"Bitch!" Franklin was lumbering towards me, his face scarlet with rage.

I was hurt, but not seriously. With an effort, I got to my feet. I raised the gun. "Please give me an excuse to shoot you, Franklin." He paused, uncertain if I meant it.

With a spray of gravel, Lonnie and the Harley skidded to a halt beside me. "Get on! We'll catch him up. I saw which way he turned."

I rammed the Smith & Wesson back into the holster. No stuntwoman, bruised and bleeding, could have done a more efficient leap onto the cycle than I did. The last glimpse I had of Franklin was him hastening towards his Jeep, the keys of which were in my pocket.

The Harley howled as Lonnie pushed it to the limit. We screamed through the quiet streets like an avenging banshee. He wore a helmet; I hadn't had time to put mine on, so I had to press my face into his back to protect my watering eyes.

"There he is!" Lonnie yelled exultantly.

I squinted over his shoulder. Emory Hastings was driving like a madman, but we had the advantage of being on a much more maneuverable, high-powered two-wheeler. Lonnie roared up behind the Escalade. Through my tears I saw Hastings look back, his face contorted. Then he swerved and the brake lights flared.

Lonnie swore, accelerating the Harley around the SUV to avoid a collision. Now we were in front of him, Hastings gunned the engine and tried to run us down.

"Kylie, hold on!" Lonnie sped up to gain some distance, then braked hard and swung into a side street so sharply that I was almost thrown off. Hastings fish-tailed, got control, and then, engine screaming, disappeared from view.

It only took a few moments for us to catch up with him again. We were about to plunge into the traffic on San Vicente. I was horribly aware that Ariana was helpless and vulnerable. If Hastings crashed, she could be injured or killed.

Horns blared and brakes squealed as the SUV skidded through a red light, the Harley tightly behind it. Driving like one possessed, Hastings clipped a car, which spun away, starting a chain reaction of collisions.

At last I heard the welcome sound of sirens. Ahead, the Escalade rushed towards the always-busy intersection with Wilshire Boulevard. The traffic lights turned green. The waiting vehicles started to move with what seemed agonizing slowness. Hastings kept his hand jammed on the horn as he swerved to go around the column of cars turning left so that he could cut in front of them.

"He's headed for the freeway," Lonnie yelled.

On the 405 freeway the Escalade could reach lethal speeds. I yelled back, "Lonnie, we've got to stop him."

The end came suddenly. The Escalade and Harley, engines shrieking, were speeding towards the freeway on-ramp. Lonnie took the Harley up beside the SUV. I caught a glimpse of Hastings' frantic face as he wrenched the wheel to block our way. Lonnie abruptly slowed, Hastings overcorrected and lost control, spinning like a top as cars ricocheted in every direction.

The Escalade came to rest in a sea of vehicles, spread out like toy cars. The wail of sirens was now a cacophony. The moment Lonnie stopped I was off and running. Emory Hastings, blood on his face, sat dazed in the driver's seat.

I wrenched open the back door. Ariana, bound hand and foot, with duct tape across her mouth, struggled to sit up. Supporting her with my arm, I carefully removed the tape. She took a deep breath.

"I knew it would be you," she said.

CHAPTER TWENTY-FOUR

It was good that I already was aware that the debriefing schedule for victims of captivity could take days, otherwise I would have been driven crazy mad with frustration. While Ariana was being debriefed, we learned about Emory Hastings' obsessions from Detective Lark, who'd interviewed him extensively before charging him with a litany of crimes, including kidnapping, attempted murder—that would be Lonnie and me—and an extraordinary number of traffic offenses. Once the evidence was in, he'd also be charged with embezzlement.

As Glenys had told me, Emory Hastings had been a passive stalker for many tears, watching women compulsively, but never doing anything too overt. Eventually this wasn't enough. His marriage, a mistake from the start, was in trouble and Zelda was spending more and more time away from him. He began to fantasize about abducting someone he could mold to his perfect woman, a woman he could teach to truly love him.

The impetus for this fantasy had come unknowingly from Frank Franklin, who had given him the movie *The Collector* to view. It was a revelation to Hastings and he began serious preparations to carry out an abduction, first by having alterations to the basement of his house to turn it into a velvet prison. He obtained several stun guns and experimented with them. Then he began his search for the perfect victim. At the top of his short list of suitable women were two names: Nancy McDuff and Ariana Creeling.

Hastings' close observation of Ariana's life had led him to believe that I was an obstacle to be removed, so, as he said to Ted Lark, he had fun trying to frighten me into leaving Los Angeles.

His preferred victim was Ariana, who had long fascinated him, but she seemed more formidable to subdue than Nancy, so Hastings decided Nancy would be his principal target, although he was prepared to substitute Ariana if necessary.

Nancy's angry comment that her rocket-scientist lover, Barry, was furious and was looking to teach Hastings a lesson he wouldn't forget, alarmed him. Hastings realized that it was likely Nancy had told other people of his pursuit of her, so she was dropped in favor of Ariana, whom he'd treated much more circumspectly.

Wearing jogging gear, a baseball cap, and dark glasses, he often ran in the Hollywood Hills near Ariana's house. He'd park downhill and make his way up on foot. He always wore a stun gun disguised as a water flask in a sheath at his waist and carried in his pocket a hypodermic loaded with a potent sedative. There was a blind corner immediately after leaving Ariana's place that no other dwellings overlooked, and concealed behind bushes, Hastings spent time there observing her movements.

Ironically, had he carried out his initial plan, which was to knock on Ariana's door, subdue her—and, if necessary, Gussie—with the stun gun, then use her own car to abduct her, it all would have been recorded on the surveillance camera.

But what had happened was that he set out from his observation area, Ariana pulled out of her garage and turned his way. There was no other traffic so he seized the opportunity, waving her down as she came around the corner. He'd told Ted

Lark how she'd reluctantly pulled over, put down the window, and asked what he was doing there.

Stun guns and tasers use high-voltage low current electrical discharge to cause great pain and muscle contractions that temporarily paralyze the victim. Hastings had dragged Ariana into the passenger seat and injected her with the sedative before she could recover.

"I never molested her," he'd assured Lark. "All I did was keep her confined in complete luxury. I treated Ariana like a queen, so she would eventually find herself loving me." And Ariana's beloved BMW? It had been in Hastings garage for several days, but he decided it was too risky to keep the vehicle. He'd gone over it to remove any fingerprints and, wearing gloves, had driven the car to the worst part of town, where he'd left it with the key in the ignition.

The night of Ariana's rescue, Frank Franklin, perspiring heavily, had been picked up hurrying along the exclusive Brentwood streets in a vain attempt to escape. Although he'd taken no part in the original abduction, when he'd realized Ariana's disappearance could be related to Emory Hastings' fascination with *The Collector* movie, he'd been intrigued and delighted.

"Sick, sick individual," said Ted Lark. "It was a pleasure to book him as an accomplice. Franklin got a charge out of forcing Hastings to put up with his company, but worse than that was how enthralled he was with the idea of keeping a woman captive and his suggestions as to what Hastings could do now that he had total power over someone."

* * *

It was a glorious Monday morning. Today I would see Ariana for the first time since Wednesday night. She'd been released on Sunday morning and spent the day and night with Janette. I'd spoken to Ariana on the phone, but our conversation had been stilted and awkward. She thanked me for saving her, I'd said it was all Lonnie's skill on the Harley that had done the trick, and then we'd been left with nothing to say—or rather too much that remained unspoken.

Looking uncharacteristically cheerful, Fran came bounding into the kitchen when I was making myself a pot of tea. "Terrific to see Ariana look so well," she said. "Why didn't you come around to Mom's last night? We were expecting you."

Before I could come up with an excuse, Fran went on, "I owe you one, Kylie, I really do. My New York agent loves *Catastrophe Survival* as the title for my book. She's already got several publishers interested. There may even be a bidding war!"

"That's bonzer, Fran."

Melodie appeared in the doorway, the oddest expression on her face—sort of a combination of deep suffering and the desire to murder someone. She let out a long, despairing sigh.

"What's wrong with you?" demanded Fran, never very sympathetic. "Toothache? Constipation? Ingrown toenail?"

"I have been betrayed, deceived."

"I'm sure Bruce and Lexus didn't mean to upset you," I said. "Besides, the engagement's off, ever since Aunt Millie threatened to disinherit Bruce."

"*My* engagement's on," said Lonnie, beaming as he squeezed past Melodie in the doorway. "I popped the question last night, and Pauline said yes! Isn't it wonderful?"

We all congratulated him, me wholeheartedly, Fran without too much enthusiasm, as she didn't like Pauline, and Melodie with the listless air of one unable to share another's joy.

"What's wrong with you, Melodie?" Lonnie asked.

"She's been betrayed and deceived," said Fran helpfully.

"I'm speaking about"—Melodie choked—"Yolanda, also known as"—her mouth twisted—"Cassandra. That snake in the grass, that double-dealing, cheating…" She broke off, unable to continue.

"What in hell's she done?" Fran asked.

"The part was mine. Everyone said so?" Her voice trembled as she added, "I was born to play that character. Born!"

Light dawned. "Chiley Dorsal?" I said.

"Stabbed in the back, sold down the river…"

"Cassandra got the part of Chiley Dorsal?"

"She persuaded them that casting a genuine psychic medium would generate favorable publicity," said Melodie bitterly. "No mention that she can't act! That she stole the part from me! The treachery!"

"My psychic abilities tell me Cassandra's moving out of your apartment," said Lonnie.

Melodie drew herself up. "If she's not gone by the time I get home tonight, I'll throw her out."

"Don't worry too much," said Fran. "Quip says the word in the biz is the show will probably fold anyway."

The faintest smile appeared on Melodie's lips. "You think?" she said.

* * *

I was in Bob's office telling him about my mum's troubles with the Platypus Posse. Mum had called last night to announce the latest problem. Due to difficulty in guaranteeing platypus sightings, the Platypus Posse had now become the Sugar Glider Posse.

She'd said with scorn, "So they're all shrieking, 'So cute! The way they glide between trees with their darling little legs stretched out!'"

"Aren't sugar gliders nocturnal?" I'd said.

"Of course they are. And the little things are even shyer than platypuses. The Posse will be lucky if they see one a month."

I was saying to Bob how Mum was expecting a slew of money-back demands from disappointed Sugar Posse members, when Ariana came through the door.

"Ariana! You're here?"

"I am."

Bob gave her a huge hug. "Welcome back."

"It's wonderful to be here." When, grinning, he released her she said, "Kylie, can I see you in my office when you're free."

"I'm free now."

Exulting, I followed her down the hall. She was too thin, but she moved with the same resilient grace.

She shut the door behind us. "Kylie, there's something I must tell you. While I was captive, I had a lot of time to think about my life and what was important to me. Without the distractions of an ordinary day, everything was stripped down to essentials. Those things that were vital to my contentment became blindingly clear. My good health, having enough money to live comfortably, the love and support of friends and family, Gussie—and you."

I was afraid to speak, to say something that might destroy the moment.

Adorably serious, Ariana went on, "That last time we made love, you said to me that you were mine, body and soul. And I froze you out. I'm so sorry for that. It all seemed too much for me, to take responsibility for your happiness. Now I see I was wrong. You were offering me a gift, not making me accountable. I'd like to offer you that gift in return."

My heart soared. "Your body and soul, Ariana?"

A smile illuminated her face. "The whole enchilada."

Bella Books, Inc.

Women. Books. Even Better Together.

P.O. Box 10543
Tallahassee, FL 32302

Phone: 800-729-4992
www.bellabooks.com